Chief Red Iron

—

The Lakota Uprising

D1615757

Front Cover: Photo provided by the author. The photo is of the Chief Red Iron statue crafted by John Lopez. The sculpture is located at the Granary Rural Cultural Center near Groton, South Dakota.

Back Cover: Photo and images provide by the author.

All interior images provided by the author.

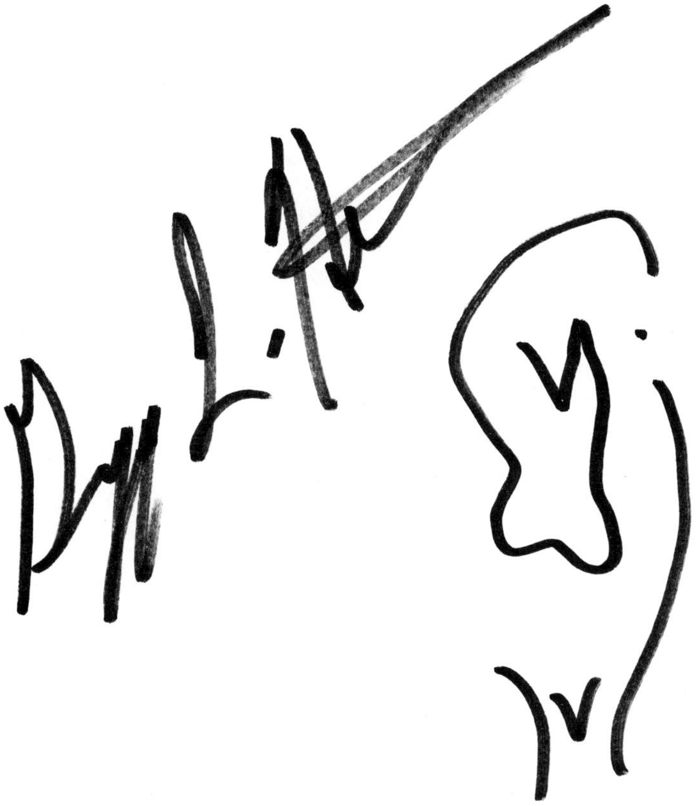

Other Books by Gregory L. Heitmann:

Fort Sisseton – Dakota Territory

The G MANN II: Pay-2-Play

Thanks to Grady for pointing me in

the direction of this uniquely South Dakota story.

Special Thanks to:

Angela

Dorene

Gwyneth

And all my family

Dedicated to the great people of the Midwest.

Part I

Blessed are the peacemakers: for they shall be called the children of God.

Mathew 5:9, King James Bible

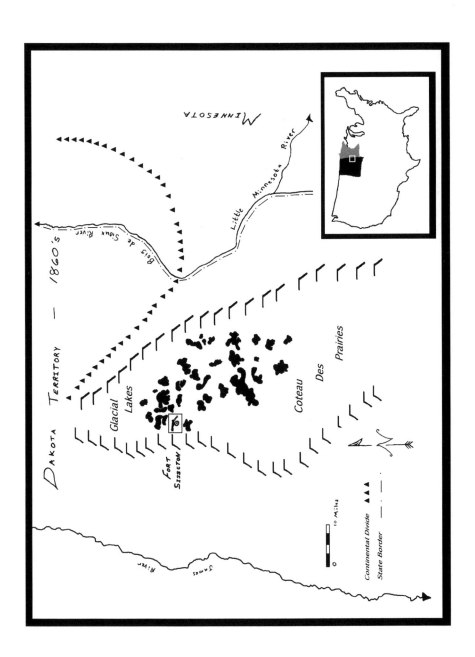

- 13 -

Chapter 1
A Boy, Red Iron

Long before there was a Dakota Territory, the land was simply "home" for the Lakota. The native people of the areas that would become the states of Minnesota, North Dakota, and South Dakota knew the land in their language as *"manil,"* the prairie. Before the time that the people of the prairie were characterized by the commonly accepted French term "Sioux," the Lakota had carved out a nomadic way of life, following and hunting the bison that roamed the plains.

1832 – Prairie

Before he was chief of his band of Lakota, he was a boy, Red Iron. In 1832, Red Iron was ten years old and a special boy on the verge of manhood. He was noticed by the tribal elders and thrust into roles reserved for young men typically a few years older than Red Iron. This boy, charismatic and clever, matched these traits with an unflappable demeanor, a youngster chosen to be groomed for leadership and with a personality ahead of his biological years.

On a lazy, summery, autumn day, Red Iron's tribe was hunting in an area that in a few short years would be established as the Dakota Territory, and later this same area would be considered the northeast corner of the state of South Dakota in the United States of America.

These hunting grounds are a part of an extremely productive area for the Lakota. Deer, pronghorn, grouse, and of course, the bison, roam this locale; the region was first known to European explorers as the Coteau des Prairies, so designated by the early French explorers. Translated, Coteau des Prairies is "slope on the prairie." This elevated rise on the flat surrounding prairie is the remnant of glacial activity ten thousand years prior. As the glaciers receded to their frozen climes of the north, it left in its wake a nearly level landscape of rich soils, now infiltrated with prairie grass as far as the eye could see. But the Coteau is different. It was an area that evaded the last flooding of the most recent glaciers, a wrinkle on the landscape. On either side of the Coteau, inland seas blanketed the earth for a few hundred years, erasing the jagged edges and smoothing much of the rough work the glaciers carved out on the land. The Coteau was untouched by the action of the sea waters, leaving an example of the raw carvings of the glacial efforts. The Coteau is its own meteorological region. The elevation compared to the surrounding flat prairies squeezes a little more moisture from the atmosphere to support an ecosystem different from its neighboring ocean of prairie grasses. The undulating hills of the Coteau are pocked with lakes, sloughs, ponds, and bodies of water of all shapes and sizes. Trees encompass these lakes, blending into an inseparable forest of oaks dotted with cottonwoods and lush shrubs and grass. The botanical varieties thrive on the Coteau and provide home to an equally impressive myriad of game animals that the Lakota tribes harvest for food stock.

Today, the young Lakota, Red Iron, holds the reins of several impatient horses in the buffeting winds; the young lad is bending in rhythm with the waves of the prairie grass in the gusts of the breeze. The boy stands on the border between the prairie grass and a grove of oak trees. He grips the horses' reins tightly as their tails twitch nervously under darkening skies. Red Iron is part of the hunting party. Selected to hold the horses for the hunters, the task may not be glamorous, but he is labeled as a hunter and envied by other boys his age and older. From his elevated position on the Coteau, Red Iron can see the storm approaching the hills. The storm front rolls swiftly across the prairie, and Red Iron braces himself just inside the tree line.

A half mile away from Red Iron, two young Lakota warriors belly-crawl. Silently they approach a doe with her fawn. The deer are bedded in the wooded shadows during the midday. A few raindrops fall on the leaves as the wind whips the tree tops, but at ground level where the hunters crawl, the wind is mostly ameliorated by the dense forest of oaks. The raindrops fall with a steady patter as a young brave slowly rises to a knee with arrow nocked on his bow string. He draws fully and releases the arrow. A dull thud resonates as the arrow finds a home in the chest cavity of the doe. The deer bolts and, after a few leaps with its fawn trailing behind, she falls mortally wounded. The fawn disappears into the trees. "You got her, Long Feet!" Single Eye calls out.

Single Eye is twenty years old. He is a serious soul for someone so young. He is dressed in plain buckskin with limited fringe on the seams of his shirt sleeves and repeated on the seams of his leather trousers. His face bears the paint markings of the hunt that also serve as camouflage. "Good shot, Long Feet. Tonight we will eat like Chiefs!" Single Eye remarks with the slightest smile, a deviation from his solemn personality.

Long Feet responds to Single Eye with a nod, satisfied with his kill. Long Feet is also twenty years old. He is the default leader of this generation of warriors. Known as the hardest worker of his age group, he may not be as naturally gifted, but Long Feet has become the leader through his constant pursuit of perfection. "Let's get the deer butchered and loaded before the rains hit," Long Feet advises stoically.

The other hunting party members emerge from the leaves and branches, materializing from nowhere amidst the cover of the undergrowth as the group moves forward to collect the downed deer. A flash of lightning illuminates the dreary forest and is followed closely by a clap of thunder. Long Feet looks skyward, extends his palm, and states, "It's too late."

A deluge of rain roars down onto the leaves of the oak trees, hissing through the forest canopy and drowning out any sound.

The lightning strike that warned Long Feet of the storm was near where young Red Iron was holding the horses for the hunting party. The concussion of the bolt knocked the boy to the ground. The psychological advantage, held by an eighty pound boy at the end of the reins of several horses, is lost for the moment as Red Iron's grip loosens on the reins and the spooked horses buck, terrified of the storm's power. The boy regains hold of the reins in his hands and bolsters his grip with his second hand, "Whoa!" he calls out to try to steady the herd. "Calm! Calm, horses!" Red Iron cries out through the hiss of the rain's steady downpour, "Steady!" Red Iron scans his surroundings, looking for a tree to fortify his hold on the reins by wrapping the tethers to a solid position.

Another lightning strike sizzles nearby with a crash of thunder that pushes the horses over their threshold. The horses bolt into the woods before Red Iron can act on fixing the reins to the trees. The team of horses drags Red Iron through the forest.

*   *   *   *   *

As Long Feet and Single Eye carefully gut the deer, preserving the heart, liver, and everything they can consume, Single Eye rises from his knee and looks deeper into the woods. "What?" Long Feet pauses from working his knife to skin the deer for a moment.

"Do you hear something?" Single Eye inquires as he strains to see through the rain.

"Like what?" Long Feet asks as he continues to peel away the deer's hide with his knife.

A faint howl pierces the steady patter of the falling rain. The howl gets louder and louder as the braves listen and exchange nervous glances as they try to understand the sound. Branches crackle and pop as the team of horses flash by the hunters with Red Iron in tow. The horses gallop near the men, and the howl is identified as Red Iron screams with a shrill and constant "Ahhhhhhhhhhh!" as he bounces behind the horses. The men stand witness to the spectacle frozen with mouths agape.

Red Iron passes the hunting party and a moment lingers before Long Feet cries out, "Let's go!"

Long Feet and Single Eye chase after Red Iron, leaving the rest of the party to stand with the fresh meat. After a few hundred yards pursuit, the two men find the boy wedged in the forked "Y" of a young tree, the horses held at bay. "Red Iron? Red Iron, are you ok?" Long Feet asks as he kneels next to the boy.

Single Eye works to uncoil the reins of the horses wrapped around Red Iron's arm. The boy breathes heavily. He is battered, bruised, and cut. "What happened?" Long Feet inquires.

Red Iron blinks rapidly in an attempt to regain his senses. I-i-i-it was the l-l-lightning," he stutters. "It spooked the horses."

Single Eye has worked to free the boy from the tethers, and Long Feet stands and extends his arm. Red Iron grabs Long Feet's hand and is towed to his feet. "Whoa," Red Iron groans as he is unsteady on his feet and staggers as he wobbles to grab hold of a tree to brace himself.

The two men laugh nervously, "You going to be ok?" Single Eye raises his eyebrows and questions Red Iron.

Red Iron gives an affirmative nod and leans on a tree for support, "Just give me a minute or two."

The two men smile. Single Eye controls the reins of the horses, jerking on their bridles to command their attention. He looks to Long Feet who is shaking his head in disbelief. "I can't believe you held on," Long Feet remarks. "We are lucky. If those horses had escaped...who knows?"

Single Eye chimes in, "Great work saving the horses! This is a feat of a future Chief!"

Long Feet smiles and tousles Red Iron's hair as the rain steadily falls in a cooling autumn downpour.

Chapter 2
Twenty Winters

1842 – Prairie

On the open prairie, the wind blows. That is a fact. The prairie dweller is more prone to notice when there is a calm settled over the area. The absence of the perpetual breeze is an oddity. This fall night was like nearly all the others. The wind had lost its brute forcefulness, bending the grass during the daylight hours, but the night breeze was there, still ruffling the sides of the teepee.

Red Iron has joined the younger warriors to convene a council. This council would send a representative to the elders advocating a position that would determine the future of the Lakota and other tribes in the area.

The eyes of the young warriors circling the small fire stared into the flickering flames. The only sounds were the hiss of moisture escaping the burning wood and the sporadic pop and crackle of the oak log. A long period of silence settles on the men as each warrior's mind turned over the arguments made earlier. The heated debate among the men had ended a few minutes ago, and silence had blanketed their midst. It was time for a decision.

Red Iron was entering his twentieth winter. It was his first council meeting with the young warriors. He was not afraid to speak his mind and share his opinion.

"I think we should sign the treaty," Red Iron offers. His eyes meet the eyes of Long Feet. The leader of the young generation of warriors is on the cusp of the entering into the elders' circle. Long Feet will deliver the consensus decision from this group to the elders. Long Feet holds his tongue as he turns his gaze from Red Iron back to the fire.

"Are you crazy? What do you think gives the White people the right to negotiate on this land?" Single Eye glares at Red Iron. His one worthless eye, cloudy and intimidating, his namesake, stares achingly at Red Iron.

The long silence again permeates the teepee. Long Feet finally provides a final opinion, "I agree with Single Eye. I will report to the elders that we prefer to stand against the White men."

Red Iron shakes his head discouraged, "How long will we fight?"

"What do you know about fighting, young Red Iron?" Long Feet chides.

"I know I am young. I know that I have been in battles for five summers, shoulder to shoulder with all of you, my brothers. Fighting soldiers. Fighting other tribes. I do not want my children to fight these same battles."

Red Iron examines the angry faces surrounding the fire. The nine other warriors, his peers, shake their heads disapprovingly as they stare into the waning fire. "I ask again, how long will we fight?"

Long Feet scowls and with gritted teeth responds, "We will fight as long as it takes to remain free!"

Silence drapes the group once again. For a few moments the tension is palpable. The flap of the teepee rustles and is flung open. A petite, pretty young Indian woman, Half-Shadow, beckons to Red Iron through the door, "Red Iron! It is time. Your babies are here, twins! A boy and a girl!" She calls with excitement from outside the teepee.

Red Iron leaps to his feet. He directs his attention to Long Feet, "Talk to the elders. You know my position. My children are here. I want peace in my lifetime. I want peace for my children."

Red Iron exits the teepee with a flourish. The wind finds its way through the flap and fans the flames of the fire momentarily before the flap is back in place. The men return their dour stares to the fire.

*   *   *   *   *

When Red Iron charged through the flap of his own teepee, his wife was lying on buffalo robes next to the fire. Two babies were clutched to her breast. With a nod to Half-Shadow, she was dismissed and exited the teepee. Red Iron was alone with his new family. He knelt to embrace his wife and children. He wrapped his arms around the trio and buried his face into his wife's tangled hair. Her labor was not the easiest, but Cloudy Moon was euphoric, enjoying the suckling babies at her breast. Red Iron pushed away ever so slightly to free a hand to gently stroke one infant then the other. "They are beautiful," he affirmed.

Cloudy Moon reaches for her husband's hand and grasps it. Her eyes lock with Red Iron's, "Yes. A warrior and a princess. The Great Father has blessed us."

The naked babies kick and squirm as they position themselves at opposite breasts under the watchful eyes of their parents. "I have names," Red Iron states authoritatively. "The boy will be called Curved Wing. The girl will go by Blue Feather."

Cloudy Moon's beaming smile brightens, "Beautiful names for beautiful children."

The wind whistles and gusts outside the teepee.

"Listen," Red Iron cocks his head, "The Great Spirit has acknowledged our babies' arrival with flurry of wind. It is a good omen."

Chapter 3
Twin Trouble

1852 – Prairie

Ten years pass in the blink of an eye. The family bonds strengthen, especially for twins. Red Iron's children are virtually inseparable as they explore the prairie's landscape, discovering new and exciting aspects of their world.   The nomadic paths of the Sisseton-Wahpeton Band of the Lakota, Red Iron's Band, has settled into their summer encampment. Here they will hunt and replenish provisions for the cold months of the year. The base camp is the hub for the summer satellite camps that will follow bison and other game to fill the caches for the winter. The elderly, the women, and the children perform the daily chores and make preparations to battle the frozen months as they have done for generations. The men, the warriors and hunters, provide much the raw food stuffs that the camp processes. It is a grind, but the early summer pace of activity is a little more relaxed as there is time to gather and prepare the necessary provisions.

The rains have restored the prairie grass to a luscious, thick carpet, providing the forage for the wild game and the horses. Berries and roots are plentiful and are harvested with enthusiasm.

The Glacial Lakes region, an area that would later become the northeast corner of South Dakota, is again proving to be the breadbasket for the Lakota people as it has always been. The area of undulating hills bearing the name the Coteau des Prairies has rich soil, the result of a series of glacial activities over several thousand years. The glaciers ground the igneous rocks into a powder that became the basis for the soil, a mixture of organic and inorganic materials that provides the bedding material for vegetation to thrive. A few hundred years of growing seasons has established exemplary humus; some of the finest decomposing plant and animal materials on earth rest on these prairie hills.

The Coteau provides a micro climate of sorts for the 20,000 square mile region of the prairie. The top of the Coteau is about 600 feet higher than the surrounding flat prairie. The abrupt elevation change provides enough of a difference in geography to shape the winds. The winds in turn shape the moisture and clouds, thus impacting precipitation amounts. The climate is just different enough from the surrounding prairie on either side. Some have deemed this area "the Buffalo Ridge" as it stands out like a hump on a bison.

The glacial activity not only left the rich soils; it left pock marks and pockets that capture and hold water, thus forming the glacial lakes, ponds and sloughs in the region. The combined effects of the elevation and climate seem to produce a consistent supply of rain and snow to keep the bodies of water full. This moisture in turn has allowed another differentiating feature to take hold of the area...trees. The empty prairie with the waves of tall grass is interrupted on the Coteau by interspersed stands of oak, cottonwood and various other trees surrounding the permanent bodies of water. Different varieties of shrubs also inhabit the area. They are hardy and tolerant to the sometimes drought conditions. They grow next to the shallower pools of water, finding their place intermittently between the rolling hills of the Coteau.

It is a beautiful place. The natives did not come upon their home and settle by accident. They chose to establish their roots in the unique area of the Great Plains, the Coteau des Prairie region. These Lakota roots run deep in the area and always will.

This summer of 1852 was not unlike all the previous summers in the last fifty years with one exception: the rare European visitor had become a trickling stream of Anglos to the Lakota's territory. The elders in the tribes were being forced to take notice, but Red Iron's twin children were oblivious to the changing times. They were in their formative years, sponges of knowledge and information of their lands and culture. Today, and every day, was a new day of learning.

*   *   *   *   *

Like the speckles dotting the back of a leopard frog, the lakes, ponds, sloughs, marshes, and even large puddles crowd the landscape of the

Glacial Lakes. The summer time also brings visiting waterfowl to the prairie. The ducks and geese make themselves at home on the prairie ponds, fighting each other for the right to breed and nest in the rushes and cattails. Once hatched, they raise their offspring in the open water preparing for their annual southern migration to warmer climes.

It was summer now and the heart of the nesting season. Curved Wing and Blue Feather had reached a milestone age of ten years old. This age came with more independence and more responsibility. With less supervision and more chores, today they found themselves with egg gathering detail. Away from the main camp, the twins trudged through the thick cattails forming a ring around a small pond. Curved Wing frowns as he pushes through the tangled blades of the reeds, forging the trail and slogging through knee-deep water. He stops and turns back to his sister and shakes his head in disbelief, "Blue Feather, I can't believe you are here with me. You should be with the women, learning their ways. This is men's work, hunting."

Curved Wing continues to shake his head as he turns and pushes forward through the mass of rushes. He re-grips his bow and adjusts his quiver on his back. He uses the bow to bend the cattails in front of him. New green stalks of reeds, lush and pliable, are mixed in with the previous year's brittle, crackling stems. The crunching prevents conversation as they move steadily forward looking for nests. Curved Wing stops again to rest. The brother and sister are remarkably similar in appearance, even as twins go. At this age, the only aid to identification are the clothes and hair. Curved Wing is shirtless, wearing only his buckskin trousers. His hair is braided; a single large braid falls to the middle of his back. Blue Feather is in her buckskin dress. Her hair sports braids; the braids fall from the sides of her head, mirroring each other and extending to each shoulder blade.

Curved Wing stares at his sister and shakes his head in disgust as he catches his breath. "Why are shaking your head at me?" Blue Feather questions. "I can keep up with you better than Black Teeth."

Blue Feather points to the hillside. Above the pond, an overweight child lying flat on his back is shrouded in the prairie grass. He dozes unabashedly, resembling a lump of doughy-mud. "I am a better hunter than Black Teeth, your supposed best friend."

Curved Wing rolls his eyes as Blue Feather continues. "I do everything you do, and I do it better than Black Teeth. All he does is eat and sleep! He never helps you do anything, but he sure takes credit at camp."

Curved Wing points to himself, "But, we are men. These are things we are supposed to do!"

"Hush, I can do these things. Mom said I could." Blue Feather stands hands on her hips. "Let's keep moving."

Curved Wing smiles, "You're right about Black Teeth. He probably should stay with the women."

They push forward, slogging through the water. A rustling in the reeds ahead of the twins catches their attention. Curved Wing freezes and holds up a hand. A hen mallard bursts from the reeds. The duck rousted from her nest, alights in the open water. "I want to get that duck!" Blue Feather shouts. She wrenches the bow from her brother's hand and pulls an arrow from his quiver before he can even react. With a quick shove to her brother, she pushes to edge of the reeds into the clearing of the open water.

"Hey," Curved Wing calls out as he stumbles backward nearly taking a seat in the water.

"Hush!" Blue Feather calls to her brother as she nocks the arrow and draws on the duck. The distraught mother duck flaps her wings pathetically as she quacks with a ruckus trying to draw the intruders away from her nest. Blue Feather aims carefully.

"Hurry! She's going to get away!" her brother calls out from behind with borderline encouragement. "Get her! You can do it!"

Blue Feather smoothly releases the arrow. She has practiced in the past, but this is her first live fire. The flopping duck proves to be an elusive target. The arrow misses cleanly. The surface tension of the water deflects the point of the arrow, perfectly reflecting the angle of the arrow's trajectory. As Blue Feather lowers the bow, she watches mesmerized along with her brother as the arrow skips off the pond surface and sizzles through the reeds on the other side. The arrow seems to have a mind of its own as it careens forward, launching itself toward a dozing Black Teeth on the hill side. The arrow targets Black Teeth's flabby leg. It superficially pierces his thigh. The feather fletching snags the skin, and the arrow buries itself in the soil of the side hill.

Black Teeth shrieks an unearthly howl as he awakens. "What is happening!" he cries with a start. He looks at his leg and finds the source of pain. The arrow has gone nearly through-and-through the soft, fleshy part of his thigh. The arrow is snagged in the ground, but rips free from the soil as Black Teeth thrashes in pain. The arrow dangles from his leg, caught and held by the stabilizing feathers on the end of the shaft. He stands howling and staring in disbelief.

Curved Wing grabs the bow from Blue Feather and silently motions for her to stay where she is. He moves forward and whispers, "Find the nest and grab the eggs. Don't move until I get to Black Teeth."

Blue Feather nods. Curved Wing pushes through the cattails. He bolts from the reeds when he reaches the open prairie and rushes to his friend's side. Black Teeth sobs; the arrow protrudes from his leg as he stands frozen in fear.

"This might hurt," Curved Wing states. He reaches for the arrow and with a flick of his wrist he pulls the arrow through the skin.

Black Teeth wails in pain and falls over. A trickle of blood pools at the wound. The pudgy Black Teeth is dressed in only a loin cloth, and the two slices in his thigh left by the arrow trace blood drops to the ground. "It's barely bleeding," notes Curved Wing.

Black Teeth is sobbing inconsolably, more from the sight of his wound than pain. Curved Wing inspects his arrow. "Good news. I can still use this arrow. Come," Curved Wing extends his hand. "Get up. I'll get you home."

"Wh-wh-what happened?" Black Teeth manages to squawk. He reaches for Curved Wing's hand and is pulled to his feet by his friend.

"It was a fluke," Curved Wing shrugs. "I shot at a duck on the water." Curved Wing points to the pond. "I was on the other side of the lake. The arrow ricocheted off the water like it was frozen and came straight to your leg." He shakes his head, "Can you believe it? I *missed* the duck. That is what is so weird."

The boys start walking toward camp. Black Teeth leans on Curved Wing and limps exaggeratedly. "It hurts," Black Teeth winces with every step.

"I think you'll be fine," Curved Wing assures.

Hidden in the cattails, Blue Feather watches her brother tend to his friend. When they are out of sight she moves through the rushes and locates the duck's nest brimming with eggs. She plucks the eggs from the feathery bowl and places them in a pouch slung around her shoulder. Having gathered enough eggs, she leaves three for the hen to hatch. Blue Feather moves to the edge of the cattails. She carefully inspects the landscape for any observers. Noting she is alone, she moves into the open prairie and steadily paces herself as she walks back to camp, careful to keep far enough back and out of sight of her brother and Black Teeth.

Chapter 4
Scolding

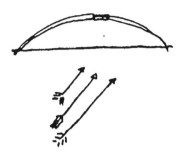

For Curved Wing, the hike back to camp was a long one. With the weight of his friend Black Teeth leaning on him, the weight of facing the consequences of his mother was equally heavy. The closer they inched toward camp, the more Black Teeth leaned on Curved Wing. The moaning from Black Teeth also increased in volume and in frequency as they got closer to home. By the time they crested the last rise and the encampment came into view, a cluster of curious women and young girls were waiting to see what was howling and approaching from just over the hill. When they identified their tribe-mates, they rushed forward to assist.

The bloated boy, Black Teeth, is playing up his injury for his maximum benefit. His moaning has lowered in volume now that the crowd had gathered. Black Teeth's mother is in hysterics. Curved Wing began his explanation of the accidental ricochet of the arrow but was halted with a slap across his face from Black Teeth's mother. "It was an accident!" Curved Wing glowers at the large, crazy-eyed woman.

She raises her hand again to strike at Curved Wing. Her sweeping blow is dodged this time by Curved Wing. The woman's momentum from the miss knocks her off balance, and she stumbles and tumbles into the tall prairie grass.

The onlookers are hushed. Black Teeth's mother gathers herself to her knees, preparing to pounce again on Curved Wing. "Enough!" a cry comes from the crowd of women as Cloudy Moon steps forward. "Tend to your son, and I will tend to mine!"

The silence is interrupted by the whispering breeze bending and swirling through the tall grass prairie. Blue Feather has closed the distance and is able to move to her mother's side, joining her brother.

Curved Wing glares back and forth between Black Teeth's mother and Black Teeth. Black Teeth's eyes are wide with fear as he lies in the grass. Cloudy Moon breaks the silence, "Enough," she reaches for her son. "His father will address this. Don't worry." Cloudy Moon turns to Black Teeth. "I am sorry, Black Teeth." She pushes Curved Wing towards Black Teeth, "Tell Black Teeth you are sorry."

Blue Feather locks eyes with her brother. Her mouth opens to speak, but Curved Wing cocks his head and gives an almost imperceptible shake of his head to discourage her.

Curved Wing lowers his eyes, "I'm sorry, Black Teeth."

Cloudy Moon puts her hands on her children's shoulders. She gives them a shove towards the camp, "Get home."

Blue Feather hesitates, "Mother, I found eggs."

"Excellent, my daughter," Cloudy Moon nods. "Take them home with you. Go with your brother. I am going to help with Black Teeth's wound."

Curved Wing and Blue Feather skirt the crowd. The mass of people presses forward assisting Black Teeth as they head to the family tepee. When they are out of earshot of the others, Blue Feather speaks, "Why did you protect me?"

Curved Wing shrugs and shakes his head, "You saw how mad everyone was." He gestures back to the crowd, "Imagine if they found out you, a girl, had done this. It would be unforgivable. You would be mocked and tortured."

They move through the village of tepees. Curved Wing shrugs, "Besides, we're twins; we got to look out for each other."

Blue Feather smiles, "I guess I owe you one, brother."

Curved Wing lovingly shoves her as he smiles, knowing he did the honorable thing to protect his sister. "Hey," Blue Feather playfully cries out as she stumbles from her brother's push. "Don't make me break these eggs."

Curved Wing is not afraid of the consequences. He knows his father will understand and be fair in meting out punishment.

Chapter 5
Fire Talk

In the calm environment of the tepee with his peers, Red Iron sits beside the fire on a cool fall night. The first frosts of the autumn have put a chill in the air, and the wind rustles the falling leaves outside. This group of warriors, the same age and training, rest tonight in camp. The hunting has been at a fevered pace to replenish the food cache for the winter. Other groups of the tribe have their own conversations around separate fires, but this restless group of men smokes their ceremonial pipe tonight, seeking blessing over the hunt tomorrow. The prayers are completed, and the casual conversation begins with Red Iron. He touches his friend's neighboring knee as the men stare into the flickering fire, "How is your son with his leg?"

Single Eye snorts and smiles, "He is fine. Black Teeth is very proud of his scar."

Red Iron nods, "He is a good boy."

The pipe is reloaded with tobacco and fired up by Long Feet. He makes the offering to the four directions and drags from the pipe, exhaling the smoke as he passes the pipe to his friend Red Iron.

"After the hunt, the elders will meet with the soldiers at the fort. Have you noticed there are many more soldiers lately?" Red Iron queries.

The group nods in affirmation. "Treaties," Long Feet states denigrating the word in disgust. "I am tired of the talk."

Single Eye wraps his arm around Long Feet's shoulder, "I hear you my brother."

Long Feet turns from Single Eye's gesture to staring back into the flickering flames. His brow furrows as the storm inside his words belies the relaxed atmosphere surrounding the fire. "Many treaties have been struck. The White man has signed treaties with tribes up and down the rivers," Long Feet continues. "Yet there is still no peace."

Single Eye smokes the pipe in turn and passes the pipe on, "Talk, talk, talk. That is all we have done. I'm tired of talk. I would prefer we settle our differences once and for all on the field of battle."

The pipe passes from man to man as Single Eye's words sink in. After a long silence, Red Iron breaks it, "We need our own treaty."

Long Feet is visibly agitated by the words, "I would rather die than meet the fate of our brothers to the east. They live like prisoners...like slaves. They have been rounded up like a herd of bison and chased from their lands." Long Feet meets his eyes with each man's eyes encircling the fire. "No, I think it's time to fight. To fight and show the White man that we will not be herded like animals, escorted from homes. Who wants to fight?"

Red Iron answers with his own question, "How long must we fight?" He stares into the fire. "We have fought the White man. We have fought our own Chippewa brothers to the north before that. Before the Chippewa we fought our Cheyenne brothers to the west. Before that, we have fought our brothers, the Yanktonai and the Winnebago to the south. What is it going to take to stop the wars?" Red Iron looks up from the fire, "It should be that our children's children will still be fighting?"

A murmur of consideration ripples through the men.

Red Iron pokes at the fire, "I'm tired of the fighting."

"We are starving!" Long Feet counters. "Where, where are the bison? Where are the turkeys?" Long Feet shrugs his shoulders mockingly at Red Iron. "Where are the deer? How do I feed my family? How do we feed our families?"

"You have heard the treaty talks," Red Iron calmly states. "We can farm the land. We can grow crops. You have seen the healthy grass and trees. The land can provide food other than animals."

Single Eye waves away Red Iron's statement in disgust, "How should we farm without tools? And seed? The soldiers promise; the White man promises." Single Eye gesticulates, "What do we have to show for the promises? Broken treaties? I say this, broken words from the White man don't feed our people."

Long Feet picks up the argument, "Single Eye is right. They are starving us out of existence. It is a peaceful way to get rid of us, the thorn in their side. Yes, to get rid of the thorn you cut it. They cut us by starvation."

Single Eye is wound up by the emotions of his words, "I don't want to be a farmer! I am a warrior! I am a hunter!" He pounds his fist into his open hand with each word. "It is time to fight!"

The men nod in agreement, except Red Iron. He is unconvinced. He stands and his eyes look to the top of the tepee as he recalls a distant memory and finally begins to speak, "I remember my grandfather telling me about his grandfather's favorite tale. I will not bore you with the details. The essence of the story does not change with details." Red Iron sighs and continues, "At the time of our grandfather's grandfathers, there were no horses. The beasts appeared among our neighboring brother's tribes and bands. Soon our people had horses. Our way of life changed significantly." Red Iron extends his finger and sweeps it across and in front of his seated brothers, "The lesson that was passed to me is that everything changes. We are at a season of change in our land. Not the trees changing color and cold weather. The White man is here. He is not leaving. The people must adapt and change, or we will disappear."

Red Iron stands before his comrades. The majority have turned their eyes down to the fire again, realizing, sadly, that he is indeed correct. Single Eye and Long Feet glare defiantly at the man standing in front of them. Each man searches his own thoughts: how can this arrogant man, younger than they, be willing to surrender their way of life. Red Iron nods, "I will speak to the elders." He pauses with a deep breath, "I will speak for peace."

Long Feet slowly rises from his cross-legged position. He extends an accusing finger at Red Iron and measures his words carefully, "You…you are not the Chief. We have had a spirited debated this evening, but we have not declared a position of this peace you refer to." Long Feet waves his arms before the group. "Warriors, tell him. Tell Red Iron we will fight!"

Single Eye stands with Long Feet, "I will fight. I will die rather than give in to the treaties!"

Single Eye and Long Feet are outnumbered. The seven other warriors sit in silent support of Red Iron. "I will inform the elders of our decision. It is peace. It is for your sons and daughters and my son and daughter to live in peace."

Red Iron begins to step toward the flap covering the tepee opening. "Red Iron," Long Feet calls out halting Red Iron at the opening. "This can't continue," he states gravely, "it won't continue."

"I know," Red Iron responds with a nod. "But, peace is what I will ask for tomorrow when we meet with the soldiers."

The men in the tepee stare at Red Iron, not understanding. Red Iron explains, "The elders have asked me to accompany them to the treaty talks with the soldiers. I have agreed to ride with them to discuss these matters. I am told that Chief Drifting Goose and Chief Struck-By-The-Reed will also be at the talks."

Long Feet is angry, "I have heard of no such talks! Why was I not informed!"

Red Iron forces a weary smile, "I do not know. These are the decisions of the elders, and I will honor their decisions."

Long Feet averts his eyes and waves away Red Iron, "Go then. Get out of my sight."

Red Iron nods to his fellow warriors, and they return the nod before he exits.

Chapter 6
Growing Up

    The bond between "The Red Iron Twins," as they were known by the tribe, grew stronger into their adolescent and teen years. Blue Feather and Curved Wing would spend hours firing arrows into the side of a hill. Curved Wing would tutor Blue Feather on the finer points of launching an arrow. Breathing properly so as not to draw your aim from the target, along with repetition of the shooting motion are what Curved Wing emphasized to his sister.

    Curved Wing would spend more and more time with the boys his age, but he would return to Blue Feather and share his new found knowledge. During these formative times, Curved Wing would push his sister away and deny her participation in the games the boys would play. But, many times he would give in and allow her to tag along behind and out of the way because he knew her stubborn ways. He could not argue with her as she would never back down. It was often easier to relent and allow her to come along. The women of the tribe stepped in as a common buffer, pulling Blue Feather back to the female duties such as drying and storing the food, repairing and making clothes. She enjoyed the skinning and tanning of the bison and deer hides, but the other light duties were not suited to Blue Feather's temperament; she wanted to be where the action was. Her fondest memories as a blossoming lady were not dressing the dolls. Her favorite times were stomping through the stream, chasing fish and grabbing them with her bare hands for the evening meal. Sharing in the competition with her brother to see who would catch the biggest fish of the day, and earning bragging rights until the next fishing adventure, were more important to Blue Feather than any of her gender prescribed activities.

"One more, one more," Blue Feather would cry to her mother as Cloudy Moon came to take her daughter back to work.

Blue Feather always wanted to launch one more arrow. To perfect the sweet science of shooting and hitting the target, that was where her thoughts rested. While she might be taken back to perform chores such as sewing, the women gossiping around her was blocked from her mind as her brain sifted through the things she enjoyed.

The fishing and the bow and arrows were important and fascinating, but her true love was horses. For Blue Feather, one of the most difficult days of her life was when Red Iron brought home a bright-eyed colt for his son. The green monster of jealousy rampaged in her mind for months as she longed for a horse of her own. That was not to be. Women did not have horses. Curved Wing was a generous brother. He knew it was killing his sister to watch him with such a prized animal. He let her help him care for that colt; after all, who wouldn't want help with caring for a needy horse and sharing the chores associated with the growing equine? More often than not, Blue Feather would provide the needed care for "Bucky" as she called him. Bucky because of his buckskin colored coat. She was paid handsomely by Curved Wing. Not in a monetary sense of goods, but in favors. Curved Wing would sneak away with his sister to some site out of observation of the tribe. Here, Curved Wing would dismount and let his sister ride free on the prairie, racing to and fro, up and down hills, slashing through the tall prairie grass. Bucky came alive under her light frame and would respond with the speed comparable to that of a hawk diving from the sky. The wind would whistle past Blue Feather's ears as she urged the horse faster. She felt fully alive when she was astride that mount.

Time turns the page on everyone's childhood and "The Red Iron Twins" were no exception. At eighteen years old, they were now "Chief Red Iron's Twins." Red Iron had been a strong leader from his youth. The tribe recognized the undeniable fact of the young warrior's charismatic personality and intelligence. He was bestowed the title of Chief Red Iron at the age of thirty-eight years old. He was a relatively young chief that could and would shape the life of the Sisseton-Wahpeton Band of the Lakota for the next three decades.

Chapter 7
The Boundary

1860 – Dakota Territory

A lone Indian stands atop a hill. He is dressed in his ceremonial eagle feather headdress. His arms are held above his body forming a "V" shape as he faces north. What cannot be seen immediately is the crowd of soldiers and Indians below him, waiting at the base of the hills. Everyone is in their formal dress. At the crest of the hill, the single Indian chief with his decorative headwear, hard earned from years of war, is Chief Watoma. He is making the final speech of the day. His solemn, weathered face faces into the light summer breeze from the north. Surrounding him in silence and listening were many dignitaries. The commander of nearby Fort Sisseton, the commander of Fort Ripley in Minnesota, and the most out of place contingent of United States envoys from Washington, D.C., stand at attention. The envoys with dark pinstripe suits and ruffled shirts stand out like sore thumbs. The men stand stiffly with one hand on their heads holding their stovepipe hats fixed against the wind, while the men periodically dab sweat from their brow with hankies as they stand in the afternoon sun.

From his high point in the Many Lakes Region, Chief Watoma can see the vast, undulating prairie beyond his audience. The blue sky dotted with puffy white clouds forms the dreams of landscape artists' canvases. The lush green grass bends in the wind with a steady swishing sound punctuating the Chief's lecture. After years of negotiations and treaty talks, today was the finale. In a moment the papers would be signed and the Sisseton-Wahpeton Reservation would be established. The two separate bands of Lakota, the Sisseton band and the Wahpeton band would share a government designated area reserve. First, however, Chief Watoma would make an offering. A young warrior with an eagle feather in his hair advances up the side of the hill bearing a leather pouch. Chief Watoma extracts the contents of the folded leather carrying case revealing a pipe. After filling the pipe with tobacco, the Chief lights the pipe and offers it to the four directions. Once the offering is completed, the young warrior retreats with the ceremonial pipe.

"Today," Chief Watoma continues, "after many seasons of negotiations, we are here at Many Lakes to sign the treaty for peace. Our generations will finally know peace. It is with satisfaction I stand here today." Chief Watoma raises his arms in a "V" once again, "I stand on this hill facing the direction of the 'Cold Wind' (the north). The boundary of our lands is this point on which I stand stretching from table lands to my left and to the big stones on my right. This is our land."

A sporadic round of applause ripples through the crowd as Chief Watoma descends the hill. The envoys begin to scurry to set up rickety folding tables. The representatives from the Indian Affairs Division under the Department of War place the tables on the flattest area they can find in the rolling hills of the glacial till. Fist-sized chunks of granite pulled from beneath the quaking grass weigh down the treaties spread over the tables. Three tables with two treaties each are braced for the parties to sign. The treaties are all the same. They are copies put forth to bear original signatures and marks of the signatories.

The first to sign is Envoy Dunkirk, Deputy Secretary of War. His prepared statement offering the thanks from President Buchanan was five sentences long. His orders from the Secretary of War were clear; keep it short and to the point. Get the treaties signed and return with papers as the ink is drying. Dunkirk followed the orders. He signed his copies with a quill pen and ink and moved out of the way. General Silas, representing the Ninth Cavalry out of Fort Snelling, quickly inked his name on the copies of the treaties making way for the chiefs to make their marks. Envoy Crowley, a weasel faced man, in his black suit bore an uncanny resemblance to an undertaker. It could not have been more coincidental that he came from a long line of morticians. His older brother had taken over the family business in Philadelphia. This allowed Sheldon Crowley the opportunity to see the world as a government agent within the War Department. Crowley was in charge of making sure each chief made his mark above the English designation printed on the parchment. Through interpreters this was finally accomplished as Chief Watoma signed first followed by Chief Waneta, Chief Long Feet, and finally Chief Red Iron. The chiefs' marks were made each according to their preference of loops, squiggles, hashes and x's. Crowley was there to

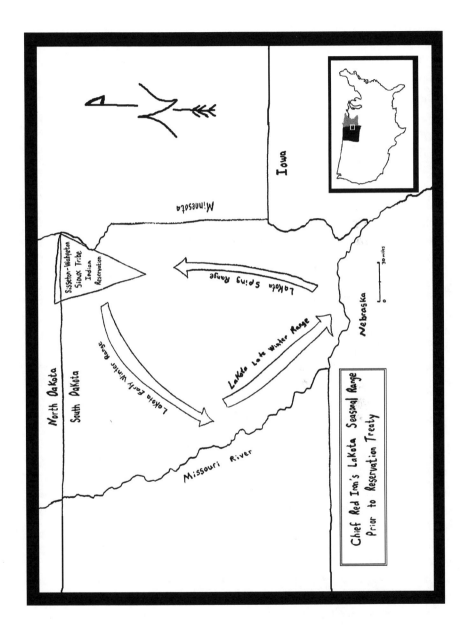

Chief Red Iron's Lakota Seasonal Range Prior to Reservation Treaty

North Dakota
South Dakota
Minnesota
Iowa
Nebraska

Sisseton-Wahpeton Sioux Tribe Indian Reservation

Lakota Spring Range
Lakota Late Winter Range
Lakota Early Winter Range

Missouri River

30 miles

witness and stamp the parchment as officially recorded, and he accomplished his assigned duty on that day.

"Congratulations, Chief Watoma," General Silas called out. Silas was an aging soldier with tired eyes bearing the dark circles of war weariness. "This is peace."

His large, bushy mustache curved slightly upward, but not enough to reveal a smile underneath. The General extended his hand to Chief Watoma. Watoma grabbed the General's forearm, and the men exchanged a firm handshake, rather an arm-shake, common among the Lakota and Native American people.

With a nod to Crowley, General Silas swept his hand toward the twenty or so wagons ringing the gathered crowd. "These wagons," the General stated, "are the first supplies the government will be providing to your people. They are filled with shovels, hoes, and other farm implements. The seed will come in the next shipment. The Lakota will be able to grow food and sustain themselves."

Chief Watoma nods approvingly.

"I am very proud to have worked with you and the Lakota. I look forward to continue working together," Silas continues as he exchanges arm-shakes with the other chiefs. "Blankets, dry goods, and medicines will be distributed to the agencies. Crowley over there," Silas indicates with a nod, "is the lead Indian agent for the Dakota Territory. He will be our primary contact to assure the delivery of all supplies granted by the treaties."

The ceremony was over, and the crowd of Indians and soldiers milled around uncomfortably for a few minutes unsure of what might be next. There was no blustery, foreboding wind gusting from the north. Only murmurs rippled through the crowd among the three hundred or so Indians and soldiers. Questions on what was next echoed among the conversations. The immediate question loomed: what should the people do? Should they now return home? And the long term question of: what was going to happen?

The immediate question was answered when the soldiers were ordered to mount up and head north, back to the fort escorting the supply wagons. The Indians followed. Most were on foot, but some rode their ponies. Horses had been decorated for the ceremony and bore the markings of celebration, a celebration of peace at last. Treaty Hill, as it was named on that day, was abandoned and empty in a matter of a few minutes. The hill would be a subject of derision by the Indians as it would later be mockingly referred to as Surrender Hill.

For most, relief came over the witnesses as they headed back to the fort or encampment, but it was an empty relief. The weight of the unknown burdened everyone's thoughts.

Chapter 8
Introductions

Prairie

The day of the treaty signing was a day Curved Wing had been waiting for. He had served as a scout for the cavalry for three years, and at the age of eighteen he was a seasoned veteran in the corps of scouts. The young man was a handsome Lakota. Lean, wiry, and tall, his outward appearance reflected his charm, wit, and extroverted personality, beautiful inside and out. His black braids bobbed as he rode his favorite horse, a paint by the name of Jobba. The ceremony was over, and he rode with his cavalry platoon dressed in his buckskin trousers and dark blue cavalry jacket. The unbuttoned jacket flapped in the breeze, exposing his traditional bone breastplate that was handcrafted by his mother. The combination of Indian dress and cavalry garb was the standard for scouts. Curved Wing topped his head with the army issue, wide-brimmed Cavalry hat with custom beadwork provided by one of his lovely lady friends. Yes, today was special for the scout. He was going to introduce his soldier friend to his sister.

"Follow me, Captain," Curved Wing called over his shoulder to his cavalry commander. "Don't say anything. Let me do all the talking," he cautioned.

The pair left the column of soldiers and veered toward a loose formation of Indian women walking north away from the ceremony. "Blue Feather!" Curved Wing calls out. "Hey, sister! Wait up!"

Blue Feather halts and shields her eyes as she recognizes her brother. Her surrounding group of women pause momentarily, but continue forward after a moment leaving Blue Feather behind. Blue Feather is a beautiful woman now. She has a striking resemblance to her twin, but her features are soft and feminine. She is an attractive woman, highly sought after as a bride by the warriors in the tribe. She is adorned in a form fitting buckskin-beaded dress emphasizing her womanly curves. She has resisted the advances of the men in her tribe still looking for that someone special. As a favor to her brother, she promised to meet the soldier that Curved Wing has bragged about so often at family gatherings. Today was the day for introductions.

*   *   *   *   *

Curved Wing and the soldier rein their horses to a halt in front of Blue Feather. The soldier is Captain Gary Hillmann. He cuts a dashing figure today in his best, fresh laundered uniform. Hillmann of the Ohio Hillmann's is a third generation American, descendent from the German Heilmanns. The Heilmann name became Hillmann thanks to hasty paperwork upon immigration. He is a twenty-four year old, freshly promoted captain, tanned and fit from his duty assignment guarding the prairie while stationed at Fort Sisseton. Curved Wing and Captain Hillmann started their respective service at the Fort the same week, Hillmann as a newly commissioned lieutenant and Curved Wing a scout. The two new federal servants to the cavalry bonded quickly and three years later were the best of friends. "Sister," Curved Wing smiles as he dismounts. "This is the soldier I have told you about; this is my commander and my friend, Captain Hillmann."

The captain slides from his horse, hat in hand. He smiles and removes his riding glove and offers his hand to Blue Feather.

"Captain, this is my sister, Blue Feather."

Blue Feather extends her hand, and the captain kisses it gently. This is the man she has been waiting for. Her attraction is overpowering, but she is able to retain her calm. "Pleased to meet you, Captain," she manages with a smile.

She turns and resumes walking, following the women ahead of her by a hundred yards now. Curved Wing waves the captain forward chasing after Blue Feather. The men tow their horses by the reins as they follow. Blue Feather smiles to herself, pleased with the chase and feigning of her disinterest. Curved Wing signals to the captain to hang back, and he hustles forward to his sister's side.

"What do you think?" Curved Wing questions his sister.

"Does he talk? He didn't even say 'Hello'," Blue Feather retorts.

"I instructed him not to talk."

"So, you are his boss now?"

Curved Wing winces, "Not exactly. He is a good man. He listens to reason. And today, the reason is you."

The twins walk together in silence trailed by the captain a good thirty yards behind.

"I have a thought," Curved Wing offers with a nod to the trees a few hundred yards ahead. "Let's stop and have lunch in the shade up ahead. It will be a cool break."

Blue Feather looks at her brother for a moment. She purses her lips, "I will stop and have lunch with you two on one condition."

"Sure. Name it."

"I get to ride your horse back to camp."

Curved Wing stops walking. He rolls his eyes and sees the mischievous glint in his sister's eye. "You can't be serious." His shoulders slump. "Why would you embarrass me in front of the whole tribe?"

Blue Feather continues to walk and answers with a shrug without turning around, "That's my offer."

Curved Wing hustles to his sister's side, "Fine," he mumbles through gritted teeth.

*   *   *   *   *

In the shade with a cooling breeze from across the lake, known as Waubay Lake, the trio enjoys a picnic packed by Curved Wing in anticipation of the planned lunch.

With a wry smile Blue Feather feeds the cordial conversation, "So tell me. How is it that your soldiers can make it back to the fort without their captain and their scout?"

Curved Wing laughs at the loaded question, "Are you implying the cavalry can get along without me and the captain?"

"I guess I am."

Curved Wing waves away the playful insult, "The captain told the platoon to stay close to the women. They know the way home."

The group enjoys a laugh at the self deprecating humor. Blue Feather leans forward, turns, and takes a long look at the captain, drinking in his fit frame and prairie, sun-tanned skin. Her eyes remain on the soldier as she questions Curved Wing, "How is the scouting business, brother?"

"Good," Curved Wing replies without missing a beat as he chews the last of his biscuit and nods to the captain. "My captain here keeps me plenty busy."

Curved Wing stands from his position seated between the captain and his sister on a large log. He sprawls in the grass, locks his fingers behind his head, and momentarily stares at the tops of the trees above before shutting his eyes. The captain and Blue Feather remain seated on the fallen tree. Captain Hillmann clears his throat and speaks, "I only pick the best scout for my missions. I say with pride, your brother is the only one I choose."

Curved Wing waves away the compliment, quickly returning his hands behind his head without opening his eyes. Blue Feather smiles and meets the captain's eyes. "Your brother is modest. He knows the territory backward and forward."

"Chief Red Iron is very proud of his son," Blue Feather remarks casually as she stands silently. She puts her finger to her lips to shush the captain as he looks on puzzled, but keeps quiet. "Thank you so much, Captain. It was a lovely lunch. I should really be moving on now."

Curved Wing lies in the grass with his eyes closed and answers lazily, "Let's just relax for a few more minutes. Let that lunch settle."

Blue Feather smiles as she sneaks to where Jobba is tethered to a fallen cottonwood tree. She unties the reins from the tree and walks the horse a few yards ahead of where her brother lays in the grass. "Go ahead, brother. Relax all you like. I'm riding your horse back to camp."

The captain watches the events with a silent smile. Jobba lets loose with a snort, bringing Curved Wing to a stiff sitting position in time to see his sister spring onto the back of his horse and begin a gallop northward.

"Hey!" Curved Wing shouts as he springs to his feet and charges after his sister. "Wait a minute!"

Blue Feather pulls the horse from a sprint after about a five hundred yard jaunt. She continues to walk the horse as her brother chases her on foot. Finally catching up to his sister, Curved Wing pants, "Wait…wait."

"Oh," Blue Feather raises an eyebrow, "Did you forget about our deal?"

Curved Wing claws at the bridle to stop the horse. The majestic paint, a blotchy combination of white and chestnut, finally comes to a halt. Between breaths Curved Wing manages, "No, no. I remember our agreement. I wanted to know what you thought of the captain." He bends at his waist and rests his hand on knee as he gasps for breath. "Do you like him?"

"I'm curious, brother, when did you become a matchmaker?"

"Do you like the captain?" he questions again. "I just think you two would make a nice couple. My best friend and my sister; that is something that would make me happy."

"He seems nice, I guess." Blue Feather dismounts and walks the horse forward. Curved Wing is recovering his breath.

They walk forward another hundred yards in silence. "Can I tell him you'll see him again?"

"I guess," Blue Feather shrugs as she mounts the horse again.

"Good. Good. Hey, one more thing...take it easy on Jobba here. He's my best horse."

"I will." Blue Feather nudges the horse forward, but stops. "You know, you should learn to negotiate a little better."

"What do you mean?"

"The captain, he is so handsome. I wouldn't have dreamed of asking to take your horse if you had told me before how attractive he is. I might have offered *you* a gift." Blue Feather smiles and waves at her brother. She digs her heels into Jobba's ribs, and the horse bolts ahead. "See you back at camp!"

Curved Wing stands alone. He throws his hands in the air as he can't help but smile at his sister. He walks forward following his sister with his eyes until she disappears over the hill and reappears further away on the next knoll. Finally she is beyond is vision even on the open prairie.

*   *   *   *   *

After a brief walk alone in the waist high grass on the prairie, Curved Wing is joined by Captain Hillman. The captain walks his horse in stride with the scout. "Good news, Captain! My sister said she would like to see you again."

"That's great, but why are you walking?"

The scout laughs, "I had a deal with my sister. She has lunch with you, and I let her ride Jobba."

Captain Hillmann nods in understanding, "I'll tell you what; your generosity will be rewarded. I will share my mount." The captain smiles, "When we get to Hump Back Lake, you can jump on board."

"That's five miles from here!"

"Yeah, you better get hoofing it," Hillmann spurs his horse forward. "We want to get back to the fort before dark."

"This is the thanks I get?" Curved Wing shouts.

"See you at Hump Back. Hurry up, we don't have all day!" the captain shouts over his shoulder.

Chapter 9
Romance

There are those that contend that love at first sight is a real phenomenon; the romance between Blue Feather and Captain Gary Hillmann was a check mark in their win column. It was not common for an Indian woman to become involved with a White man, but not unheard of either. What was unusual was that the daughter of a Chief would make time with a soldier. The rare occurrences of interracial relationships that produced "half breeds" were frowned upon by both races. The couples and offspring were often shunned from both societies. This was a first. The daughter of a Chief involved in a relationship with a White man, not to mention a soldier! Chief Red Iron would listen patiently to the discriminatory complaints of this nature brought before him. Warriors, elders, women, and medicine men at different times came to bend Chief Red Iron's ear, lamenting the travesty he was allowing to occur. With only a gentle conversational tone, the chief would remind the objectors of the Great Spirit's message, and that was, "Be one with the earth."

The naysayers would scoff, and Chief Red Iron would elaborate, "The People and the White Man, are they not both flesh and blood? Are they not both placed here on Mother Earth by the Great Spirit? Who am I to object to the Great Spirit?"

The contentious naysayers would have no argument and would leave the chief's side unhappy and bewildered. They, however, would leave thinking new ideas, with a new consideration of a differing, thought provoking viewpoint.

For Captain Hillmann his romantic intentions were not hidden from his fellow soldiers or the Indians. Leaving Fort Sisseton on the first patrol since his introduction to Blue Feather, the Captain halted his platoon outside the nearby Indian encampment. The mounted patrol waited as the Captain delivered flowers to Blue Feather. He interrupted her work amongst the Indian women in the process of mending leather tepees. This caused quite a stir amongst the tribe. But, it paled in comparison to the controversy that was rumored to have broken out over the captain's orders for the soldiers to assist in the gathering of the bouquet of flowers. Captain Hillmann defended his decision as a simple botany lesson for his troops when confronted by his commander. The commander, a jovial Lieutenant Colonel laughed off the treasonous charges from a disgruntled sergeant. The commander wished Captain Hillmann, "All the luck in the world."

Over the weeks of summer and into the fall, Captain Hillmann delivered a variety of bouquets as the seasonal blooms came and went. With the help of his platoon, the bouquets became larger and larger; eventually bouquets were handed out to all the women around Blue Feather on each delivery. It was never underestimated how much goodwill was purchased from the tribal women through the flowers.

After a few weeks, on the platoon's down days, Captain Hillmann would steal Blue Feather away from the working women, with their approval, of course, for an unchaperoned horse ride. She would sit behind the captain atop the unsaddled horse and hold him tight as they rode to one of the surrounding lakes. Often Blue Feather would talk the captain into letting her ride his horse while he relaxed with his bare feet in the cooling lake. After her rides they would walk together bare foot, holding hands on short stretches of sandy beaches that are found sporadically surrounding the larger nearby lakes.

By the fall, while walking amongst the yellow and orange oak leaves surrounding Pelican Lake, the topic of marriage was broached for the first time, out loud to their ears. Captain Hillmann spoke the words of a wedding to his own surprise. Three years ago, a lifetime it seemed now, he never imagined finding a love. His parents had been heartbroken when he informed them he was going to be a soldier. Their heartbreak continued when he left for Indian Country. Now, they would be devastated that their son would be married, not in their midst or in their vaunted Lutheran Church.

Captain Gary Hillmann asked the question, "Will you marry me?"

"Ask my father," Blue Feather responded.

It was a loop of circular questions between the couple that was answered and sealed with a shared kiss after five minutes of manic consideration between themselves. The real issue as to what Chief Red Iron's answer might be followed in healthy debate.

"You'll just have to ask my father and find out," Blue Feather ended the conversation with a smile.

Chapter 10
Permission

Chief Red Iron's Camp

On a cool early November day, when no more flowers bloomed and the autumn winds had denuded the trees of the dried, colored leaves, Captain Gary Hillmann led his patrol from Fort Sisseton. The First Sergeant, Sergeant Hendricks, was befuddled when he heard the captain call, "Halt." At the edge of the adjacent Indian encampment, the patrol halted, and Sergeant Hendricks quickly guided his horse to the captain's side. "What is it, sir? There are no more flowers to gather."

"Yes, Topper," Captain Hillmann smiled at the top ranking non-commissioned officer he respectfully referred to as 'Topper.' "But, today I have important business with Chief Red Iron. Hold the boys here for a few minutes."

Hillmann reined his horse into the midst of the tepees. He tipped his hat to the Indians he met and passed as he moved into the center of the camp. Here the largest domicile housed the chief.

Before dismounting, Captain Hillmann gathers himself with a few deep breaths and looks to the blue sky and passing clouds overhead, a breathing exercise to calm himself. Having heard the hooves on the ground outside his tepee, Chief Red Iron peers from the flap spotting the captain astride his horse staring skyward. "What is all the huffing and puffing, Captain?" Chief Red Iron looks to the sky to try to spy what the soldier might be viewing.

The startled captain quickly dismounts, "Chief Red Iron!"

The chief steps from his tepee and drops the flap, "Good day, Captain. To what do I owe the honor of your visit on this pleasant day?"

Captain Hillmann removes his hat and clutches it to his chest, "This is a personal visit, Chief Red Iron."

"I see," Chief Red Iron nods, looking the soldier up and down. He calls to children playing nearby, "Youngsters, come! Hold the soldier's horse."

The children approach reluctantly. The captain hands the reins to the sturdiest child as Chief Red Iron motions Hillmann forward while lifting the flap to the tepee. "Come in. We will smoke and discuss your urgent matter of personal business."

Inside the tepee the light and sounds from outside are muffled and muted. "Come, sit by the fire." A small flame meanders inside the rings of the rocks as a plume of smoke rises out of the top flap of the tepee. "We will have a smoke."

Captain Hillmann sits nervously. "Now then, Captain, I see you and your men were heading north on patrol?"

"Yes,"

"Is there trouble?"

"No, sir. Just a routine patrol."

"You have stopped to visit though; you must have some urgent personal business to discuss with me," Chief Red Iron gestures toward the platoon halted at the edge of camp, "to hold up the whole patrol."

"Yes."

Chief Red Iron pulls a pipe from a leather pouch, "Here it is. This is my favorite pipe. We will smoke." The chief fills the bowl with tobacco and with a small stick fires the pipe. Smoke billows from the pipe, and he offers smoke to the four directions before inhaling himself. He exhales and hands the pipe to the captain, who accepts it with a nod of thanks. The captain inhales as best as he can. It is all he can do to avoid coughing.

"I have been expecting your visit," Chief Red Iron gestures to the surroundings. "The camp talks and gossips."

The captain nods and hands the pipe back to the chief, who inhales and holds the smoke momentarily. With one hand he waves smoke from the bowl of the pipe over his body before exhaling. "My son has told me you are a man of integrity. I know this myself as we have dealt with issues between soldiers and the People."

The captain receives the pipe again from Chief Red Iron. He inhales deeply and mimics the chief the best he can waving the smoke over him as he holds his breath before exhaling slowly. Hillmann cannot read the blank expression frozen on the face of the man. The chief stares back at the fine looking soldier. "You have my blessing to marry my daughter. I welcome you to the family."

The captain is caught off guard with the chief's statement. He begins coughing uncontrollably. Chief Red Iron smiles, "Yes, it is some powerful tobacco. We will finish smoking, and you will be on your way with your patrol."

The chief takes the pipe from the captain still coughing uncontrollably. Captain Hillmann points to the door unable to catch his breath. Chief Red Iron nods. The soldier rises and stumbles to the door. "Yes, please rejoin your patrol. I will inform my daughter of my decision."

Captain Hillmann nods as he bursts through the flap of the tepee into the fresh air, gasping and coughing in a struggle for breath. His breath is taken away by the smoke and by the realization of the decision by the chief. The children holding his horse drop the reins and run from the man stomping and coughing in a giant spasm. His curious horse steps a couple of cautious steps in retreat, but the captain makes a flailing dive at the reins and catches the leather straps. His breath now returning, he finally manages a few seconds of normal breathing between fits of coughing. He leads his horse through the camp back toward the waiting patrol. Every few yards he has to stop in a fit of gasping that attracts the attention and disapproving looks of the Indians.

Chapter 11
Union

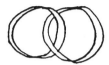

Chief Red Iron's Camp

The skeins of geese crossing the gray sky nearly interrupted the ceremony on the last day of November. The honks and squeals overhead from the migrating waterfowl provided the musical notes of a joyous occasion. It was a mild day, beautiful weather for a late autumn wedding. On a typical November day, the Glacial Lakes region on the Coteau des Prairie might see snow. Not today, the occasion was blessed with weather befitting the event.

The exchange of vows between Captain Gary Hillmann and Blue Feather was a private event. The gossip surrounding the scandalous marriage in the eyes of many members of the tribe overwhelmed the services. The specifics of the idle prattle included the soldier's offering to the chief for his daughter's hand in marriage. The five beautiful horses, a stallion and four mares, became the jealous talk of warriors and women alike. "Was it enough for a daughter of a chief?" they asked without shame.

"Too much," some would argue. "A maiden of the Tribe who would marry a White man was not worth a single horse!"

No matter, Chief Red Iron had accepted the gift and immediately dispersed of the honorable offering. He handed the sorrel mare back to the captain as a gracious thank you. The other horses were awarded to the families in most need of a good steed for hunting and hauling. Most of the tribe had started to break the fall camp. They were preparing to move south and take shelter from the winter winds in draws and ravines. Some members would remain encamped near Fort Sisseton, battling the elements side by side with the soldiers. These hardy souls were the families of the Indian scouts and other natives in relationships with soldiers. The wedding reception would be a nice break for everyone working hard to strike camp.

In a ceremony incorporating both cultures, a medicine man named Poor Moccasin, chosen by Chief Red Iron, and the Fort Sisseton Chaplain Jorgen Strauss, officiated. Captain Hillmann's best man in place at his side, Curved Wing, beamed with pride. Taking credit and reminding everyone on that day, that it was he...he was the one that had introduced the soldier to his sister. The tables turned quickly each time though as he was confronted about his life. The questions about him settling down came often now that his sister was committed. Curved Wing deflected the questions easily, "This is Blue Feather's day. Let her enjoy it." That simple comment seemed to soothe a questioner's curiosity and get the attention focused on the wedding, away from Curved Wing's personal life. Not that he didn't have his share of would be brides vying for his affection. Curved Wing had a friend. She was a Cheyenne. She lived far to the west, and through his scouting travels he had come to find what he was looking for. He did not promise her marriage yet. He was still learning the ways of the world, still living an adventurous life. He was young and not ready to settle for a routine life of children and the pressures of dependents. Curved Wing found this hard to explain.

The maid of honor was Blue Feather's friend since as long as she could remember. Standing Deer was a distant cousin to the twins. She was round and pleasant. She had made overtures toward Curved Wing but was dissuaded from further pursuit by the relatives; very much to Curved Wing's relief. She had settled into a comfortable relationship with Curved Wing's old friend, Black Teeth.

The small, private ceremony included less than thirty witnesses; equal parts Indians and soldiers. Among the guests were troops from the captain's platoon. Following the tradition of the cavalry, parallel lines of soldiers formed a canopy of raised swords. The bride and groom ducked their heads and moved beneath the tunnel of steel blades emerging as a married couple for the first time and being announced to the guests as such. The sun broke through the wisps of clouds for a few moments, providing a serene blue sky as the guests granted well wishes in the receiving line as the happy couple made their way to the reception.

The wedding reception was a far cry from the ceremony. Most of the tribe and half of the soldiers from the fort attended. A steer and a hog were slaughtered and cooked in the ground providing a feast for the wedding revelers. Music, singing, drumming, and dancing were shared into the night. The darkness kept at bay for awhile as dancing continued around bonfires.

The celebration wound down, and the happy couple retired to their new living quarters, a tepee provided by Chief Red Iron. The captain would now make his new home amongst his neighboring in-laws. His adopted family would be the band of Indians known as the Sisseton-Wahpeton Lakota.

Chapter 12
Change Agents

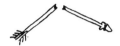

January 1862

Government treaties were in place with tribes in Indian country; the bureaucracy soon followed. In order to meet the promises the federal government put in writing, agents assigned by the War Department were dispatched; hundreds of agents were sworn in and sent west to discharge the duties they were ordered to uphold. Reporting to Washington, D.C., the general welfare and state of the Indians' conditions were the main assignments. The primary task of the agency superintendents, as they became known, was to distribute commodities and goods to the tribal members. As part of the distribution system, a census of the Indian population was made, and the Indians were identified and counted. From the census, the members were enrolled in their respective tribes, thus establishing their entitlement as outlined in the treaties.

The burdensome, unwieldy, and plodding government was never more evident than when it attempted to execute its own self-imposed rules and protocols. One might argue that the men in charge of conducting the business of the War Department were not competent. If a person would make that contention, he would be partially correct. It was a willful neglect of duty that described the incompetency. Fueled by greed and as large organizations are sometimes subject to, graft permeated the delivery system put in place to assist the native people.

"Crowley's Gang" was well known for its abuse of power within the War Department. Sheldon Crowley had found a special place in Washington, D.C., as a Deputy in the War Department. His willingness to travel to the nether regions of Indian country had won special admiration of his fellow bureaucrats in the halls of the Capitol's buildings. He was considered an expert in the emerging and problematic field of Indians and their culture. He had parlayed his success into establishing a network of pals appointed within a small branch under the War Department, Indian Affairs. Crowley recommended and approved all the Indian agents assigned to the remote areas of Indian country. With his handpicked minions, Sheldon Crowley skimmed, embezzled, and stole his way to riches. The Indian Affairs Division of the War Department was nothing more than an afterthought in Washington, D.C. Politicians threw money at the "Indian Problem," assuming it would cure whatever was ailing it. Kickbacks, payoffs, and appointments to Indian Affairs' positions purchased by less than reputable men lined Sheldon Crowley's pockets. This is the method he used to pillage the entitlements owed to the tribes. Mr. Crowley became a wealthy public servant in no time.

A most recent appointee of Mr. Crowley was a despicable man, Jon Coverdale. He had been assigned to one of the most remote locations in the United States, the Sisseton-Wahpeton Agency in the Dakota Territory. Mr. Coverdale was a devout disciple of the ways of the Crowley Gang. The tribute required of Coverdale for his appointment was a tidy sum of two thousand dollars. He had begged, borrowed, and stole to get the funds to pay Mr. Crowley. Now, just a few months later via train and horse drawn wagon, he was in the cozy, albeit frozen, Agency Village. A few hundred yards from Fort Sisseton and adjacent to the Indian encampment, Agency Village had sprung forth from the empty prairie. Consisting of little more than five buildings that included a warehouse and his office, it was the closest thing resembling a town within a radius of seventy miles; this was Jon Coverdale's Empire.

Chapter 13
Jon Coverdale

January 1862 – Agency Village

Winter has set in at full force, but today was a slight reprieve. The sun was shining, reflecting with a glare off the glossy snow drifts. The temperatures were crisp, hovering in the single digits. The environment was deceptive. The sun shone brightly and would confuse a man's body into believing the temperature was warmer. This fits Jon Coverdale. He is a cold man. On this afternoon the sun has reached its apex and is waning, providing the strange yellowish winter-tint to the atmosphere. Coverdale locks the warehouse door with an oversized padlock. Another convoy of wagons has delivered goods in preparation for the upcoming first of the month distribution. The warehouse holds stores of dry goods: flour, beans, corn, and numerous sacks of food stock. Along side these supplies, tools for farming are stockpiled for distribution in the spring. The warehouse itself is the largest structure at the agency. It is a hastily raised amalgamation of stone, brick, and wood; yet it has a particular feel and look of government stodginess.

Jon Coverdale smiles as he signs for the goods and sends the wagons away. The wagon train will spend the night at the fort before heading east to Minneapolis and Fort Snelling for another load and return trip. With no wind the breath of the men at the reins and the horses pulling the wagons hangs momentarily in an eerie steamy mist before evaporating. Coverdale signs the last paper and imprints, next to his signature, his embossed seal. With a wave Coverdale dismisses the wagons, "Farewell, gentleman. Until next month, snow drifts willing."

The wagons move away revealing several Indians observing the goings on. Jon Coverdale has grown used to the Indians hanging around the Agency and ignores them as he pulls his overcoat tighter. He is dressed for the milder temperatures of the East Coast climes. His pinstripe suit and ruffled shirt and ascot provide little in the way of insulation against the harsh temperatures on the prairie. His stovepipe hat does nothing to protect his ears. He stands out on the prairie as a buckskin clad Indian might stand out in the halls of Congress. "Gentleman," Coverdale tips his hat to the Indians. He reaches for the padlock once more and yanks at it to assure that the door is secure. He begins to move the short distance across the dirt and snow covered trail to his office shack a few yards from the warehouse.

"Sir," the Indian known as Spring Water pleads, "we are starving. Can't we get flour and blankets?"

The Indian called Brings to the Fire steps in to impede Coverdale's path. "Sir, we saw the supplies being loaded into the warehouse."

Jon Coverdale is in his early thirties. He is angry. Coverdale is angry at himself for having been foolish enough to accept an assignment in what he could only describe as the ends of the earth. His idea and plan to recover his two thousand dollar investment and begin his profiteering has been slow to develop. Siphoning off supplies for black market sales had not been as described to him over poker games back east. With a roll of his eyes, Coverdale begins to quote his regulatory guidance, "Section five of statute ten, under the..." he shakes his head and stops the recitation. "Gentleman, I'm sorry. By order of the Secretary of War, these supplies are not to be distributed until the first of the month." With a big sigh Coverdale continues, "I know it is cold, but it is only the twentieth day of January. We still have eleven days until the first. My hands are tied. I cannot release the supplies. It would be a violation of the law."

Brings to the Fire pleads, "The treaty says you will provide supplies."

An annoyed Coverdale shakes his head, "I am following the treaty and the orders of the Secretary. If you will excuse me." Coverdale sidles by the Indians and continues to his office.

Spring Water shouts at Coverdale's back, "We are hungry. What are we supposed to eat?"

Jon Coverdale stops. He turns slowly to face the Indians while brushing aside his unbuttoned overcoat, exposing a pistol on his belt. He shakes his head and sneers as he points to an area of prairie grass exposed and cleared of snow by the blustery winds. "I don't know. Eat the grass. Come back on the first of the month. We will distribute the commodities then." Coverdale disappears into his warm office.

Chapter 14
March Winds

March 1862 – Dakota Territory

The winds of March alternate in a pattern of warm winds from the south one day, melting the snows, followed by a frozen wind from the north, bringing a bone chilling temperature. The saying on the prairies is: "March comes in like a lamb and out like a lion."

There is a reason this cliché was coined. It is true. The grip of the winter is loosened with the longer hours of daylight as the calendar rolls into March. The heating power of the sun changes the air flows, and the weather becomes unstable. Thus when the calendar leaves February behind, we are able to fulfill the prophesied forecast, and they held true to form this year.

A blanket of new white lay over the prairie as a lonely soldier trudges through the heavy, wet snow. In the blinding sun and whipping south wind, the soldier makes his way from Fort Sisseton to the adjacent Indian encampment. His path meanders through the knee deep snowfall. The shortest distance between two points is a straight line, but when plowing your way through the snow, a quick glance back at your trail is all the evidence you need to understand that straight lines don't exist in the snow. The drifts and the hazards below the snowfall make a human being unable to travel that shortest distance when snow is involved.

The single soldier locates his destination, a tepee on the fringe of the Indian encampment. He ducks inside; Captain Hillmann is home. The flap is replaced and the whistling wind in his ears is finally silenced in the shelter of the tepee.

"You're here," Blue Feather pronounces sleepily as she stirs from her nap, awakened by her husband's entrance. She is noticeably pregnant and struggles to sit upright with her newly acquired girth.

"Yes, the colonel ordered me to come check on you. How are you?" The captain sheds his heavy overcoat and scarf. He pauses as he waits for his eyes to adjust to the darkened tepee after entering from the blinding snow-reflected sun. He works to remove his boots.

Blue Feather works her way to her feet. She holds her hands on her swollen belly, "How nice of the colonel."

Captain Hillmann moves to his wife and holds her in his arms, placing his hands atop hers as she caresses her stomach. "The colonel asked how much longer it would be."

"Still four months, but look at me. I'm huge!"

"Maybe it is twins. You were a twin. It runs in families."

Blue Feather shrugs, lost in the arms of her man. The captain pulls away with a sigh, "I had to walk from the fort. I did not want to bring the horse from the shelter of the stables and barns. The snow is deep and heavy."

"Come, sit by the fire and rest," Blue Feather orders.

Captain Hillmann sits, following the command only to spring back to his feet at the commotion at the entrance. "Anybody home?" a shout echoes as the flap is flung open, and a bundled man enters. The intruder unfurls his scarf covering his face and hat, revealing the smiling face of Curved Wing. "Mmm, I can smell something is on the fire." Curved Wing fastens the entrance flap and removes his overcoat.

Hillmann guiltily looks to his wife, "Honey, I forgot to mention your brother might stop by."

Blue Feather smiles, "Welcome, brother! We have stew."

"I am starving. That snow just takes it out of a man."

"It's already melting under the warm wind. It will probably be gone within the week," Captain Hillmann returns to his seat by the fire. He drinks water from a bladder and offers some to Curved Wing.

"Sit," Blue Feather orders to her brother, "I will serve the stew."

Curved Wing sits and warms his hands over the small fire. The men sit quietly as Blue Feather busily prepares to serve the men.

*   *   *   *   *

Everyone is served and eats wordlessly enjoying the stew while lost in their own thoughts. Blue Feather finally breaks the silence, "Gary?"

"Yes, my love."

"I wanted to talk to you about Superintendent Coverdale. It's happened again. He did not hand out the apportionments at the first of the month. He told everyone again that supplies are low. We need to ration distributions. Because of the weather, the wagons were not coming from the east on time."

"I know that the supply wagons have not been on time. That is true," Captain Hillmann nods between mouthfuls of stew.

"He is withholding supplies," Blue Feather continues. People are hungry and cold. There are blankets in the warehouse. I have seen them. This winter has been harsh. A lot of the people did not break camp and move south this year." Blue Feather locks eyes with her husband, "People are starving and freezing, and Coverdale is holding supplies that would help the people."

Curved Wing sets his empty bowl down and wipes his mouth with his sleeve, "Coverdale. He is a bad man. He has no respect for any man, Indian or soldier...it doesn't matter."

Captain Hillmann turns from his wife to Curved Wing, "Tell me. What do you know about Coverdale?"

Curved Wing scratches at his head and pulls down on his braids to straighten them considering what to say. "Coverdale. He is a crook. He is selling supplies on the black market. If you want something, you just have to pay for it."

"You've seen this?" Hillmann questions.

"Yes. He is trading food, blankets; whatever he can for guns, alcohol, and other illicit goods. I know he is."

The captain stops eating, "Why am I just hearing about this now?"

Curved Wing and Blue Feather look at each other and shrug. The fire crackles and pops as the captain looks back and forth between the twins. "I really don't know what to say. I'll check into it."

"People are getting desperate. I fear what might happen. I should have said something sooner, but I was hopeful." Blue Feather's eyes well up with tears. "The last thing I want to do is make trouble, but I'm afraid."

Captain Hillmann eases to his wife's side. He rubs her back and comforts her. "I will discuss this with the colonel. There, there, take it easy."

"I'm scared of what the people might do. They've reached a breaking point," Blue Feather's voice cracks as she wipes at tears. "Mr. Coverdale has threatened the people. He carries a pistol on his belt, and he makes sure the people see it."

Captain Hillmann catches Curved Wing's eye, and he confirms the claim with a nod. "Talk to Spring Water and Brings to the Fire. They were there when Mr. Coverdale told the people to eat grass."

Captain Hillmann pulls his wife close and wraps his arms around her engulfing her. He kisses the top of her head as she softly whimpers into his chest. "Don't worry. I'll see that nothing bad becomes of this."

Chapter 15
Indian Agent

Fort Sisseton Indian Agency

It was a promise kept by Captain Hillmann. As requested by Blue Feather, the captain had reported the plight of the Indians suffering through the long winter to Major Randolph. Major Vladimir Randolph was an amiable man and brought the captain with him to discuss the situation with the colonel.

Inside Lieutenant Colonel Ed Hagen's toasty office, the captain, the major, and the colonel spoke. Major Randolph spoke first, but not of the current situation, "How are things back home, Colonel?"

"Wonderful," Colonel Hagen smiled and nodded. He gestured to the wall where a framed sketch hung; centered and featured on the empty wall, the sketch of a woman and two young ladies all in their best dresses smiled down upon the men. "My wife has provided me a drawing of who waits and prays for me back home." The colonel is in his mid-forties. He is graying and distinguished. His wise and even temperament has earned him respect throughout the territory.

The captain and the major nod. "It is a beautiful picture," the major acknowledges.

The men sit in silence for a moment, each with their own thoughts of home. The stone building housing the headquarters of Fort Sisseton contains the commander's office. Colonel Hagen's modest office is comfortable enough. The man in charge of the outpost has some luxuries. He has a wood burning stove in his office, and the heat keeps the last of the winter chill at bay. A few scattered books line the shelves and multiple racks of deer antlers line the rest of the wall space.

Colonel Hagen brings them back to the business of the meeting, "Major, you had some information you wanted to share?"

Major Randolph startles with a twitch as his mind returns to the military conversation. "Yes, the captain here," Randolph gestures to Captain Hillmann, "informed me that there is dissension in the ranks of Indians." The major leans forward and rubs his knees; he unconsciously massages the muscles above his knees as he continues describing the situation. "The captain here is married to the chief's daughter."

"Yes, I am fully aware of that fact, Major," the colonel responds as he glances between the two men seated in front of him across his desk.

"Blue Feather, the captain's wife has reported tensions rising. The Indian Agent, Coverdale, is behind in handing out supplies."

The captain picks up where the major leaves off, "Coverdale is claiming the weather is delaying the supplies from Minnesota."

The colonel shakes his head, "I would tend to believe Coverdale. The snow's been deep this year."

"My wife is very nervous. The rations are tight, and Coverdale has supplies of food and blankets he won't release. The Indians know this and resent not receiving what the treaty calls out."

Major Randolph picks up the conversation again as the colonel listens, "That's what frightens me. Hearing about resentment amongst the Indians. A lot of these young braves are just itching to fight. They're lookin' for a reason, and this could be it."

It's the captain's turn again, and he sighs before continuing, "The tribe is not used to staying here on the exposed prairie during the winter. They usually move further south into the timber along the Missouri River. They're not accustomed to these harsh conditions. That's shortening their fuse."

Colonel Hagen raises a hand to halt the discussion. "I hear you, gentleman. What do you say to a ride over to see Mr. Coverdale?" With a smile and a nod, the colonel dismisses his visitors, and the men stand.

"We'll have the horses brought around," Major Randolph salutes his commander as he snaps to attention alongside Captain Hillmann.

The colonel returns the salute.

* * * * *

The ride from the Fort to the Indian Agency Superintendent's office is brisk. The soldiers' horses tread carefully between snow drifts and slick, iced-over puddles. The March wind is extending the winter on this day; it blusters from the north, heaving and howling through the naked trees. The officers are joined by Captain Hillmann's platoon as an escort for the short jaunt from the fort. The platoon's guidon banner, carried by the sergeant in charge, flutters and pops in the wind as the riders advance. In no time the cavalry descends upon Indian Agent Jon Coverdale's home and office.

The contingent reins their horses to a halt. The officers dismount. Major Randolph gives the order as he tosses his reins to the sergeant in charge, "Take our horses out of the wind," he points to the warehouse. "We will be out shortly."

The sergeant nods as two other soldiers gather the colonel's horse and the captain's horse. The platoon moves off across the way, leaving the officers on the porch. The commotion has drawn the attention of Coverdale, and he has come to the door. He stands with a frown on his face, peering from the open door assessing the soldiers and pondering their visit. He turns his frown into a pained, fake smile and invites the soldiers inside, "Come in, come in. Get out of the cold!" He waves his hand motioning the men to enter the building. "To what do I owe this honor of a visit from the cavalry on this desolate winter day?"

"Hello, Jon," Colonel Hagen responds as he crosses the threshold, removes his hat and extends his hand.

Coverdale shakes the colonel's hand as he directs him with his handshake toward the wood burning stove. "Warm yourselves by the stove. It's chilly out there. Winter won't release us from her grasp." Coverdale's face begins to ache as he forces his smile. "Can I get you coffee? Jackson! Get the officers some coffee!"

Jackson James is Coverdale's assistant. A young man in his twenties, fresh from his Eastern education, Jackson took the assignment out West to look for health. His life had been, to this point, without vigor. He often struggled with asthma brought on by the pollution of the crowded cities. He was enjoying a renewed vitality on the windswept prairie. Jackson was a diminutive, bespectacled man, physically fitting the image a bookkeeper might fulfill. "Yes, Mr. Coverdale."

Jackson James leapt from his post at his desk, marking his page with a stiff, flat piece of metal as he closed the ledger. He scurried to the pantry and kitchen area and produced a coffee pot. He filled the pot with water and placed it upon the wood burning stove. "Coffee will be ready in just a few minutes," Jackson announced to the group with genuine glee.

He was happy to have visitors breaking the monotony of balancing numbers in books or transcribing Coverdale's letters all day. After a brief moment in the midst of the soldiers, Jackson retreated to his desk and stood by observing.

"Well, gentleman," Coverdale crisply speaks, "how can I be of service?"

Colonel Hagen gets to the point, "Jon, I have emergency orders for you to take care of." He loosens his coat, reaches into his breast pocket and hands Coverdale a packet of folded papers.

Jon Coverdale takes his time flipping through the papers as he reviews the documents, nodding one moment then proceeding to shake his head disapprovingly the next. Jackson James broke from the safety of his desk area and approached the stove bearing cups. He poured coffee, handing each soldier a steaming, pungent brew. Jackson held the final cup waiting for his boss to finish reading, not wanting to disturb the man and possibly face Coverdale's temperamental wrath. Jon Coverdale's serious, furrowed brow was transformed with a smile as he finally looked up from his reading material. With a nod he accepted the cup of coffee from James, who retreated back to the refuge of his desk to watch the goings-on.

With a careful sip and an "Ah," Coverdale hands the papers back to Colonel Hagen. "This is all very interesting, Colonel, but I do not fall under the authority of your military command."

Colonel Hagen is surprised by Coverdale's dismissal of the request as he pushes the bundle of papers back into the hand of Coverdale. "I'm not sure you understand, Jon. These orders are from Fort Snelling and General Terry himself. The Indians are cold, restless, and hungry. We need to tap into supplies to bridge ourselves to spring. If we're not careful, pretty soon we might have a real problem on our hands."

Colonel Hagen locks eyes with Jon Coverdale, and they stare at each other for a full minute before Jon retreats ever so slightly. Coverdale squeezes the papers in his hand and sips his coffee as he turns to Jackson, "Jackson, could you check and see what supplies might be available for release?" Coverdale turns back to Colonel Hagen, "Colonel, my monthly assignation with the natives distributes prescribed commodities. We have been behind in shipments of supplies. I am reluctant to stick my own neck out for fear of an emergency."

"Mr. Coverdale," the colonel straightens, "this is the emergency you are worried about. If you and I don't take action, you may not have to worry about what's at the end of your neck that you refuse to stick out."

Coverdale swallows hard and glances at the serious expressions on the soldiers' faces. The gravity of the situation registers with the man. "Jackson, what is your ledger telling you?"

"Sir, we have grain and blankets in reserve."

"Very well," Coverdale nods. "I see. If it was anyone but you, Colonel, this might be different. I will do my best to help."

Colonel Hagen nods, "You have my gratitude and my word that if there are ever any questions on your conduct, you will have my support."

"I appreciate that, Colonel." Coverdale turns rigidly, stinging from his capitulation to the soldiers. "Jackson! Get my hat and coat. I am going to the warehouse to check on the stocks. Get the word out that we will make an emergency distribution tomorrow."

"Yes, sir!" Jackson scurries to grab his own coat and hat before retrieving his boss's garments.

*　　*　　*　　*　　*

The Indian agent and his deputy followed the soldiers outside and waved goodbye to the cavalry as the platoon directed their horses back toward the fort. Coverdale was silent as he completed the short walk to the warehouse. He dramatically removed his key ring, found the correct one for the lock, and unshackled the door. The two men moved inside out of the wind, but the building was cold and empty.

"Where is the stock?" a puzzled Jackson observed.

"Mr. James, that seems like a question you'd be able to answer. After all, you're the one with the ledger."

His naïveté evaporated like the fog of his breathe in the cold storage warehouse. Jackson's eyes were opened in that instant. His boss's reluctance to release food stores to a desperate Indian population was revealed. Coverdale could not hand out supplies that weren't there.

"Wha-wha-what are we going to do? We just told the colonel that we would provide emergency rations."

"Mr. James, it appears we have had a break in. Thieves have visited our facility and depleted our provisions." Coverdale pushes back his coat, revealing his holster with pistol as he surveys the vacant building. "You'll have to make out a report."

Jackson James stares at the exposed pistol lost in thought. "It's hard to believe this all happened on your watch," Coverdale smirks as he turns to look at Jackson.

Jackson is focused on the gun hanging from Coverdale's belt. "Huh? I beg your pardon."

"I said," Coverdale continues, "it's hard to believe this happened on your watch."

The first beads of sweat appear above Jackson's lip and on his forehead even in the frozen room.

Coverdale moves toward the door. He extends his gloved hand and slaps it down on Jackson's shoulder. Jackson James flinches. "Come on, Mr. James. Let's get back to the office, and you can work on the paperwork documenting the loss."

Jackson's slackened jaw moves to close, and he swallows hard as his shoulders slump. He follows his boss out the door, wondering what to do.

Chapter 16
Spring Passion

The winter tests one's faith, but believers know that spring is rebirth. Along with the first signs of the green grass prompted by the increasing power of the sun, spring provided a baby boy for Blue Feather. The Indian mid-wife placed the baby in the mother's arms and all was right in the world.

Amidst the backslaps and handshakes from his fellow soldiers, Captain Hillmann handed out cheap cigars to his cavalry brothers. The trading post in Lake City provided the traditional, yet affordable, tobacco announcement of celebration for the new father. Soldiers and Indians reveled in the resurrection of the prairie and its inhabitants as the days got warmer and longer. It was but a temporary pardon from the tensions building. The reservation lifestyle was not taking hold amongst the tribe. The rift formed from the supply shortage during the winter continued to deepen. The trust and reliance of the government had come into question at the elder's councils.

The supply wagons began to steadily stream in from the east leaving plenty of goods in the warehouse. However, agricultural tools and seeds for crops had not been distributed and nerves were taut. A domesticated life was not an existence in which the Lakota were familiar. It was not a surprise to anyone on a sunny spring morning that tempers flared. During a routine supply delivery, as the wagons were off-loaded under the supervision of Indian Agent Coverdale and his able-bodied deputy, Mr. James, the shouting began to rain down from the on-lookers.

Gone were the historic duties of a Lakota warrior. The hunting was now steeply limited due to the unmanaged harvest of the game animals within the reservation. The herds of bison the Indians had followed in their traditional way of life had migrated west, away from the burgeoning settlements of man. In the past, a young man of Indian blood had also wiled away his time defending or conquering his neighboring brothers in constant territorial wars. These times had fallen by the way side. The young men on reservations were without a purpose and loitered around the settlements, bored and restless.

Farming was the activity prescribed by the federal government; however, an agrarian lifestyle was foreign to the natives. Government issued pamphlets and instructions for using tools and seeds required to establish the crops did not sit well with the warriors. No, it was not a surprise that the evolving, mashing, and combining of cultures was only planting the seeds of conflict.

Groups of young men milled around the Agency warehouse. They watched and waited for something, anything to happen as time eased by. The native men, Lakota mostly from Hahn-shkay Ble (the Long Lake) area, were now transplanted to the nearby Indian settlements. All of them had adopted a modern dress of wool trousers and cotton shirts. They wore brimmed hats; some displayed slouch hats offering protection from the sun. Some still wore a combination of buckskin clothing, shirts, trousers fringed with leather strips, and jackets. It was the young Lakota known as Sapa Wapaha (Black Lance), who wore a beaten slouch hat and discarded cavalry blouse that started the shouting. His friends quickly joined their voices with his to express their discontent.

"Coverdale! Coverdale!" Black Lance shouted at the men unloading the wagons into the warehouse. Coverdale refused to acknowledge the raised voice. "Where's our tools? Where's our seed?"

After each barked question from Black Lance, his companions would provide a chorus of affirmation of their own questioning cries. After several minutes of ignoring the onslaught of verbal abuse, Jon Coverdale's mouth curled into a mock smile as he finally acknowledged his jeering section. He handed his clipboard to his deputy with a nod to keep the operation moving. Coverdale ambled from the side of the wagons to a distance halfway between the warehouse and the shade of an ancient oak tree where the would-be warriors gathered. The distance between Coverdale and the antagonizing men was a mere fifteen yards. Coverdale didn't raise his voice in response to the insults that were directed at a steady pace as he stood in place. He folded his arms in a motion that pushed back his black duster revealing a pair of pistols held by a double holster. Gone from Coverdale's wardrobe were frilly collared shirts and East Coast pinstripe suits. Replacing his prissy threads was a tailored, black, woolen suit, white cotton shirt, and a string tie. The tie was an after thought of Coverdale's, a last vestige of his refined upbringing and his call for respect to his position. Topping his "uniform" was the finest, wide-brimmed, black hat, a precursor to the Stetson, found and delivered from Minneapolis. Coverdale now envisioned himself as some sort of gunfighter, a delusion fueled by the trickle of illicit funds he had steadily pocketed from his skimming scheme. Full of this newly found confidence, as false as it may have been, Coverdale confronted his verbal assailants. The young men finished the attack with a final assault of cursing towards Jon Coverdale's mother.

"Are you done? May I speak?" Coverdale shook his head as a mocking smile curled across his lips. He scanned the group of young men numbering ten as he counted. In his mind Coverdale surmised he could still plug all of them with the Colt revolvers strapped to his hips if need be...with two rounds to spare, or heaven forbid if missed, he still had his Derringer in his boot. "Listen to me. My boss, the big Chief in Washington, D.C., has not ordered the release of supplies."

Black Lance laughs condescendingly at the dark figure standing before his group. Coverdale's attempt to pose in an intimidating fashion has only brought forth puzzled looks on the young men's faces. "Look around you, Coverdale." Black Lance lifts his hand above his head. "This tree? It is growing new leaves. The grass. The grass below your feet is green as well as the hillsides. It is time to plant! The government has told us to grow crops, but how can we without the supplies we've been promised?"

Behind Coverdale his deputy, Jackson James raises his hand to stop the unloading process. He sets his clipboard down and moves behind his boss. Jackson has not followed the fashion-conscious lead of his supervisor. He is dressed in his East Coast garb. His silk shirt bears the frilly collar through his pinstriped suit. His head is topped with a derby-style hat that is eventually on its way to evolving into a true stovepipe top hat, but the fashion world of the territories lags a few years behind the United States. The pale, waif-like man looks more a child than a man. His wire rimmed spectacles age his face, providing the only contradiction to his youthful appearance.

"Sir?" Jackson's inquiry spins Coverdale a quarter turn as he flinches toward the unexpected voice behind him. Jon Coverdale's hands bounce to the handles of his pistols. Jackson puts his hands in the air as he absorbs a glowering look from his boss. The subordinate lowers one hand slowly and points to the warehouse, "Can't we at least release some of the tools and seed? It is getting late in the spring planting season. We have fresh stores of both available. Just off the wagons. Can't we make an exception?"

"Jackson, Jackson, Jackson," Coverdale relaxes and heaves a deep sigh of exaggerated disgust toward his underling. "Mr. James," he continues clucking his further disappointment and performing these theatrics on an imaginary stage before his audience of young Lakota men. "We...we," Coverdale points with both hands at his chest, "are in charge. We decide when and what to deliver. We give the orders." The man in charge flings back his duster once again to display his hardware strapped to his sides. He looks again at the Indians eyeing his performance. "Yes, Mr. James, you need to remember who is in charge around here. Do you want to be a deputy the rest of your life?" Coverdale does not take a breath in his melodramatic speech, "I should think not. I'm sure you have great aspirations. Dreams of being in charge...like me. Someday you may find yourself in that position, but you have to learn the lessons I'm trying to teach you."

Jon Coverdale feels his oats and draws a paper from his pocket. It is a blank piece of folded paper, but he creates non-existent orders handed down to him. He unfolds the paper and reads: "From Washington, D.C.," he pauses, "I quote 'To Indian Agents of the Western Territories...seeds and agricultural tools are to be distributed on the fifteenth of the month and no sooner.' Signed by Alvin K. Rodgers, Deputy Secretary of War."

Coverdale waves the paper dramatically in the air before folding and returning it to his inside jacket pocket with a flourish and spin. A gathering crowd of two dozen or so Indians in the vicinity have joined the young men to see what the commotion was about. Jackson James speaks up again, "Mr. Coverdale, what can it hurt? It's just five days before the order; it will keep the natives busy. They can work the soil and sow the seeds."

"Mr. James," Coverdale responds ashamed of his deputy. "Have you not heard a word I said?" The Indian agent turns to the crowd and holds up his hand, fingers extended. "In five days," his voice booms, "we will begin handing out the tools and seeds. Come back in five days to garner your supplies." He pushes his hand higher, "Five days! There's no sense in just hanging around here. Come back in five days!"

A mixture of resentment and excitement resounds from the Indians gathered in numbers reaching four or five dozen. Some are happy to hear the news of seeds and tools; others sense absurdity of the arbitrary and capricious timelines that they are at the mercy of. The soldiers assigned to assist the cargo offloading react nervously to the encroaching crowd.

Jackson James also feels the tensions and discomfort as he returns to his clipboard and accounting responsibilities.

Chapter 17
Restless

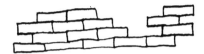

With her husband by her side and her brother sitting across from her in the tepee, Blue Feather serves a late supper to the men. The baby coos in the background, happy to kick and stretch its limbs in the flickering fire light. "What's wrong?" her husband finally asks.

"Hmmm?" Blue Feather returns her attention back to the task at hand, serving the meal.

"You're very quiet tonight. Is something on your mind?"

"It's Coverdale. I was out with Bradley. We had gone to walk. He was fussy, and I thought a walk would put him to sleep." Blue Feather ladles more stew into Curved Wing's bowl. Her brother smiles and mouths a "Thank you," as she continues her story.

"There was a loud confrontation near the warehouse today. The supply wagons continue to come in, and soldiers were unloading the wagons." Blue Feather shakes her head. "I arrived in the middle of the shouting between a group of young men and Mr. Coverdale. The leader of the men was Black Lance. I know him. He is my age. He is from the west of here, the Long Lake area."

Blue Feather holds her hands up moving her thumbs and fingers in a motion like mouths talking, "There was an exchange between Black Lance and Coverdale. The supplies, the tools and the seed, won't be released for five more days." Blue Feather shrugs, "It's going to be too late to plant."

Curved Wing joins the conversation, "I have heard this also. Coverdale rubs people the wrong way."

"That's the other thing," Blue Feather recalls with a shrill flinty voice. "Coverdale, he is dressed all in black with a long duster. He dramatically shows his fancy pistols on his hips. He seems to want to use them."

Curved Wing nods, "The people are restless. They have nothing to do. Planting would keep them busy." Curved Wing looks to Captain

Hillmann, "Do you think we could hire Black Lance as a scout? It would give him something to do rather than stir up trouble."

The captain shrugs. His eyes meet his wife's pleading, brown, doe-eyes, "Can you talk to the colonel again? Please, Gary? Talk to the colonel -- for me."

Her husband shrugs and forces a weak smile, "Yeah, I can say something to Colonel Hagen again. It will have to be next week." Captain Hillmann's eyebrows rise sheepishly, "Your brother and I, we have orders to Fort Ripley. That's why we are so late for supper tonight. We were getting things ready. We leave at first light."

"Oh, I see," Blue Feather drops her eyes to the fire and pokes at the flames with a stick.

"We are escorting arms and ammunition back to the fort," the captain cringes trying to explain to his wife and her hurt feelings. "I'm sorry. I should have mentioned it sooner. It's our protocol. We have to have an extra security squad for arms escort."

"I know. I understand," Blue Feather replies without looking up.

Silence settles over the tepee for a few moments. Curved Wing soaks up the last of his stew with a crust of bread. He leans forward and pats his sister on the shoulder, "Thank you for supper."

She smiles politely back. "Speaking of having orders, I have a favor to ask," Curved Wing states seriously as he stands and prepares to leave.

Blue Feather acknowledges her brother's grave tone with a frown, "Sure, what do you need?"

"It's not that serious, sister," Curved Wing smiles. "It's Jobba, my paint. He's come up with a lame foot. I need you to look after him while I'm gone."

"No problem," Blue Feather heaves a sigh of relief.

"Don't ride him," Curved Wing explains, "Just walk him a couple miles a day. That's what the Doc said. Jobba's at the fort, so you'll have to walk over and get him."

The captain chimes in, "You can put Junior on your back and get out and walk. Get out of the stale air of the tepee and get some of that fresh spring air."

Curved Wing gestures toward the fort, "I told the stable hands to expect you. We'll be back in a week." He looks to the captain, who affirms the statement with a nod.

"I'll do it. I look forward to Jobba's company." Blue Feather stands. She moves forward and hugs her brother. "Be careful...and take care of my husband."

"I will." With a point of a finger towards the captain, Curved Wing exits, "See you in the morning, boss."

Chapter 18
Abercrombie

Fort Abercrombie was another "gateway" to the Dakota Territory. Located on the southeastern tip of what would become North Dakota only two and a half decades after settling, Abercrombie was a busy outpost. Fort Abercrombie was named for Lieutenant John J. Abercrombie, the founder of the fort. He was responsible for the location and construction of the wooden garrison located along the Red River. His selected location proved troublesome due to the habitual flooding of the Red River nearly every spring, but the military post served adequately for a useful twenty years.

Colonel Abercrombie went on to serve with gallantry for the Union in the Civil War following his wilderness deployment to the Dakota Territory. Wounded at the Battle of Seven Pines, he served in less tumultuous commands near Washington, D.C., the rest of the war. Abercrombie eventually retired, brevetted to Brigadier General. Nonetheless, some may argue that a fort named in your stead, may be the highest honor a military man can receive, even if you named it yourself.

In the spring of 1862 Fort Abercrombie was a point of gathering for nations. The Indian nations of the region had come to meet with special envoys from the federal government. The envoys were to hear the complaints of the natives...specifically the conduct of the Indian agents throughout the territory and their poor administration of the treaty requirements agreed upon in the formation of the reservations.

The parties gathered around the expansive wooden table in the commander's office. The table was imported from the East especially for these high level peace talks. It was out of place with the rudimentary furniture of a military fort surrounding it. Also included in the summit were the territorial governors, appointees of the federal government. These men sat at the table with the native Lakota leaders. Chief Red Iron addressed the lead envoy from Washington, D.C. He was a man by the name of Wilhelm Tate. Mr. Tate did not want to be at the meeting. He in fact, preferred the modern confines of the Washington office, but here he was listening to a man dressed in feathers and leather, a savage in his mind. "We have held the peace, but the government has not held its promise." Chief Red Iron paused and surveyed his audience. His mind was taken back to a time in his childhood when no White man breached the Lakota lands. Now he cast his gaze on men wearing uncomfortable, useless clothing. It did not seem possible to have an intelligent discussion with such shameless men. "As my brothers have testified, the Indian agents you have sent to us are not honest. And now you ask for more intrusion on our lands?"

Chief Little Crow picks up the point of Chief Red Iron's statement and question. Chief Little Crow is still the most feared warrior amongst the Lakota and the U.S. Army. As one Cavalry colonel from Fort Ripley had put it, "Chief Little Crow is out of patience. It's not if he will revolt; it's how much damage he and his warriors will do once they start."

It was all rhetoric for Chief Little Crow, and he did not hold back his disdain for the meeting or the men he conversed with on this day, "I cannot speak for Chief Red Iron and his band in the Upper Agency." Chief Little Crow gestured toward Chief Red Iron before balling his hand into a fist and pounding firmly on the table. "The Lower Agency will not stay quiet."

A gasp followed by murmurs rippled through the envoys, governors, and soldiers. As silence returned to the room, Chief Red Iron stood, "The Upper Agency is suffering at the hands of its superintendent. You all know this man, Mr. Coverdale. I have asked for tolerance and peace from my people...but, patience has limits."

Chief Little Crow rose to his feet and joined his fellow Lakota leader. Chief Little Crow was bored with the speeches. With a sneer he spoke, "We have shared our words with you. Time for talking is now over."

For Chief Little Crow, the time for talk had passed months ago; his best warriors were not to be denied. Plans were in motion while the chief had attended the empty talks.

The envoy, Mr. Tate, stood cuing the rest of the attendees to stand, "Thank you, Chief Red Iron. Thank you, Chief Little Crow. I appreciate your candor. I have already asked the governors to send investigators and auditors to review the superintendents' work."

The two chiefs nod in acknowledgement as Mr. Tate continued, "I assure you that I will personally deliver your message to the President in Washington." With a wave of his hand, Tate directed attention to large crates placed near the doors. "We have gifts for you." Mr. Tate maneuvered around the table and signaled to a young man. The man approached carrying two small wooden boxes. "We have medals for the great chiefs to commemorate our talks. These are sent from the fathers in Washington to honor the Indian leaders." Mr. Tate opened one of the boxes displaying the molded silver medallions.

Chief Little Crow waved his hand, refusing the gift and moving toward the door. Chief Red Iron nodded and received the medals. "Thank you. I will see that Chief Little Crow gets his medal."

Chapter 19
Fort Ripley

Fort Ripley, Minnesota Territory

One hundred and forty miles east of Fort Abercrombie, Fort Ripley stood as a nondescript military installation established in the late 1840's. In typical fashion of the day, the fort's mission was primarily to act as a buffer between Indian tribes and the ever increasing White settlers. Rather uniquely, Fort Ripley also was a mitigating factor between feuding factions of Native Americans. The Lakota, the Ho-Chunk, and the Chippewa all had a claim staked in the area surrounding the Minnesota Territory lands. Ripley was the name that was eventually settled upon for the name of the fort after briefly answering to the call of Fort Marcy, then Fort Gaines. Gaines and Ripley, both soldiers having served with distinction in the War of 1812, the moniker, Fort Ripley, won out for unknown reasons and stuck as the name of the garrison in the mosquito infested deciduous-forest wilderness of what was the Minnesota Territory at the time.

Fort Ripley is a hub, bustling with activity. Soldiers march in confined areas, drilling for readiness. Cavalry teams mill around on horses that dance in place, itching for a chance to stretch their legs. In close quarters with the supply stores, the surrounding soldiers encompass Captain Hillmann's platoon, loading the munitions supplies for their wagon train back to Fort Sisseton.

Captain Hillmann whistles loudly between his teeth to get Sergeant Chaffee's attention. Chaffee spins around and nods to the captain. "Chaffee!" Hillmann calls out, "How much longer to load the wagons?"

Chaffee ambles to the captain's side and picks at his teeth with a sliver of wood from one of the boxes of the crated weaponry. Sergeant

Chaffee still drags his words with his Irish accent, "'Tis imminent, Captain. The wagons will be fully loaded and secured within the hour."

"Very good, Sergeant," the captain nods. He dons his riding gloves, leather gauntlets, "Prepare the men to move."

"Aye, sir."

The Captain moves to review the first of three supply clerks' clipboards, noting the receipt of the goods. From the paperwork review, he moves to inspect the crates stability in the wagons. The overland wagon ride will be a grueling test of strength for the transport equipment. With his gloved hands, the captain pushes and pulls on the wooden boxes, testing the chains and straps. All is well, and Captain Hillmann retreats to the supply officer's quarters, a clapboard shack attached to the log constructed warehouse for a final word.

Chapter 20
Jobba

Fort Sisseton, Dakota Territory

In the mid-morning sun, Blue Feather carries her baby on her back as she passes through the Fort Sisseton gate, across the parade area, to the fort's stables. The soldier in charge of the stables is Corporal Mancuso. He is a stocky man of dark-complexion with roots in the Roman Empire. His face lights up as he spies the beautiful woman with a baby, announcing boisterously, "Ahhh! Here she is! This must the captain's wife. And without a doubt, the sister of Curved Wing." He doffs his cap and bows deeply.

Blue Feather smiles and blushes at the introduction and display, "Yes."

"Well then, we've been expecting you. I am Corporal Mancuso. Carmine Mancuso. You may call me Corporal, Corporal Mancuso, Mancuso, Carmine...I answer to any and all of them."

"It is nice to meet you, Corporal."

"I see you have the little one with you today, very nice."

Blue Feather smiles proudly, "This is Bradley. He is named after his grandfather, a General in the U.S. Army."

"You and the captain must be very proud," the corporal and Blue Feather stand in silence a moment. With a sigh and a heave of his shoulders, he steps forward, "Come, let's get Jobba."

Blue feather follows Corporal Mancuso through the stables to the corral where Jobba, the beautiful paint waits for company. His head bobs and his lips sputter at the sight of the pair approaching him. The corporal gathers Jobba and attaches a long lead rope to his bridle. Jobba limps. His front left foot gingerly bears the weight of each step. The soldier walks with Blue Feather toward the gate across the parade grounds. Blue Feather breaks the silence, "Do you think this will help? Me walking Jobba? He is such a beautiful horse, I hate to think this is the end."

"Prepare for the worst; hope for the best. That's my motto," the corporal shrugs. "Horses are beautiful, powerful animals. They are also delicate. One misstep or badger hole, and they are lame. With all the weight over their narrow legs, it might be said that the design of the horse was to look at, not to use."

Jobba nickers behind them at the end of his rope. Blue Feather smiles, "He knows you're talking about him."

Mancuso can't help but laugh, and they continue walking. The pair reaches the fort's gate. "Thank you, Corporal, for your help. I'll have him back in a few hours. We are going to walk to the East Lake and back. I'll be back everyday this week while my husband and brother are gone to Fort Ripley."

Mancuso nods, "Yes, that's the munitions run. That is a full week's ride. The wagons are slow on that route; that cargo is heavy."

"Thank you again."

"It's my pleasure. I know if anyone can help Jobba recover, it's a beautiful attendant like you." The corporal nods to the guards at the gate and waves Blue Feather through toward the beaten path away from the fort. The green grass lining the trail waves and curls in the breeze. Blue Feather walks slowly in the warmth of the sun, towing the ailing horse at a leisurely pace. The baby on her back fidgets a bit and cries. Blue Feather softly sings a soothing Lakota lullaby. Jobba nickers in appreciation.

*　　*　　*　　*　　*

Fort Ripley, Minnesota Territory

With the wagons loaded, secured, and covered in canvas, the order is given to move out, and a dozen wagons exit the gates of Fort Ripley pointed south by southwest. Alpha Company, commanded by Captain Hillmann, escorts the wagon train with twelve mounted soldiers; including the teamsters driving the wagons, the unit is 24 men strong.

Chapter 21
The Hunting Party

Four Mile Lake, Dakota Territory

Four miles nearly due north of Fort Sisseton, a depression carved by the glacier of ten thousand years prior is now filled with water forming the lake designated as Four Mile Lake. The derivative name was a not-so creative naming device of the soldiers first surveying their surroundings. Several of the glacial lakes held similar names, names corresponding to the distance from the fort as the crow flies, Nine Mile Lake, Six Mile Lake, Two Mile Lake, etc. The natives had often referred to the lake as No Shore Lake because of the limited access due to the steep slopes bordering the water.

It was a constant conversation among this particular hunting party comprised of four Lakota men and led by Black Teeth, Curved Wing's long time friend. The twenty-something year old warriors, now turned exclusively to hunters, ventured today on a hunt bordering the area surrounding Four Mile Lake. Black Teeth was the accepted leader of this party that hunted together. They were friends and formed their exclusive party choosing to limit participation to just the four of them. Black Teeth had grown to be a man hardened by his childhood. The derision of his youth addled by the taunts and teasing from peers and adults regarding his weight and his name, Black Teeth formed an outcast of a man. The difficulty of youth forged this man into a steeled and mean soul. The Lakota knew of his anger and dared not cross Black Teeth, but rival tribes would face his anger in a flash if they provoked him. Rage was a useful trait for war, but in peace, rage was a burden for Black Teeth and everyone surrounding him. Compound the personality of Black Teeth with the overall cultural shift the Lakota were undergoing and you have the recipe for upheaval. The Lakota culture was in flux. The nomadic lifestyle was gone. Now confined to the reservation, this was not anything the people had ever seen before. No one knew how to react and adjust to the permanency of the sedentary, new lifestyle.

Crown Fire was another member of this tight knit group. He was the youngest member of the team and a follower. He would do as he was told. Crown Fire enjoyed listening to the rambunctious debates when Cold Water and Black Teeth would spar with their words. He would not join in on the verbal jousting, but that did not mean his passions did not run deep. His resentment for the conceding to the reservation life and the continued maligned treatment of the people by the Indian agents fueled his fire.

Cold Water had married up in life, lifting his station several notches in the Lakota band. Cold Water was married to Black Teeth's sister. By this association, Cold Water had received the automatic bid into Black Teeth's circle of friends. This did not necessarily mean the two braves were copacetic soul mates. In fact, it was quite the opposite, but it benefited both men. Each used the other to be the sounding board for ideas. They were each others devil's advocates. Their constant arguments vetted ideas and philosophies that indubitably would best solve any problems the hunting party crossed.

Rounding out the hunting posse was Rock Knees. The young brave, Rock Knees, was a cousin to the twins of Chief Red Iron, Curved Wing and Blue Feather. He was the son of the twins' mother's sister. He was a big boy, athletic and always up for a physical challenge. Rock Knees had grown up happy-go-lucky in his family, excelling in the challenges of children's games and exhorted by the adults to continue his success. The life he lived and his friendships with his cohorts was something Rock Knees reveled in; the optimistic view was his station in life.

Dressed in buckskin and riding painted ponies for the hunt, the crew trotted across the prairie, braids bouncing rhythmically to the hoof-steps of the horses. Overlooking the steep slope to the waters of Four Mile Lake thirty feet below, Black Teeth reined his horse to a halt. His mates gathered by his side as he surveyed the surroundings and spat forth epithets bent towards the lack of hunting success. The men held their tongues and refrained from making eye contact with their leader, although the corners of Cold Water's mouth tugged upwardly, not able to suppress a smile. As Black Teeth stared into the distance he shook his head in disgust, "I am sick of this. No deer. No pronghorn. No turkeys. We said goodbye to the buffalo years ago. This will not do."

"My wife and child starve." Crown Fire whines, "We find no game. Yet, we all know for a fact, the superintendent sits on stores of food, seeds for planting, and other supplies."

Black Teeth turns to Cold Water and spies his smirking brother-in-law leaning forward resting in his saddle, "Why is this amusing to you? Something has to be done!"

"You've heard Chief Red Iron," Cold Water shrugs, "we are at peace. We are farmers now."

"Do you not listen to what I say?" Crown Fire whines again, "How can we be farmers with no farm equipment or seed?"

Cold Water scowls at Crown Fire, "I heard you! Quit your belly-aching!"

Black Teeth turns his horse and moves between the two men, "Peace!" he gives a nod toward Cold Water. "Chief Red Iron says 'peace.' What does he even know about war to talk about peace?"

"Hush, all of you!" Rock Knees plows into the fray. "Quit your complaining. Come on. Let's hit the trees. We'll find some turkeys." He motions with a nod to the thick stand of oak trees, extending over the hundred acres running along the southwest corner of the lake.

"Fine. But, when I get back...I'm going to give that Indian agent a piece of my Lakota mind!"

Cold Water sneers, "Are you sure you should do that? You don't have a lot to spare." He spurs his horse forward ahead of the group trying to get a distance between himself and Black Teeth before the insult sinks in.

Two men snicker and Black Teeth frowns with a wounded scowl as he digs his heels into the ribs of his roan horse in pursuit of Cold Water. The hunting party rides into the light breeze headed for the oaks. They dip into a wooded ravine and disappear from sight.

Chapter 22
Concessions

1862 – Sisseton Agency

The increasing frequency and volume of Indians gathering each morning outside the agency superintendent's office should have been a tell-tale sign of the discord between the Indians and the new dependent culture being forced upon the tribe. Whether Mr. Jon Coverdale, superintendent, chose to ignore the warning signs of dissension or was oblivious, did not matter. Many natives had reached their breaking point. It was not necessarily a choice for them; it was a last ditch alternative needed to survive.

Jackson James was constantly distracted by the random shouted threats emanating from the crowd outside. He could not concentrate on his appointed duties: the record keeping for the stores of supplies filling the warehouse across the way. As Jackson peered through the window panes, he saw wavy images just twenty or so yards away. The glass in the windows was not high quality and the funhouse images of tall, lanky Indians, next to squat men and women alternated depending on the pane of glass he cast his gaze through. Each day Jackson noted the dress of the gathering crowd. It was always the same; the dark canvas clothes the government issued. Large brimmed, flat-crowned hats were the typical style covering the heads of both the men and women in the so-called street between the warehouse and the agency office. The gauge pronounced by Coverdale was as follows —"As long as the Indians aren't in their buckskins they donned for war clothes, we are ok."

Jackson James came to appreciate a keen eye for fashion as sported by the Indians outside his window. For several minutes Jon Coverdale watched his assistant. The young man stared out the window the whole time. "Mr. James," Coverdale called across the one room office, "What is it that has you so fascinated outside the window that you cannot work?"

"Nothing, sir," Jackson James dipped his pen in ink and ran his finger to the ledger and entered a number.

"Nothing?" Coverdale inquired as he rose from his chair and approached the lad. "You don't seem to be getting much work done."

Coverdale positioned himself between the window and Jackson blocking the view. Coverdale turns his attention from his assistant to the window. "I see a few more unfriendly faces this morning."

"Yes, sir," Jackson replies without looking up from the ledger.

"Still, no buckskin or headbands."

"I don't like it, sir."

"What makes you say that?" Coverdale queries, an eyebrow arched and with his hands clasped behind his back, he looks over his shoulder at his deputy.

"Permission to speak candidly, sir?"

Coverdale waves his hands, "Of course. You are my deputy; I need you to tell me what's on your mind."

"There's more of them out there," Jackson nods toward the window. "Everyday...there's more. We are at the middle of August, and they never got seeds or equipment for planting. The shouting is more frequent. Frankly...I'm scared."

"I see," Coverdale moves forward and puts his hand on his deputy's shoulder. Jackson flinches to the touch, "What do you suggest?"

Jackson flips a few pages in his ledger, "We have plenty of dry goods." He runs his finger through rows and columns of his entries in the large book. "We could release beans and flour..."

Coverdale pats Jackson's shoulder and gives it a squeeze as he interrupts, "Mr. James, you are a good deputy. I think we will do as you say." The superintendent releases his grip on his deputy and turns his attention back to the window and the crowd outside. "I just have one question for you, Mr. James. On whose accord do we release these supplies? We have orders to follow. The regulations state that disbursements shall be made at the first of the month."

"Sir, I have been brushing up on the regulations," Jackson jumps at the chance; he grabs a hardcover book and flips to a dog-eared page. "Right here," James Jackson reads, "The superintendent of the Indian agency shall have broad discretionary power to carryout the appropriate discharge of his duties to provide contingency operations deemed necessary." The deputy looks up at his boss inquisitively.

"And?" Coverdale shrugs.

"And, you are in charge to do what you see fit. That is what the regulation says."

"But, what is the contingency? We have our standing orders to disburse on the first of the month."

"Sir, I beg you. What good are disbursement orders if there is a revolt?"

Jon Coverdale paces casually around the room as he thinks, stopping at each window and surveying the gathered Indians before continuing to pace around the room. He circles the room several times as his deputy observes, afraid to interrupt his superior.

Coverdale finally halts in front of the back door of the agency office. He opens the door and the heat of the August day permeates the room through the breach. The stone building manages the heat well, remaining cool into the late afternoon, but the open door is the opportunity for the thermodynamic balance of the inside and outside air. "You may have a point." Coverdale peers out the back door toward the fort a half mile away. "Yes, you have provided an excellent argument as a good deputy should."

Jackson James nods as his boss turns his head and locks eyes with the lad. "We will make some concessions. Go. Go to the fort and retrieve some soldiers to help us hand out some supplies. I will proceed to the warehouse and announce a mid-month distribution to occur immediately." Coverdale smiles and has his expression reflected by his deputy, "This should provide some calm."

Jackson springs to his feet, lunges for his derby, and jams it on his head. With a wave of his hand he ducks his head under his boss's arm as he bolts out the back door headed for the fort.

Chapter 23
Boiling Over

At the nearby East Lake, Blue Feather leads Jobba along the shore. The narrow strip of sandy shoreline is a perfect area for exercising Jobba's sore leg. The stallion's limp has eased noticeably. The horse playfully trudges along the beach, alternately splashing in the cool water, then on the hardpan, wave-compacted sand, and finally stepping comfortably through the fluffy sand. This area of the shoreline stretches for a half mile or so. The prevailing winds have eroded the glacial boulders and piled the fine sand along the southeastern shore. Baby on her back, horse in tow, Blue Feather enjoys the cool shade of the overhanging oaks as she walks. Enough breeze provides a steady lapping of small waves onto the sandy shore. After this shoreline walk through the sand, they step up onto the grass covered bank that surrounds most of the lake. The stretch of sandy shore is replaced by cattails and tall phragmites. Each quadrant of the lake seems to have its own botanical signature established by years of winds and erosion. On the opposite shore, Blue Feather can see the steep cut bank. The exposed dark soils contrast to the green grass above and the blue sky reflecting off the lake. She stops under the last oak. Under the shade of the tree she inhales deeply as a breeze rustles the leaves overhead. Turning her head skyward with her eyes closed, she breathes in the air, cooling her from the inside out. A smile comes across her face as she opens her eyes and pulls the lead rope towing Jobba close. "How are you doing, boy?"

The horse blows, lips flapping. Its huge head bounces in response to Blue Feather's caress across its nose. "Let's stop in the shade and sit a spell before we head back."

Jobba's tail flicks and flops, whisking away a bevy of flies gathered along the sandy beach. Blue Feather scratches his nose, and Jobba gently nibbles at her fingers. "Grass? Ok, then." She extends the rope to its full length and fastens it to a large fallen limb. "There you go, boy. Have a snack," Blue Feather grunts as she heaves her papoose from her back to check on her son, "Then we'll turn around and get you back to the stables."

Blue Feather inspects her son as she sits in the grass. She removes her moccasins and dangles her feet in the water enjoying the peace and quiet. After deciding to give her weary feet a quick rub down, she lays back in the grass. Head to head with her son, each staring up at the blue sky peeking through the spaces in the old oak tree leaves, Blue Feather sighs. Her son kicks his legs and reaches his hands toward the sky, testing his new found and growing strength of his limbs. "I wish it could be like this forever...peaceful," Blue Feather whispers. She closes her eyes and dozes off.

*   *   *   *   *

With a startled twitch, Blue Feather awakens. Her dream has made her flinch to consciousness again. She looks at the shadows, noting she had only been asleep a few moments. She cocks her head and sees Jobba grazing contentedly. With a sigh she pushes herself to her feet, "Better get back."

Jobba lifts his head as he sees the woman stand. He moves closer to her step by step, nose to the ground, pulling on the tender grasses in the cool shade. As Blue Feather loads her son on her back and is settled, the horse is by her side. His tail brushes her as he flips the coarse whip at the cloud of flies and mosquitoes now gathered. He stamps rhythmically to shoo the pests. "Come on. Let's get moving." Blue Feather releases the loop from the log, and she leads the horse back along the sandy beach. Jobba splashes through the water with each step, happy to get a reprieve from the insects.

Chapter 24
Ignition

Less than a mile and a half from where Blue Feather's horse-healing, walking therapy was occurring, the Indian agency was boiling. The angry momentum of the gathered natives had sunk to a mob mentality. The distribution began in disorder with Indian Agent Jon Coverdale at its center. Coverdale with his loyal deputy by his side checked off the supplies, dispersed with the help of a handful of soldiers, against the names on the clipboard. Scuffles broke out amongst the Indians themselves as they jockeyed for position in line. "People!" Coverdale cried out, "There are plenty of supplies!" The scuffling bodies surged forward, pressing and jostling the Indian agents sorting out the goods. "Please, have some patience as the distribution process commences."

The yelling was fruitless. The first inkling of panic had enveloped Coverdale. He leaned over to his assistant, "Jackson, I need you to go to the fort. You have to summon more soldiers for security." Coverdale held his position against the masses pushing against the doorway to the warehouse. Coverdale and James formed the thin line between the stores and a run on the supplies. With a nod, Jackson James handed over his clipboard to his boss and departed. He pushed through the crowd using all his strength to worm his way through the smallest gaps of the riled natives. The mob was thirty to forty people deep at this point. Coverdale watched his deputy disappear instantly into the heaving sea of humanity.

The Superintendent of Indian Affairs stood on a crate that was assisting in blocking the warehouse door. He screamed and waved his arms over his head, "People! People!"

The clipboard was knocked from his hand. Coverdale's hands went to his waist, "Damn it," he whispered. In his haste to get to the warehouse he had forgotten to strap on his gun belts, a mistake that could not be corrected.

*   *   *   *   *

Jackson James was hustling. He was repeatedly looking over his shoulder as he ran, so much so that he nearly crashed into Blue Feather and Jobba halfway to the fort. The near collision spooked Jobba and the horse danced and bucked at the end of his lead rope as Blue Feather held on to the restraint with two hands. "Mr. James? What's the rush?"

Jackson James hunches over, his hands resting on his knees out of breath. "I'm sorry, Blue Feather," he gasps. "There's trouble at the warehouse. I'm going to get more soldiers."

"More soldiers?" Blue Feather queries as she finally reins in Jobba, "There are already soldiers there?"

Jackson straightens with his hands on his hips still gulping for air. "We were handing out some interim supplies...things just got out of hand," he wheezes. "Please stay away from the Agency until calm is restored. I have to go." Jackson bolts away, but shouts a final warning over his shoulder, "Stay away!"

Chapter 25
Hoofprint

Blue Feather stared at the back of Jackson James gliding through the edge of the woods, finally breaking into the open prairies heading for the guard post at the gate of Fort Sisseton. She tried to absorb the information imparted to her from the Deputy Indian Agent. It didn't make sense. Jackson was clearly out of his mind. She heard a single gun shot in the distance and the eerie howl of simultaneous screaming from afar.

Jobba, calm now, sidled to her and bumped her shoulder. The baby on her back was displeased, and his cries gurgled. She bounced to distract the boy. She towed Jobba to the edge of the stand of trees towards the knoll blocking her view of the agency a half mile away. The breeze had died, and the noises emanating from the disturbance at the agency sounded other worldly. As Blue Feather topped the hill, the agency came into view, and she saw a full-on riot before her eyes. Her mind balked at registering the alien noises and vision presented to her from this distance. The mob moved as one, heaving and swelling like a strange monster. Men and women darted away from the warehouse, hunched over carrying heavy loads on their backs.

Distracted by the scene playing out before her, Blue Feather did not see a disheveled Jon Coverdale running toward her out of breath. "I need your horse!" he commanded as he lunged toward the lead rope.

"No!" Blue Feather sidestepped the man's grab.

"Gimme that horse! I order you to hand over that horse for government security!"

Blue Feather dodged another attempt to commandeer the horse, "This horse is injured and not fit for riding!"

Coverdale's shoulders heaved up and down as he stepped back and glanced over his shoulder to see the pillaging of his warehouse. The three soldiers that had been assisting him with the distribution were high-tailing it across the prairie, back to the fort. He turned his attention back to the matter at hand. Through gritted teeth he growled, "Woman, I need this horse now!" Patience by the wayside, Jon Coverdale lunged at Blue Feather, shoving her to the ground. Her grip steadfastly riveted to the lead rope, the horse's head jerked sharply, following the path of the bridle. The horse spun awkwardly as the baby on her back cried out. Blue Feather screamed out her one-word response, "No!"

Coverdale took a quick look over his shoulder at the horde surrounding the warehouse. In his mind it was not too late to save things. Jobba was not too pleased by the excitement playing out before him, especially the twisting and turning of his lead rope. The aggravated horse fought the halter. He bucked stiffly before kicking up his heels, head drawn down by his lead rope. The series of kicks by Jobba as he fought the rope got wilder and wilder. As Coverdale turned back to the horse, a flailing hoof caught him across the bridge of his nose. The hollow, sickening thump of hoof to head left no doubt...Jon Coverdale dropped stone dead.

Blue Feather screamed. Jobba, fueled by her screams, cries from the baby, and the dead man under foot, bucked wildly. Blue Feather could hold on no longer. The horse broke free and galloped into the woods. "Jobba!" Blue Feather cried in vain. As she pushed herself to her feet, she stared at Jon Coverdale's bloody and mangled face. The skin was peeled back in a hoof print, a u-shaped flap floating in the oozing blood. Yes, Coverdale, Indian Agency Superintendent, was dead, his body lying in the waving prairie grass. Down the hill, his emptied warehouse erupted into flames. Blue Feather took a last look at the corpse, and her eyes were drawn from the body to the flames of the burning building. With her boy firmly strapped to her back and screaming incessantly, she decided she would pursue Jobba. She walked toward the stand of trees while unstrapping the baby from her back. Rocking and shushing the infant she provides comfort to the wailing boy. The shock of what has happened drives her to her knees. She disappears into the tall grass and cries softly, holding the baby tightly in her arms. A few moments pass and the baby is comforted and quiet. Blue Feather gets to her feet. She straps the baby to her back and moves in the direction she had last seen Jobba running. Away, her mind presses her, away from the tumult of the riot playing out at the warehouse. Maybe, just maybe to find Jobba and return, it will have been a bad dream. She moves forward numb.

Chapter 26
Caravan

Agency

The rebellion at the agency has dissipated. Soldiers from the fort survey the damage. The warehouse burns slowly and steadily. Soldiers stare into the flames lost in their thoughts, pondering the future. No effort was made to fight the warehouse fire; it was empty and not worth salvaging. The burned wooden roof could be replaced over the stone walls in the future if the situation would ever warrant it. The agency office of Jon Coverdale was ransacked and bore scars of torches, but it had refused to burn. The chaos distracted the would-be arsonists, and they left the building, retreating with supplies from the warehouse and whatever could be taken and used. The Indians have retreated to their tepees and homes; the men have left the women and children. The warriors have disappeared into the coulees and ravines, banding together to fortify against the soldiers and government they know will soon be seeking answers, justice, and revenge.

The afternoon shadows of the prairie grass wave across the scarred and bloody face of Jon Coverdale. As soldiers move about the agency, assessing the damages, they come across Coverdale's corpse. A soldier leans down and checks for any sign of life. "He's dead. Load him on the wagon. We'll haul his body back to the fort for burial."

"Aye, Sergeant," the two privates respond as they turn and make their way back to the agency for the wagon.

The sergeant stands over the body from the same position, where just hours before, Blue Feather had stood. The sergeant scans the area and the bustling soldiers gathering at the agency buildings. More soldiers on horseback arrive from the fort. The two privates commandeer the wagon tied outside the agency office. He can see the soldiers pointing to where he stands and in a moment the two privates are driving the horse drawn wagon toward him. The sergeant sighs, "It's going to get rough."

*   *   *   *   *

Captain Hillmann rides alongside his friend and chief scout, Curved Wing. They are a couple hundred yards in front of the caravan of wagons. The convoy is returning with its cargo of munitions from Fort Ripley. Slow moving under the heavy loads, the wagons rumble and creak beneath the pale blue afternoon sky. The captain turns to his scout, "What do you think? Should we call it a short day and establish camp here?"

"It's still a full day's ride to the fort. I'm sure the men would appreciate the early day."

The captain nods, "I'll call it then. We'll set the camp there," he points to a grove of trees.

"Looks good," the scout concurs as he turns his horse to face the wagons a few hundred yards away. A wry smile crosses his face, "Race?"

The captain eases his horse to face the wagons as he tries to fight back a smile. The horses beneath the men can sense the tension on their saddles as the men's legs tighten over the animals ribs. "On your mark, Scout. Say the word, and we're on!"

The men hold their horses back. The mounts are ready to run. Curved Wing rides his black stallion, a three year old character, fast and lean. Curved Wing had named the black colt, "Soot," as in the color of charred stains of a fire. He calls out its name soothingly to calm the horse. "Soot, soot, soot," he whispers, mimicking a bird call.

Captain Hillmann sits atop his squat, muscular buckskin stallion, Bucky. Bucky quivers and stomps as he fights the bit and reins, ready to burst forward.

Curved Wing gives a nod to the captain, "Go!"

The men spur their horses and rip forward through the prairie grass neck and neck, racing toward the wagons. The tall grass skims the horses' bellies. The legs of the steeds are obscured by the lush vegetation on the rolling hillsides; this gives the appearance of schooners skimming across the prairie.

Curved Wing pulls into the lead and finishes strong as the winner of the race. The stampeding arrival brings forth curses from the Non-Commissioned Officer In Charge, also known as the NCOIC, Sergeant

Chaffee. "Durn blast it, Captain! You two come charging back here hell bent for fury; it scares the troops, including yours truly."

Captain Hillmann smiles meekly, "I apologize, Sergeant. The scout keeps getting the better of me in these races. I want to try to finally win one of them."

Sergeant Chaffee shakes his head in disgust. "What's the word, Captain?"

"We're knocking off early," Captain Hillmann points to the grove of trees. "Head the wagons over to the trees and set camp for the night."

"Aye," Chaffee salutes.

Part II

"*A man can choose to make war or a man can choose to make peace. I choose to make peace.*"

- Chief Red Iron, 1859

Chapter 27
Farmer Kaufman

Kaufman Farm

Outside of their rough hewn barn Paul Kaufman hitches two horses to the wagon. The sun is setting and his wife, Amy, wrings her hands nervously, "Why do you have to go now? It will be dark soon."

Paul and Amy Kaufman are first generation Americans. Their parents homesteaded the land near the community that would eventually become Brown's Valley, Minnesota. Paul Kaufman ran the family farm since his parents had passed. Paul along with his brother, Karl, who lived less than a mile away, broke more sod every year and were making a successful go of an agrarian life. Having learned to farm at their father's knee in Germany, the boys watched their parents suffer the ruin of the lands purchased by naïve German land barrens and the Rhineland aristocracy. The Elites evicted sharecropping tenants for no other reason than to return the lands to the wilderness for sport hunting reserves. Farm lands were left to nature, and food production, along with the agricultural jobs, dwindled to nothing.   The Kaufman family, having heard of the American opportunities being shared by neighbors, packed up their worldly possessions and immigrated to the burgeoning country of possibility. In a short time, the fertile soils of the Minnesota Territory had been tapped by the Kaufman clan. Through their experience and hard work, they prospered.

Amy was the progeny of the neighboring German enclave by the name of Schmidt. Amy and Paul were married by seventeen and were full partners in the farming operation that Paul inherited just a few years later.

"Karl and I need to leave immediately. We need to have the winter wheat in the ground this week if we are to manage any chance of a harvest next summer. They have what we need in seed stock just outside of Fort Ridgely."

Amy pitches in and fastens the buckles on the harness dangling from the horses nearest her, "Can't you wait until morning? It's...it's just nothing good can come of traveling in the pitch black. What if something happens?"

Paul stops his work and moves to his wife's side. He is tall and wiry. Some would say he looks malnourished. He might agree in some ways with that claim, not because of his wife, but because of his work habits. Paul is the type of man that will not break for a meal. If a job has to be done, it has to be done, no exceptions. Hunger, weather, sickness be damned, the chores are chores, and they have to be done. Amy appreciated her husband's pause. She knows it takes all his power to stop mid-task to come to her side and cradle her in his muscular arms. He hugs and kisses her. He pushes her to arm's length, "Thank you for the clean clothes."

Paul runs his hands through his beard and brushes down his dungarees and Henley. He readjusts his suspenders and straightens his floppy hat. "My clothes probably could have taken on a life of their own."

Amy smiles, "I'll take care of them while you are gone. They won't stand up by themselves when I'm done with them." Amy smoothes her own heavy skirt and striped cotton shirt; her outfit is soiled from her efforts of attacking chores all day.

"I'll bring back supplies also. Maybe some fabric for you." Paul kisses his petite, pretty wife on the forehead.

Amy forces a smile, "I just don't like you traveling at night."

"Don't worry. I'll be back in a couple days. You have Josey and your cousins are just over the hill if something happens."

"Paul, I just..." Amy's voice trails off as her husband pulls her close again.

"Traveling at night is good for us. It'll save us daylight for when we get back. It's like buying an extra day when I am able to accomplish this task at night. You'll see come harvest. We'll get a good return on this investment."

Amy releases a final sigh of submission. With a kiss on the lips from her husband, Paul returns to fixing the last fasteners of the hitch. She hands him a tied kerchief of sandwiches for the trip as he sits down in the wagon, reins in hand. A twitch of the leather reins jolts the horses forward. With an exchange of waves, Paul disappears into the graying evening twilight, leaving Amy with her two boys and a farm to manage for the next few days.

Chapter 28
War Party

Four Mile Lake

The sun sets, leaving the pale pink sky as dusk settles. The wind has relinquished for the day, allowing the chirps of frogs and crickets to resonate among the stand of timber surrounding Four Mile Lake. Black Teeth and his hunting party relax in the twilight as the flickering campfire hosts a portion of the spoils from the day's hunting expedition: a roasting turkey turns at the hand of Black Teeth. He sits, hypnotized and robotically rotating the crude spit to evenly cook the bird.

With the horses fed, watered, and hobbled for the night, the rest of the party tends to their equipment in preparation for tomorrow's continued hunt. The Indian warriors are each in their own world. Cold Water works to sharpen his knife. Rock Knees works the hammer on his single action rifle; he had suffered the indignation of a misfire in the earlier turkey shoot that netted six birds among the four warriors. It was an embarrassment in his failure to contribute, but the shame was compounded by the idea that his peers would consider this disappointing malfunction as a sign of irresponsible character. A failure to maintain equipment may be the first step in sullying a reputation. A warrior's greatest fear was to be thought of as someone who could not be depended upon. He must carry his own weight and be ready to carry more than his share for good of the group.

So, this is the way it was, no one spoke of the incident. Rock Knees' companions knew this could easily happen to them, thus there was no sense in piling on the humiliation. Each sat quietly tending to his task, secretly rejoicing that it wasn't him who failed...this time. It would be forgotten as soon as the hunt started the next morning, but it was a long night for each man to wrestle with his own insecurities.

The thoughts of earlier events were erased in a heartbeat as a commotion in the trees splits the silence of the darkening evening. "Who is there?" shouts Cold Water as he rises to his feet, knife at the ready, blindly grabbing for his rifle as he stares into the shadowy timber.

Rock Knees is immediately in a defensive position, rifle at the ready. He hands Cold Water the elusive rifle that he had been grasping for in the dark. Rock Knees works a cartridge into the chamber as Cold Water sheathes his knife and follows suit. The smooth click of the metal rifle actions pierces the night.

"I said, 'Who is there?' Answer!" Cold Water repeats.

At the threshold of vision from the light provided by the campfire, five Indians on horseback emerge from the trees into the small clearing. "It's me, Fox in The Grass," replies the Indian on the far left of the formation. Fox in The Grass is about forty years old. He is tall and dark skinned. His buckskins reflect the firelight, but his dark complexion appears even darker in the contrasting light. "I'm with my brother, White Blanket. I also have my cousins, Two Bears, Night Eyes, and Goes Quietly."

"I know you," Rock Knees lowers his rifle. "What's the idea of sneaking through the trees? We have a fire. We are not trying to hide." Rock Knees reaches over and pushes down the barrel of Cold Water's rifle still pointed at the group, "A man can get himself killed sneaking around a camp like that."

"You haven't heard, have you?" Fox in The Grass nods. "The people have risen up. We are at war with the White man." Fox in the Grass dismounts. The rest of the party follows his lead. Fox in The Grass hands his reins to his cousin and approaches the fire.

"What are you talking about?" Cold Water insists incredulously.

"You might want to dampen your fire. Who knows what patrol of soldiers might be out there."

Black Teeth nods imperceptibly as he pokes a stick into the burning logs to begin to dismantle the fire. The shocking news from the intruding brethren soaks into the hunting party. "Can we join you? We are hungry," Fox in The Grass questions.

Black Teeth snaps back to the moment, "Yes, by all means, join us. Please tell us what happened."

The visitors remove their gear from the horses and move toward the fire. White Blanket is left to tend to the horses as the men settle near the fire and the sizzling turkey with its enrapturing aroma.

Fox in The Grass sits next to Black Teeth. Black Teeth gives a nod of approval to Fox in The Grass as he continues to turn the spit and tend the fire. "The agency warehouse was emptied by the people and burns as I speak," Fox in The Grass meets the eyes of each man near the fire with his eyes before continuing. "The Agency Superintendent...dead."

The men unconsciously lean away from the news as if softening the blow. Cold Water responds, "Coverdale is dead?"

Fox in The Grass nods affirmatively. "Good," Cold Water responds matter-of-factly. "Couldn't have happened to anyone more deserving."

Rock Knees speaks up, "What did Chief Red Iron say?"

Fox in The Grass points to the north, "He's not around. He's up north with the governors and other chiefs making more talk. More talks of treaties and peace."

Black Teeth glares as Rock Knees, disgusted by the question of Chief Red Iron. He turns his attention to Fox in The Grass. With a nod of his chin toward the warrior he questions, "And you? What is your plan?"

Fox in The Grass shakes his head and shrugs, "All the men have fled the settlements. We are looking to rally as many warriors and figure out what to do."

Black Teeth slowly shakes his head side to side and emits a low whistle. Rock Knees speaks again, "Chief Red Iron is not going to like this."

"Who cares what Red Iron thinks?" Black Teeth snaps.
Rock Knees recoils at the rebuke. Black Teeth's rage is surfacing in his scowl. "All Red Iron has ever done is talk, talk, talk! All at the expense of the people! Peace at the expense of the people!"

Black Teeth searches the eyes of the men surrounding him. He has their undivided attention. "I will not sit back anymore and be told what to do. Not by Red Iron, soldiers, superintendents...no one will tell me what to do...No one." Black Teeth growls his last few words and holds his index finger in the air.

A few grunts of agreement are shared from the men listening. Black Teeth's emotional speech is having the effect he desires. It incites the warriors, and he continues, as he rises to his feet, "I say we go out and take back what is ours! Are you with me?"

The warriors cheer in agreement.

Fox in The Grass stands and extends his arm, "I will ride with you."

Black Teeth grabs the man's elbow, and Fox in the Grass grasps Black Teeth's arm sealing the partnership.

"Rest tonight. Enjoy the turkey. Tomorrow is our day," Black Teeth orders with authority.

Chapter 29
Horizon

Prairie

    Twenty-some odd miles north and east of Fort Sisseton, an area just off the edge of the Coteau des Prairie along an old oxbow that once carried the flows of the Bois de Sioux River, the cavalry company digs in for the night. This is the river that runs north forming the border between the Dakota Territory and the state of Minnesota. Having crossed the river late in the day, Captain Hillmann and the caravan under his command called it an early day. This would be a chance to relax, dry the uniforms, and ease into the confines of Fort Sisseton at a reasonable hour the following day.

    As the sun sets, the first watch is in place, protecting the wagonloads of munitions. The soldiers have been fed and now relax. Captain Hillmann makes a pass on foot through the encampment, greeting the soldiers and checking one last time before dark, the company of men under his command. The soldiers are gathered around the fires; groups are separated into their friends for conversation and final tasks of the evening performed with the aid of firelight. A steady chorus of "Good Evening, Captain," chimes in from each cluster of soldiers.

    The captain provides his own standard response of "As you were," in order for the men to stay in their relaxed positions rather than come to attention. With this informal inspection complete, the captain reaches his own accommodations on the edge of position. The scout, Curved Wing, materializes from the graying light, "Captain, you need to see this. Bring your glass."

    Captain Hillmann cocks his head. He moves to his saddle pack stowed in the lean-to shelter and removes a leather case. He follows the beckoning Indian to a rise forty yards from the canopy of the grove of trees they have settled in for the night. From this elevation change, the men can see over the tops of the oaks. Curved Wing points to an ominous column of smoke outlined against the orange hue of the setting sun. The smoke column has taken on a purplish tint mimicking the scant clouds in the sky. The wind has diminished along with the light of day, and the still air carries the night sounds of the crickets, insects, and a few straggling birds getting to their roosts. In the distance, soldiers muffled laughs and shouts can be heard. "Uh-oh," are the only whispered words shared between the captain and the scout as they contemplate the origins of the wisps of smoke torn apart at the higher elevations.

The captain opens the leather case he has carried to the top of the knoll. He expands a telescope pulled from its protective sheath. He peers through the tube, holding his breath to keep steady. Finally exhaling, he glances toward his scout, "Do you think it is from the fort?"

Curved Wing shrugs, followed quickly with a nod, "I don't know what else it would be."

Captain Hillmann hands the scope to Curved Wing. The blanket of silence is pock marked with a raucous outburst of laughter from the camp behind them. Curved Wing scans the column, fighting the fading light. "I'm worried," Curved Wing breathes his words, "It can't be a wildfire. It's just one narrow column of smoke."

"I'm going ahead tonight to check it out," Captain Hillmann announces.

Curved Wing nods in agreement, "I will go with you. You might need some navigation help in the dark."

The men ease their way down the slope of the hill. "I will go inform the sergeant, get our horses saddled," the captain orders.

With a tip of his hat, Curved Wing peels from the captain's side and lopes toward the picketed horses.

Chapter 30
Cattail Lake

Southeast Shore of Cattail Lake

Nearly three miles from Fort Sisseton and the Agency Village, far enough away to seem like another world secluded from the burning warehouse, Blue Feather followed the tracks of the runaway horse, Jobba. Cattail Lake during times of high water combines with Kettle Lake. Kettle Lake is part of the defensive positioning and strategic protection of the location of Fort Sisseton. The combined lakes cover about 2,700 acres, but more impressive is the meandering shoreline of more than 8 miles in circumference during moisture rich years. In the dry years, individual sloughs and potholes separate from the single body of water, but this year was a wet year, and the lake was a formidable pool. The high waters flooded some of the sandy beaches surrounding the lake and saturated the soils and vegetation ringing Cattail Lake.

Blue Feather followed Jobba, the skitterish stallion some three miles from the outbreak of the revolt. The trail was not too difficult to track. Paths blazed through rushes and hoof prints in the soggy soils marked the horse's free run. As the sun set on the evening, the wind had calmed. During the heat of the day when the wind had gusted and swirled, Jobba had bolted at each passing burst of breeze, sending himself into a headlong sprint away from his pursuer, Blue Feather. A distant glimpse of the horse now and again pushed her spirit on. She was not to be vanquished in her quest to recapture the horse. She had resolved to bring Jobba home. The one step in her mind that might move things back to normalcy and not what she feared, a full-on Indian revolt.

But now, in the breathless air and fading light, Blue Feather found her quarry. Jobba grazed calmly near the southeast shore of Cattail Lake, a point as far from the fort as you could be, but still be adjoining the facility via the body of water. "Easy, Jobba. Good horse," Blue Feather whispered soothingly as she eased forward. The stallion's tail twitched erratically, and his skin quivered, shedding the evening's contingent of flies and mosquitoes out in full force into the calm night air.

"Easy, boy. Easy now," Blue Feather cajoled as she tip-toped forward on tired legs. "That's a good boy."

Blue Feather touched the side of Jobba and ran her hand gently across the steed's ribs. His head remained down, snipping blades of the cool lush grass. She ran her hand forward toward Jobba's thick neck, approaching his massive head. A cough from her baby strapped to her back snapped Jobba's head to an alert position, ready to bolt. It was too late for the horse to continue its freedom run; Blue Feather had her foot on the lead rope still dragging in the grass. The horse felt this pressure on his halter and relaxed. "It's ok. It's ok," Blue Feather continued. She moved her hand stroking the horse's neck, finally moving her hand to his nose and rubbing gently. Jobba peeled his lips back in what one could consider a makeshift smile. He sighed deeply with lips flapping. "That's right. You're safe now. Let's go home."

Blue Feather turned and took her first step toward her home. She saw the column of smoke in the distance and stopped. It was her first reminder of the earlier carnage she witnessed a few hours earlier. The trek around the lake searching for the lost horse had been a pleasant distraction for most of the afternoon, but now she was again aware of the harsh reality of what the future held. She pulled on the lead rope and quickened her pace. The smoke in the distance made her aware that the chase had taken her farther than she realized. She would be heading home in the dark; traveling in the night would be difficult. It was best to try to make the most of the diminishing light.

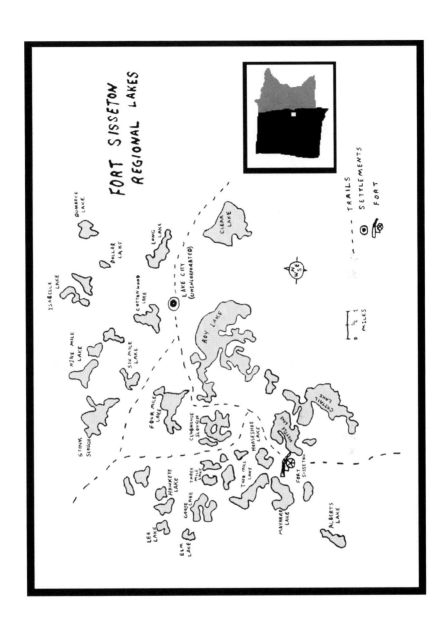

FORT SISSETON
REGIONAL LAKES

TRAILS
SETTLEMENTS
FORT

DUMARCE LAKE
DOLLAR LAKE
LONG LAKE
CLEAR LAKE
ISABELLE LAKE
COTTONWOOD LAKE
LAKE CITY (UNINCORPORATED)
NINE MILE LAKE
SIX MILE LAKE
ADY LAKE
STINK SLOUGH
FOUR MILE LAKE
CLUBHOUSE SLOUGH
HORSESHOE LAKE
CATTAIL LAKE
HAWKEYE LAKE
THREE MILE LAKE
TWO MILE LAKE
KETTLE LAKE
FORT SISSETON
LEE LAKE
GRADE LAKE
ELM LAKE
MAYNARD LAKE
ALBERTS LAKE

0   ½   1
MILES

- 125 -

Chapter 31
Night Ride

Prairie

Alpha Company's cavalry camp had quieted when Captain Hillmann returned to the enlisted population's campfires, marching through to track down Sergeant Chaffee. The captain's curt hellos and crisp salutes dampened the evening's revelry. The soldiers understood something was afoot. At the opposite end of camp from the lone officer, Captain Hillmann, the NCOIC's bivouac was found. This was the bunk of Sergeant Chaffee.

Captain Hillmann found Chaffee relaxing with an evening cup of coffee. Simon Chaffee was a gruff career soldier. His English accent was left over from his emigrant roots some thirty-five years earlier as a six-year old orphaned-boy stepping off the boat with his uncle, having crossed the Atlantic Ocean from just outside Leeds, England. His red hair and ruddy complexion give away his mixed English-Irish heritage. The no-nonsense sergeant sat on a log next to the fire. He stood immediately as the Captain approached, showing respect this late in the evening, even as Captain Hillmann commanded, "As you were."

After an exchange of salutes, Captain Hillmann laid out his observations, "Sorry to bother you so late, Sergeant."

"It's no bother at all, Captain. What's on your mind?"

"Curved Wing spotted a column of smoke. We talked it over and feel pretty confident that something has happened at the fort or the agency."

"Mmm-hmm." Chaffee grunted.

"We're going to ride ahead tonight and try to reach the fort," the captain concluded.

Sergeant Chaffee nodded and sipped at his coffee, hesitating before speaking, "What do you think it is?"

"It's not a wildfire, but it looked like it could be a substantial structure fire at the fort or Agency. I'm not sure, but I'd rather we don't charge into something willy-nilly."

"I see," the sergeant grimaces. "Best not tarry then...be on your way."

"You are in command as the highest ranking soldier in my absence. Your orders shall consist of delaying departure until noon tomorrow. You will double the watch."

"Captain?" the sergeant's face scrunches in full question.

"I don't want all these supplies coming into the fort if there is trouble. When I arrive, I will send reinforcement escorts to meet you. They will tell you if it's all clear."

"Aye, Captain," Sergeant Chaffee affirms his understanding of the commands.

With a flourish, Curved Wing appears on his mount, the captain's horse in tow.

"You have your orders, Sergeant. We'll be on our way."

Sergeant Chaffee gives a nod as Captain Hillmann mounts his horse. "One other thing, Sergeant. I have left my camp in place. Please see that it gets stowed tomorrow."

"Yes, Sir!" Sergeant Chaffee salutes crisply.

Captain Hillmann salutes. Curved Wing spurs his horse west into the last remaining light, and the captain follows suit.

*   *   *   *   *

It was a roller coaster of a ride for the captain and the scout as they traveled from the convoy's camp toward the fort. The degree of difficulty was increased by the darkness and the high clouds that rolled through as a front pushed its way east across the prairie. The moon was blocked by a thin veil of haze and the weakest hint of moonlight and starlight attempting to bore through the atmosphere provided the only illumination. Up and down the men rode at a cautious, but steady gait. More than once the pair dismounted their horses, not to provide a rest for the steeds, but to scale a steep slope of the Coteau's rolling hills. The uneasy ride through the glacier carved hills was a challenge, but the men were up to such a test on this evening.

Not necessarily at breakneck speed, the men cover the roughly thirty miles in just under five hours. Walking their horses side by side as they ride, Captain Hillmann and Curved Wing discuss a plan in near total darkness. They can see each other's silhouette, but not much else. "There is no sign of any flames," Captain Hillmann remarks.

"You can still smell the lingering smoke. The fire likely burned itself out by now," Curved Wing notes.

"I'd like to check on Blue Feather before we do anything. I want to make sure she is ok. She may be able to tell us what happened," the captain whispers. "Best we keep the tones hushed as we get closer. Just in case."

"Yes," Curved Wing grunts.

The men move stealthily in the darkness. Curved Wing guides the pair to the edge of the Indian encampment. Curved Wing halts his horse and reaches back. He grabs the bridle of the captain's horse to stop him. In a tone barely audible, Curved Wing breathes, "We walk from here."

The men dismount and lead their horses through the first cluster of tepees on the outer edge of the settlement. Curved Wing again halts the captain, this time grabbing his arm. Curved Wing points, and whispers, "I see Jobba. He is hobbled outside the tepee."

Curved Wing arm bars the captain from moving forward while he thinks. "Blue Feather was going to exercise Jobba, but why would she not return him to the stables?"

Captain Hillmann pushes Curved Wing aside, "I'm going to find out right now."

*   *   *   *   *

It was still dark. Only a hint of the first inkling of light in the east indicates the dawning of a new day. Captain Hillmann tosses the reins of his horse to Curved Wing. As Curved Wing secures the horses to Jobba, the captain flips open the flap of the tepee. A dozing Blue Feather with her baby by her side is startled by the intrusion. In the dim light of the embers warming a pot of stew, the captain witnesses Blue Feather scramble for the rifle opposite her child. "Easy! It's just me!" the captain cries out as he puts his hands in the air and sweeps his hat from his head.

Blue Feather holds the rifle aimed at the doorway. Curved Wing pokes his head inside the opening, curious to find out about the commotion inside, "Sister, what has happened?"

Blue Feather relaxes and eases the rifle down as Captain Hillmann moves to her side. He drops to his knees and engulfs her in his arms. The silent sobs and shoulder shakes wrack Blue Feather's body while her husband tries to dampen her pain. "Shhh, there, there," the captain offers soothingly. "We're here now. It's fine. You're going to be fine."

Curved Wing eases his way into the tepee. He moves to the baby and squats next to his nephew. He dangles his finger in front of the child, and the child reaches for it. After a few moments Blue Feather has composed herself. She pushes back from her husband as she wipes her eyes and tries to explain, "I don't know what happened. I was walking Jobba for his exercise, like I promised. I hadn't noticed that many more people had gathered around the warehouse and agent's office. There was a rumor that some supplies were going to be released, but as far as I know, it was just a rumor."

Blue Feather wipes her eyes and blows her nose into a kerchief before continuing, "Something happened at the warehouse. I could hear yelling, whoops, and cries, even though I was several hundred yards away."

Blue Feather holds her hands up and shrugs her shoulders, still in disbelief. "Before I knew it, Jon Coverdale was approaching me demanding to take Jobba."

Curved Wing and the captain hang on her words as she pauses. Blue Feather's bottom lip begins to quiver, and her husband reaches out and places his hand on her shoulder, "It's fine, my dear."

Tears stream down her cheeks as she looks past her husband, staring into nothingness, remembering the sickening chain of events that resulted in the death of the Indian agent. She moves her mouth, but no words come. Gary tries to pull his wife close, but she resists. "I want to...I need to tell you what happened."

Curved Wing nods and the captain catches his eye. He turns back to his wife and nods for her to continue. "He again demanded the horse." Blue Feather stares at the wall of the tepee, a far away look in her eye. "I said, 'No.' He pushed me," Blue Feather motions as if holding the rope. "I lost my balance but held the rope as I fell."

Her face scrunches as the memories flow, "When I fell, it jerked the rope attached to Jobba's halter." Her eyes meet her husband's, "Jobba, he's skittish as it is. You don't even need a commotion." Blue Feather's lips curve into a momentary smile before she turns back to the wall and mimes reaching and gripping the rope. "The jerk of the rope swung Jobba's head sharply. Coverdale stepped back as he looked at me on the ground. He turned back to the horse, who had swung around. Jobba bucked wildly and kicked...just once." Blue Feather shudders and sighs, "Jobba's kick caught him square in the face."

Both men's jaws drop. Their eyes widen. Blue Feather stares at the wall, "All the men have left camp. The warriors are preparing for battle."

"Coverdale is dead?" Captain Hillmann questions in disbelief.

Blue Feather turns her attention to her husband, annoyed at the question, "Yes, he's dead! I lost my handle on the rope, and Jobba took off. I spent hours trying to find him. Trailing him. Tracking him. Finally finding him and coaxing him close enough to catch him and bring him back."

The sound of horses' hooves distracts the conversation momentarily. Curved Wing stands, "Someone is outside. I'll go check."

Curved Wing moves to the flap of the tepee, sliding it and revealing the breaking light of dawn. Curved Wing does not exit, but listens as Blue Feather continues. "I didn't even realize how bad things were. I thought I saw the warehouse catch fire. It was a blur. I was so intent on catching Jobba. I wanted to get the image of Coverdale out of my mind. The sound...the sound of the kick..." her voice trails off.

From outside the tepee a terse command is shouted by a soldier, "Everyone inside the tepee, show yourselves!" Major Taber repeats his command.

Curved Wing already poised to exit, emerges from the flap. Sergeant Chilton, one of the members of Major Taber's squadron shouts, "There he is! Get him!"

Chapter 32
Arrested

Indian Camp

    An unsuspecting Curved Wing offers no resistance to soldiers bailing off their horses and tackling him. He is thrown to the ground in a heap and restrained. He is too stunned to vocalize a protest immediately. His head is forced into the ground where he ends up with a mouthful of grass. Curved Wing wrestles and manages a strained, "Hey!"

    Captain Hillmann bursts from the tepee portal and emerges to mounted soldiers and several more soldiers battling a resistant Curved Wing, squirming on the ground.

    "Let that man up, now!" Captain Hillmann orders. The authoritative command freezes everyone momentarily.

    Curved Wing breaks free from the grasp of his captors and bolts to his feet. He escapes to the side of the captain. "What is the meaning of this attack? I demand answers!" Captain Hillmann shouts.

    Major Kip Taber dismounts from his horse. At the recognition of his superior officer, Captain Hillmann comes to attention and salutes, "Major Taber. Good morning."

    Major Taber tugs his gauntlets from his hands and eases over to the captain. He takes his time in returning a salute to Captain Hillmann. "At ease, Captain," Taber motions to the captain with a steadying, palm up gesture. Major Taber is tall, fair-haired, and of Scandinavian descent. He is thirty-plus years old and proudly sports a long, blonde, curled mustache that he is quick to comb with his fingers and twist into shape, an unconscious habit. "Now calm down there, Captain. Let's talk about this."

    Taber moves in front of Captain Hillmann in slow, gliding strides and halts. He tucks his gauntlets into his belt. As Blue Feather emerges from the tepee curious to understand the shuffling and shouting outside, she catches her husband's eye. The captain quickly turns his stare back to the major, absorbing his every move. The major gestures over his shoulder at the soldiers on horseback and to soldiers still catching their breath after wrestling with Curved Wing. "These men were performing their duty. I have orders to arrest the Indian scout, Curved Wing, for the murder of Jon Coverdale."

Blue Feather gasps when she hears the accusation. "No! Has the army lost its mind? I was there! Mr. Coverdale was kicked by a horse!"

Blue Feather charges toward the major and is intercepted by her husband, preventing any physical assault directed toward Taber. Captain Hillmann points to Curved Wing, "You are mistaken, Major. This man is my top scout and my brother-in-law. I can personally vouch for his whereabouts over the last twenty-four hours. We were escorting a supply wagon train. We had camped for the night, we saw smoke, and he and I came directly through the dark of night to this camp." The captain points his finger to the ground.

Major Taber has what some would say an aggravating quality. His most neutral expression is often misinterpreted as a smirk. This is the expression that crossed his face as he processed the information shared by the captain. It was enough to enrage Blue Feather all over again, and she had to be restrained by her husband as one arm held her baby and the other arm flailed inconsequentially at the major. Taber stood in silence eyeing Blue Feather, Curved Wing, and then back to the captain as he mulled over the situation.

Captain Hillmann broke the silence, "Did you hear me, Major? Do you understand what I am telling you?"

The major nods almost imperceptibly, "Well, then," the captain continues. "You know you have the wrong man. Let him go."

The major nods affirmatively and shrugs as he pulls his gauntlets from his belt, "I'm afraid I can't do that, Captain. This man was identified by multiple soldiers as they retreated from the warehouse riot yesterday. We have eyewitnesses." Major Taber points to Jobba. This Indian was with that paint. It is a very distinguished-looking horse. It would be difficult to mistake that horse for another." Major Taber moves toward Jobba. He extends his gloved hand to touch the horse. The horse whinnies and bucks against its hobble, and the major withdraws his hand quickly as he retreats several steps. With his back to the captain, the major points toward Curved Wing, "Regardless of all our talk, I still have my orders. Sergeant, you and your men arrest that man." Major Taber turns back toward the captain, "You understand this, Captain."

Captain Hillmann nods ever so slightly. The sergeant acknowledges the order with a quick salute, and with the soldiers, he moves toward Curved Wing.

Blue Feather riles again as she is held by her husband. "How dare you? You are wrong! I was with the paint! The horse kicked the agent; he kicked him in the face! I was there! You should arrest the horse if want an arrest!"

Captain Hillmann squeezes his wife's wrists to restrain her as she bursts into sobs. The soldiers surround Curved Wing, ready for a fight. Curved Wing looks toward his friend and brother-in-law. A slight shake of the head from Captain Hillmann is enough of a silent communication for Curved Wing to understand the situation. He throws his hands up, and the soldiers bring the shackles forward, clamping his wrists and ankles. Blue Feather spits toward the sergeant. The sergeant, Sergeant Chilton, a diminutive man, known to bear a chip on his shoulder for his inferiority complex related to his size, points at Blue Feather, "Oh, that's very clever, woman. Do you know who Jon Coverdale was? He was appointed as an agent because he knows very important people back East." Anger flares up in the sergeant's eyes as he points a crooked finger at Blue Feather. He moves closer and wags the finger in her face, "Woman, you need to understand; somebody's going to pay for killing an Indian agent, and it sure as Hell ain't gonna be no horse."

"At ease, Sergeant," Major Taber orders. "We have the Indian; he is coming with us."

"Please, Major, don't do this," Captain Hillmann makes a final plea. "This is a mistake."

Major Taber moves to mount his horse. He finds his stirrup with his foot, but before swinging his leg over he offers, "If it is a mistake, we will sort it out." Taber mounts his horse, "Put the prisoner on a horse!"

Blue Feather breaks her husband's grip and runs to the major on his horse. "No! Arrest me! I was there. It was me! My brother did nothing!" Blue Feather is frantic as her brother is lifted atop a horse.

She turns back to her husband, "Gary, stop them! Do something!"

Curved Wing calls down from his horse, "It is nothing, Sister. It is just a misunderstanding. I have done nothing."

Blue Feather falls to her knees, head in hands, sobbing uncontrollably. Captain Hillmann moves to her and kneels down, wrapping his arms around her heaving body. "It's ok. We'll get this figured out."

The soldiers move out with their prisoner in tow as Major Taber hangs behind. "We are taking him back to the brig at the fort. I'm sure the colonel would like to talk to you as soon as possible."

The major spurs his horse forward and rides quickly to catch up to the squadron as Captain Hillmann watches from his knees, his wife's head buried in his chest.

Chapter 33
Messenger

Fort Abercrombie

Just outside the military post where a small community had sprung forth to serve the soldiers, the peace talks between the Indians, State, Territorial, and Federal Governments were proceeding. In the only establishment suited for such a gathering, the boarding house and hotel known as the Willows, hosted the conference. Refined was a relative term on the prairie. The Willows was as refined as it came for this part of the Dakota Territory. Actual china was available as serving porcelain, carted in by wagon from the relatively adjacent city of Minneapolis and the current end of the line for the railroad. The attendees had come in large part to discuss the westward expansion of the rail.

The scheduled four day peace talks had entered the third day. Chief Red Iron had found a man of similar interests in Lieutenant Governor Cashman. Graham Cashman was appointed as Lieutenant Governor of the Dakota Territory. This week he was serving in the governor's stead in the negotiations. Red Iron and Cashman had spent nearly all their free time enjoying each other's company and discussing a shared philosophy on life and humanity. Lieutenant Governor Cashman had just turned forty years old. He was an up and coming politician. His jet black hair and fine features gave him a celebrated and confident look, the envy of many men in his circles. Graham Cashman may have been from Back East, but he had assimilated to the West. He had shed the derby, ascot, and stuffy clothes you would see worn by the federal contingent from Washington. He was accepted by the soldiers, Indians, and citizens of the budding territory. He was a man able to get things done for the people he represented.

Thus it was that the two men, Chief Red Iron and Lieutenant Governor Cashman, were seated next to each other at the table with a view of the street. The pair shared a quiet side conversation while diplomats from Washington, D.C., rambled incoherently citing doctrine and policy, attempting to relate the new Territories to "civilized" parts of the world. The men were the first to see the messenger, a soldier, blaze recklessly down the street occupied by a scattering of merchants, soldiers, and other civilians caught off guard by the messenger's unabashed entrance into the town. The brows of both Chief Red Iron and Cashman furrowed upon the sight of the rider's stark actions perpetrated on the sleepy settlement. Through the wavy images of the simple glass windows of the Willows meeting room, the men could see the messenger throw himself off his horse and sprint through a gathering crowd of curious onlookers at the entrance of the boarding house.

After a brief pause the messenger appeared behind another soldier, a lieutenant, who proceeded to approach the table where a sleepy looking colonel leaned back to listen to a whispering lieutenant. The colonel's face lost all color and nearly fell back in his chair upon the news from the messenger. The colonel, acting solely as host and military observer from the nearby Fort Abercrombie, bolted to his feet. He wavered slightly before steadying himself against the table pausing to gather himself. A low level attaché in the diplomatic party sneered, "If you don't mind, Sir, we are still in conference."

Lieutenant Governor Cashman, ever the professional statesman, provided encouragement to the colonel, "Are you ok, Colonel? What has happened?"

The colonel stammered slightly, but quickly regained his composure, "I-I-I...I have just received a message. I'm sorry to report that we have word from the Fort Sisseton Agency. There has been an Indian rebellion. Indian agent, Jon Coverdale is dead. The warehouse has burned."

Audible gasps circle the table as the news is absorbed. "That's all the details we have," the colonel continues.

Lieutenant Governor Cashman turns to Chief Red Iron. Verbal communication is not needed. The men exchange nods and lead the assembled group away from the table. The other chiefs from the neighboring bands along the Minnesota and Bois de Sioux Rivers, noted leaders Chief Flat Badger, Chief Counts Many Oak, and Chief Dry Rain, excuse themselves and quickly rally with Chief Red Iron away from the group with a noted exception; Lieutenant Governor Cashman sees them off.

Chief Red Iron bows his head, "We all know who is behind this."

They all nod in agreement. Chief Red Iron continues, "The noted absence of Chief Little Crow would seem to speak loudly. He had threatened this for some time, and he has chosen our talks to time his revolt. If it is his actions that have instigated what has taken place in the Upper Agency, *in my People's territory*, we will not tolerate this foolishness."

The Indian leaders stand silently. A simple nod from Lieutenant Governor Cashman acknowledges the gravity of the situation. "We must return to our people," Chief Red Iron makes a final declaration.

"Yes, Chief," the Cashman agrees solemnly, "Please go."

With understated grace, the leadership of the Lakota bands along the Minnesota River and Bois de Sioux River watersheds depart the formal meeting room, each man fearing the worst.

Chapter 34
Collision Course

Prairie

The teamsters driving the supply wagon train, loaded with munitions, are ready to move at first light. Under the command of Sergeant Chaffee the wagon train does not move. Captain Hillmann's orders had been clear: "Don't move until noon. A party will be sent to meet you. I don't want the munitions moving into a trap."

The words rattled around Chaffee's head, exciting every nerve. He had ordered the men to be on high alert. Hasty fighting positions had been dug into a makeshift perimeter. Yes, old Sergeant Chaffee would be prepared. His second in command, Corporal Jones was also of the same ilk, no nonsense. Jones was a young, rail thin, sandy-haired Southern boy. He had ignored the national rumblings of the nation divided and bolted for the furthest western outpost to serve in the military. He had found it and quickly climbed the ranks to corporal. In Sergeant Chaffee's mind, as well as Corporal Jones' mind, they were as ready as they were going to be. "The wagons are ready, Sergeant."

"Very good, Corporal. Tell the men to stand fast. Our orders are to move out at noon."

"Aye, Sergeant, but the men are ready now. They are itching to move."

"We have our orders. Move at noon. We'll feed 'em early, but nobody's gonna move until noon."

"Yes, Sergeant," Jones steps away to start passing the orders, but returns before the sergeant. "Any idea what's going on?" Jones drawls in a more informal conversational pace now that orders have been commanded.

Sergeant Chaffee blows out a deep breath as he checks over his service pistol. In a slow even tone, "None...what...so...ever."

Jones shakes his head from side to side.

Sergeant Chaffee looks up from his pistol to meet the corporal's eyes, "The scout and the captain, they had a gut feeling something was afoot."

"Hmmph," Jones grunts.

"Go on. Pass the orders," Sergeant Chaffee waves away the corporal with a flick of his hand holding the revolver. "Tell the men to be alert. I trust the captain has it on good account that something ill is in the wind."

"Will do, Sergeant." Jones hightails it away from Chaffee, hustling to each man with the orders.

*   *   *   *   *

Near Four Mile Lake

The Indian war party under the leadership of Black Teeth, and camped near Four Mile Lake, begins its preparations at first light. Each man has applied the war paint to both faces and horses. Silently, the rituals are completed and equipment inspected and made ready for battle.

Black Teeth applies the final white circle around his horse's eye, duplicating the one borne across his left brow and cheek. It is an offering, a prayer for vision and full cognizance of surroundings in battle. He whispers to his horse, and the beast responds to its long-time friend and rider with a low nicker. Black Teeth repeats his whisper again louder, "It is a good day to die." The horse bobs its head as if in agreement.

A branch snaps in the deep shadows of the trees holding back the dawning sky. The war party, already on edge, reacts. The metal on metal click clack of rounds chambered into rifles echoes along the line of warriors. They are eager and ready for conflict. The soft hooting of a barn owl calls out. Black Teeth smiles and laughs. He recognizes the bird call. "Father?" he calls into the shadows.

A painted war party of twenty Indians materializes from the shadowy refuge of the trees; the warriors are on foot, painted ponies in tow. Chief Single Eye smiles wryly at his son, "I see you are painted."

"You, as well, father."

"It is a good day to die," Single Eye offers.

Black Teeth nods. He whistles a sharp, two note trill that repeats and gestures for his men to gather. In a moment, the war parties have joined. Thirty warriors strong they gather around their father and son leadership team. Black Teeth speaks first, "Today, we are ready to take back what is rightfully ours." He defers to his father and steps back into the ranks of the other warriors.

"My brothers, it is a glorious day. Soldiers are sitting still with a wagon train of supplies. They are just a short ride to the northeast." Chief Single Eye points northeasterly. "They sit unprotected...a blemish on the hillside. We will take those supplies for the people." Chief Single Eye surveys the warriors surrounding him. "We have a plan. Now mount your horses and ride with me as we strike."

Black Teeth echoes the order, "Mount up!"

The expanded war party of thirty-odd Lakota warriors weaves its way silently through the shadowy forest. Finally they break out into the full light of a rising sun, moving through the low areas of the rolling hills. They ride in silence, only the sound of the hoof steps of the horses emanates, muffled in the breeze and the soft soil along with the dampening effect of the tall grass. Invisible in the shade of the long shadows of the hills etched by the rising sun, the war party makes its way on a collision course with the stationary wagon train.

Chapter 35
First Engagement

Prairie

Under the capable leadership of Sergeant Chaffee, the wagons were arranged strategically on a small knoll on the open prairie. The long views on all sides provided the early warning the contingent would need in an assault. Except for Sergeant Chaffee and Corporal Jones, the men were skeptical of such precautions, most wondered why they hadn't moved out heading back to the fort. Resentment surrounded the soldiers' "make work" attitudes and questions: "Dig more fighting positions? Why can't we just mobilize back to the fort?"

The morning dragged by for the soldiers, who found shade under the wagons, kneeling, sitting, or sprawled in the grass, rifles within reach. The wagons shield the men from the sun, and the breeze was steady, cooling the pleasant morning. Private Kendall along with Private Rankin occupy their post under one of the dozen wagons encircling the hill. Two hours into the stint with two hours before the prescribed time to move out, the soldiers' attention spans were waning. "Geez, this hurry up and wait garbage gets old," Private Kendall offers.

He reaches for his rifle from his cross-legged seated position and pushes himself to a kneeling stance, leaning heavily on his weapon. "I don't know why ol' Sarge just doesn't get us back to the fort. I could use a good night's sleep back on my bed. Lumpy as it is, it's better than the ground."

Kendall rocks back and forth on his knee as he scans the hills for any signs of life. Private Rankin is sprawled out on his back in the shade under the wagon, eyes closed. "I hear ya. It's like nobody actually knows what is going on. Couple more hours, we'll be headed back."

Two horses with riders appear in the distance, and Kendall spies them with a start, "Rankin, I got two riders way out there. They are kind of headed in our direction."

Rankin stirs from his position and joins Kendall, rifle in hand. He kneels next to his buddy, "Who the Hell is it?"

The riders adjust their route paralleling the wagons about a half mile away. "I think it's a couple Indians," Kendall whispers.

Rankin turns and hollers over his shoulder, "We got a couple Indians over here!"

Heads of other soldiers pop up from their positions, and a couple men join Kendall and Rankin under their wagon. "What do you think they're doin'?" Rankin questions.

"They must have seen us and rerouted. They're not comin' up here," Kendall responds. The riders cross the far hillside. The horses walk slowly, easing through the grass rubbing their equine bellies. They disappear momentarily behind a rise before reappearing. "Watch this," Private Kendall grins as he eases his rifle up. He thumbs the rear site to full extension and aims at the Indians over a half mile away. Steadying himself for a kneeling shot he continues to aim.

"Don't do it," Private Rankin advises.

"Take it easy. I'm just gonna try an' scare 'em. I'll shoot way over their heads." Kendall continues to aim.

Rankin shakes his head in disgust, but with a wry smile. He knows nothing he says will change Kendall's mind. "Sarge is gonna be pissed off."

Kendall continues to hold his aim, "Relax already. This is just for a laugh." He squeezes the trigger and touches off the shot. The report echoes over the low hills in the morning silence. A second report, the crack of the bullet hitting the far hillside quickly follows. Whoops and laughter ripple through the soldiers' positions as they can see the two riders break into a gallop.

"Did you see that?" Kendall laughs the words as he lowers the sight on his rifle.

Rankin stands, pulls off his hat, and laughs heartily into the brim trying to fight off the contagious laughter all around him. "You sure scared 'em!" Rankin finally manages through his chortles.

A shot rings out, and Rankin drops dead at the feet of the kneeling Private Kendall. There is no time to react, by the time Kendall looks up, he is felled by a rifle shot. The air is sliced by rifle fire as the Indian war party attacks opposite of the diversionary riders they have sent. It is a rout. Sergeant Chaffee calls out, "Fall back! Fall back!"

There is no place to retreat. No secondary plans were put into place. No attack was expected. The soldiers are cut to pieces by the war party's hail of gun fire. The two dozen soldiers are dead. The Indian attackers suffer the loss of one warrior killed and two other casualties, riders thrown from their horses.

The Indians gather at the wagons and inspect their spoils. "Well done, men," Chief Single Eye lauds his warriors. "We have struck a first blow to our enemies."

Whoops and cries rise up from the warriors. "The Great Spirit is with us today. The wagons are full of rifles and munitions. It is a sign for our cause to continue," Black Teeth offers. "We will deliver the weapons to the People, so we can fight for our freedom."

With a nod to his father, Black Teeth hoists a rifle from a crate over his head. "Enjoy the victory, men!" Chief Single Eye reaches into the crate of rifles and begins tossing the weapons to his cheering warriors.

Chapter 36
A Snake in the Grass

Kaufmann Farm

Ten-year old Daniel Kaufmann plays with his five-year old brother Nate. The boys have constructed a makeshift lake and canal on the shore of the pond near the barn. They float small, hand-carved wooden boats. "Watch this," Daniel tells his brother.

Daniel has dark hair and eyes. He is thin, but healthy. He looks older than his ten-years would indicate. He pulls down his wide-brimmed hat firmly on his head as he digs in the pocket of his bib overalls. He backs up a few paces and begins tossing the pebbles from his pocket at a floating boat. The third stone launched is a direct hit on the biggest boat and it tips over in a splash. "Wow!" Nate calls out, "Can I try?"

Nate is a miniature version of Daniel and mimics his brother in every fashion. From the heavy, canvas, hand-me-down bibs to hat, Nate is just a reduced copy of Daniel. "I need more rocks," Nate states after exhausting the supply provided by his brother.

A middle-aged Indian man appears behind the boys holding a shovel. The boys engrossed in their war games do not notice the man.

"Here you go," Daniel places a handful of pebbles into Nate's grubby paw.

The shadow of the Indian man catches Daniel's eye. The Indian has the shovel raised ready to strike. "Look out, Nate!" Daniel cries.

Daniel shoves Nate to the ground as he dives out of the way. The Indian strikes the ground with the shovel. He turns and shakes his head at the boys sprawled in the grass. He reaches down and picks up the lifeless body of a decapitated rattlesnake. "Geez, Josey! You scared the crap out of me!"

The Indian laughs as Nate's lip quivers. He's on the verge of tears. "Danny, don't use those bad words," Nate's voice cracks, but he does not cry.

Daniel stands and extends his hand to his brother and pulls him to his feet. He brushes off his younger brother's overalls, "There you go. You're fine."

Josey smiles wryly at the youngsters, "How many times have I told you kids to pay attention to your surroundings?"

Josey is about forty-years old. Formerly known as Cuts the Cane, Josey left the Lakota way of life to pursue his interest in farming. He found a willing employer in the Kaufmanns and was learning the skills of modern agriculture in hopes of someday farming on his own. He still sports long, black braids under his tall-crowned, wide-brimmed, slouch hat. He is dressed in a mixture of buckskin shirt and heavy canvas dungarees of a farmer. "What if this snake had gotten you? Your mother would never get over it."

"I'm sorry. You're right, Josey," Daniel acknowledges demurely, but with a quick recovery he turns the table on Josey. "Do you have to sneak up on us like that? You are always sneaking up on us!"

Josey smiles a broad smile and taps his chest, "It's what I do. I am an Indian, I sneak!"

*   *   *   *   *

Amy Kaufmann hangs out the laundry on a line near the house. Josey and the two boys approach the house in the mid-morning sun. Amy spies the trio, "You boys ready for lunch?

"I have supper for tonight, Ms. Kaufmann," Josey holds up the rattler.

"Another rattlesnake? He looks like a big one."

Josey looks down at the boys and back to Amy, "You gotta watch your step. They are thick around here this summer."

Amy smiles, "Mr. Kaufmann should be home in time tonight for some rattler stew. Can you skin it for us, Josey?

"Sure thing."

The Kaufmann farm situated in the fertile valley cut by the Minnesota River helps represent its share of the land of ten-thousand lakes. With sloughs, swamps, ponds, lakes, potholes, and any other name for a body of water, the region is dotted with them. The farm is surrounded. Wetlands are just a stone's throw from the barn, and a nice lake with a sandy shore rests just a quarter mile from the front door.

Amy sets out lunch on an outdoor rough hewn table with logs for stools. Josey joins the boys and Amy for a meal of chicken and fresh bread in the shade of a cottonwood tree, leaves rustling soothingly in a soft breeze.

"What do you boys think?" Amy loads a question, "Should we go to the lake this afternoon?"

The boys cry out in unison, "Yeah!"

"Do you have your chores done?"

"Uh-huh," the boys nod.

Amy smiles at her boys, "Let me ask Josey if he can confirm that you finished your chores, Josey."

Josey smiles, "Yes."

Amy probes, "You don't need their help with the cows?"

"Nope," Josey confirms, "I will be working the team on the south forty. Mr. Kaufmann wants it ready for seed immediately, as soon as he gets back with the wheat stock."

"Alright then, I'll take my sewing and the boys to the lake."

"Can we take the fishin' poles?" Daniel asks.

"Sure. You can swim, fish, and play."

*   *   *   *   *

With lunch over, Amy and her boys venture to the island beach. The beach is located on a finger of land that juts out into the lake, an isthmus that at the present is inundated by the high-water. The family has to doff their shoes to wade across calf deep waves. The short piece is underwater; a moat protecting their prime, sandy beach location. In the cool shade, aided by the breeze off the water, Amy watches her children swim and play in the sand. She sews as the kids frolic in the water. When fatigue sets in, Daniel and Nate turn to their fishing poles. With their bobbers and hooks baited with worms, they lift a steady stream of perch from the lake. The boys fill a bucket with their catch in no time. "Mom," Daniel yells back, "We'll have to have snake stew tomorrow. We got to fry this fish for supper tonight."

"You have to clean them!" Amy calls back.

In a flash Daniel has his knife out. He grabs the bucket and heads to the "butcher block" log his father put in place for filleting the fish. Daniel is proficient even at a young age. He empties the bucket of fish and works the knife, filling the empty bucket with slabs of glistening filets.

Time passes and the supper hour nears, "Come on, boys. It's time to head back," Amy sings out.

"Awww, Mom," Daniel whines. "Can't we fish a little while longer?"

Amy looks back toward the farm, "I guess. Your father's not home yet." She packs up her sewing. "Give me the fish. I'm going to head back and start supper."

She stops stowing her supplies as Daniel hands over the bucket of fish. She wags a finger at the boys, "No swimming. I'm not going to be here to watch you. You can stay and fish, but swimming is over."

The boys nod. Nate adds, "Yes, Momma."

Amy musses the boys' hair, "You listen for the dinner bell. When you hear it, you come straight home."

Both boys respond in unison, "Yes, Momma."

*   *   *   *   *

Amy Kaufmann wades through the water as she departs the island and hits mainland. She dons her shoes and continues her short trek back to the farm loaded down with her sewing and the bucket of fish. The farmyard comes into view and she abruptly halts, still hidden amongst the trees. Near the chicken coop, Josey stands conversing with three young Indian warriors on horseback. Her first qualms manifest in the pit of her stomach. She tenses and looks back to the island where her kids are fishing. The children are out of view from her perspective and facing away from the farm, hidden from the Indians. She makes her decision to continue to the farm.

*   *   *   *   *

Josey is waiting with the Indians as Amy approaches. She has never seen Indians clad as these young men are. They are dressed in buckskin trousers, shirtless, and traces of painted symbols decorate their bodies and faces. The horses are also sporting traces of paint. The paint on the horses and men seems to have been rubbed off or suffered the distortion of perspiration. Amy's senses are on high alert. "Hi, Josey, what is going on?"

Josey removes his hat and holds it with two hands tightly to his chest. His nervousness is obvious to Amy. "Ms. Kauffmann, good evening," Josey announces formally. "These men were wondering if you could provide them some eggs and chickens. They are hungry?"

Amy shrugs, "I would think so. We have plenty to spare." She moves to the adjacent chicken coop and makes eye contact with the warriors towering above her on horseback. "We'll just check for some eggs, and I'll grab a couple of young chickens."

She opens the door of the coop and enters. "I'll help you," Josey calls out and follows after her. Behind her back he gives a nod to the warriors. He draws a pistol from his back stashed in his belt. The door closes behind the pair. The group of warriors watches, still silent.

Inside the chicken coop Amy moves to grab a basket, while quickly sweeping under the closest hen and grabbing an egg. She deftly places the egg in the basket and moves to the next roost. Behind her, Josey has stowed his pistol in his belt. He reaches for a hatchet on a hook. With the smooth action of an experienced butcher, Josey grabs the first hen and lops its head off in the blink of an eye. Blood pours from the decapitated chicken's body, and Josey begins to cover Amy with red, frothy blood. Amy wheels around, screaming at the strange action, "Josey! Stop!"

It is perfect. Just as Josey had planned. He covers her mouth with his hand. He leans close to Amy struggling away from his grasp as he covers her with more chicken blood. Josey hisses, "Those men out there are here to kill you. There has been an Indian revolt."

The terror in Amy's eyes flutters her lids. She's light-headed and starts to go limp. "No, no, no," Josey whispers. "Stay with me."

Amy recovers and Josey takes his hand from her mouth. He whispers, "I am going to fire my gun." Josey tosses down the hatchet and chicken and draws his pistol. The darkened coop dug into the hill side is cool and muggy. Dust swirls in the light of the single window pane. Josey points to the door, "You are going to stagger out that door, out of this coop, and fall down, pretending to be dead." Josey pauses, "Do you understand?"

Amy is dumbstruck. She has no reaction. Josey grabs her wrist with a vise-like grip. He whips her arm and her body follows in the manner a wave travels down a taut line. "They will kill you...you understand."

The jolt through her arm and body aids in the registration of the words, and she nods fearfully. She reaches for the twitching chicken and dabs more blood on her white, cotton top. "I'm going to fire the pistol several times. Inside the coop and when you are out on the ground in plain view of the Indians, I will fire beside you to 'finish you.' Stay still after that. Do not attempt to see what happens after that. Don't look; don't try to find your boys. I'll lead the warriors away from the area."

Josey cocks the pistol, "Scream," he orders Amy.

She screams a blood curdling howl, and Josey fires the pistol, pauses, and fires again. Bursting through the door and down to the ground, she crawls meekly away. A war whoop goes up from the warriors still on horseback twenty-five yards away. Josey steps out the door, sidles over to the flailing woman. Aiming carefully beside Amy's body, he pulls the trigger and she stops moving. Chickens stream from the broken door of the coop, emerging and running underfoot of Josey.

The warriors already have makeshift torches fashioned from rags and oil from the house lamp. A spark from knife on flint ignites the first torch and the others are lit. Two incendiary devices are for the house. The oil lamp dumped on the floor accelerates the burn as the first torch hits it, followed quickly by the second. The third torch is tossed into the hay bales stacked in the barn. The warriors are satisfied with their work. Josey saddles a horse and rides with them. The next farmstead is in their sites just over the hill as flames curl and engulf the house. A black column of smoke towers to the heavens.

Chapter 37
Alone

Kaufmann Farm

It wasn't until the final gunshot that Daniel and Nate were alerted to the situation at the homestead. The boys had been engrossed in fishing. The bite had been strong for almost an hour, and the boys had landed several more nice fish for supper. The shot was an ominous sign. Daniel and Nate had been counseled by their father and Josey many times on gun safety and the value of the bullets. If a gun was fired it had better be for a good reason; that reason was most likely for putting food on the table.

The fishing poles are set aside and Daniel leads Nate to a position on the island where they can see the house. "Was that a shot, Danny?" Nate questioned.

"Shhh, get down," Daniel orders. "I think it was a gun shot." Daniel stares at the scene before him. The shrubs obscure Nate's view as he is unable to see over the scrub oak. He attempts to part the branches, but the vegetation is too thick to see clearly. Nate sees what he thinks is an Indian with his hand on fire, but can't comprehend what his eyes are seeing.

Daniel ducks down and is hidden as he watches the Indian warriors lighting bundles of reeds and tossing them in the house, flames bursting from windows. It is a nightmare. Daniel wants to turn away, but he watches. He sees Josey saddle a horse and join the warriors as they ride away over the opposite hillside.

Daniel sinks down to his knees, eye to eye with his hissing brother, "Danny, what's happened? I can't see. Tell me what you see," Nate pleads to his brother.

Daniel is unresponsive. He is in shock. Nate takes this as a cue to move. He stands and runs, calling for his mother, but Daniel grabs him after just a few steps. Daniel stifles Nate's yells for their mother, covering his mouth with his hand. Nate is frustrated and fights, not understanding why Daniel is wrestling with him.

"Just wait!" Daniel yells in a raspy, hushed tone. "Something has happened at the house. The house is on fire. I can't see Mom or Josey."

Nate's eyes are overflowing with tears, "Let's go home! I wanna go home to Mom!"

Nate pushes away from Daniel and can see the billowing black smoke. Daniel grabs his brother again when he sees he is about to bolt.

"We can't go home. We have to try to get to Uncle Nicky's." Daniel replies without thinking. His head spins.

"What about Mom? Nate questions.

Daniel is smashed by his thoughts, "The gunshot," he mumbles to himself. He knows his mother is dead. The gravity of the situation is throttling his breath; he gasps for air. "We can't...can't," Daniel tries to get control of himself. "We can't stay here," he manages to wheeze. His grip on his brother's arms becomes noticeable; Daniel is aware of his hands squeezing into his brother's biceps and his consciousness sharpens.

Nate is full-on bawling now, "Where's Mom," he blubbers in between heaves.

Daniel lies, "I think she is going to try to get help."

"I want to go with her!" Nate wails.

"We can't, Nate," Daniel offers trying to soothe his brother, "She always told us if something happens, we should get Uncle Nicky. Come on. We have to get moving,"

With nothing but the clothes on their backs, the boys ventured off the island, sneaking in the high reeds of the edge of the sloughs. After about fifteen minutes of slogging through the muck and tangled cattails in silence, Daniel found a fallen tree they could take refuge on. The boys were soaked and soiled from hiding in the weeds. There was still plenty of summer sun, and it was warm. They sat trying to catch their breath when Nate broke the silence with a whisper, "I'm scared, Danny."

Daniel's eyes met his brother's, "Me too."

"Where's Josey?" Nate questioned softly. "Did the Indians take him."

Up to that moment, Daniel had thought that Nate did not see what happened. He had heard Nate call out that he couldn't see. He didn't realize that Nate did witness the events. "What Indians?" Daniel asked to confirm what he feared.

"The Indians that burned the house," Nate replied.

Daniel frowned. He did not know how to respond. Nate continued, "Do you think the Indians took Josey?"

"I don't know," Daniel replied. "Why would the Indians take Josey? He is an Indian."

"Why would the Indians burn our house?" Nate questioned further.

"I don't know. Something must have happened to make them angry," Daniel shakes his head and sighs. He looks to the sky and can see narrow ribbons of smoke from the waning fire above the cattails waving before him.

"Do you think that's why they took Josey, because they are angry?" Nate asks.

Daniel turns his glance to his brother, then quickly back to the sky. He pulls his knees to his chest as he balances on the log. After a long pause, he simply answers, "Yes."

Daniel had always heard the stories of Indian attacks, but it never had made sense to him. The tales he had heard were likened to Grimm's Fairy Tales, The Big Bad Wolf. Wolves existed, but they didn't wear clothes and attack people inside houses. Yes, Daniel had listened to many ugly exaggerations of wild Indians killing settlers, but it was not something his mind could comprehend. Josey, one of his best friends in the world, was an Indian. Josey was a person just like his mom or dad. Daniel shifted. He lay down, his back on the log, hands behind his head and stared at the blue sky, while his thoughts churned. Should he head back to the farm? The curiosity was almost overwhelming. He couldn't though. The Indians may come back. Going to Uncle Nicky's was the thing to do. What had happened though? Why was there a gunshot? Where was Mom? The questions bounced and rattled in his brain.

"Let's go," Daniel bolted upright. He had made the decision to keep moving rather than have his mind keep spinning. "We still have daylight, and we need to use it"

"Why do we have to be in the weeds? I'm wet." Nate whined as he followed his brother, carefully, slowly moving through the reeds.

Daniel patiently turned to his brother, "We need to stay hidden because the Indians might come back. Do you understand? The Indians are still angry, and I want to keep you safe, so we have to stay in the weeds."

Nate shook his head in understanding. Daniel is about to step forward in the ankle deep water, but hesitates. "It will be an adventure. We have to go to Uncle Nicky's, but we have to be as quiet as possible and stay out of sight." Daniel manages a smile, and his brother reflects it.

The boys slink their way through the weeds until they come to the edge of the cattails and a clearing. The clearing is prairie grass, but it has been clipped down to near bare ground by the grazing of the livestock. About twenty-five yards away is another pond. It is encircled by a wide stand of cattails. Remaining in the cattails, Daniel scans the area looking for anything or anyone. He is satisfied they are alone, "Ok, Nate, I'm going to count to three. When I say three, we are going to race to those cattails over there." Daniel points and Nate nods. "One, two, three!"

The boys burst from the weeds and sprint across the open pasture. They dive into the reeds of the adjacent pond and out of sight. They move around this pond the same as before; hiding in the cover of the towering cattails, trudging and tripping through the tangled plants. Feet soaked and fatigued, they push forward, leapfrogging pond by pond, advancing toward Uncle Nicky's.

After two hours of moving steadily, the sky grew pale and the boys rested in a grove of thick shrubs. They were granted a temporary reprieve from the swamp, but they knew they would be back in the water shortly. "I'm hungry," Nate whined to his brother.

"I know. I am too. We have to keep moving. Uncle Nicky will have food. Just try not to think about it."

When they were ready to move, Daniel parted the branches and leaves of the scrub oak. In the distance he could see smoke. Far away on the horizon he could see an Indian war party presumably leaving more casualties and smoking wreckage in their wake. Soon it would be dark, and they could move freely, but fear had repositioned its grasp on the boy. Daniel's thoughts turned to his uncle. What if the Indians had been to Uncle Nicky's? It hadn't dawned on him until now and the realization burned painfully into his consciousness. His head ached from this idea. The physical exhaustion and hunger compounded the throbbing of his head. What else could they do? The plan was to go to Uncle Nicky's. Josey and the Indians had gone in the opposite direction, hadn't they? That's right; it was a good idea. Just keep moving. The brush pile was a familiar place, and Daniel had gotten his bearings. This thick stand of trees and shrubs had always been a good place to bring his slingshot and hunt birds and squirrels. He hadn't had much luck harvesting any game with his trusty slingshot, but what he wouldn't do to have it with him now! He was hungry, and he imagined placing a perfect rock into a rabbit and feasting. He smiled to himself. He gave the signal, and he burst forth from the brush, Nate in tow, and they ran to the cattails encircling the next slough.

The leapfrog exercise of slough to slough ends as night falls. Under the cover of darkness Daniel and Nate move onward. Daniel is confident in his direction even under the faint star light. "I think we are almost there. Just stay with me. Keep up."

"I'm hungry!" Nate whines, breaking from his zombie-like state as he trudges through the prairie grass.

"Me too. We'll have food soon. Uncle Nicky's always got bacon." Daniel's mind wanders as he thinks of food, any kind of food. He shakes the thought from his mind. "Let's keep going."

Daniel looks for a distraction. Something, anything to get their minds off their hunger. He doesn't have to look far, "Listen, do you hear that?"

In the still night, surrounded by the abundant wetlands, the mosquitoes thrive. The high pitched whine of their wings in such great numbers produces an eerie, piercing buzz. It drowns, muffles, and blends with the other sounds of the night; the crickets, the frogs, the hoots of an owl, all diminished by the incessant buzz.

The boys slosh through another swampy area, out of sight in the darkness under the carpeting of grass. "I hear it. The buzzing," Nate questions, "What is it?"

The boys unconsciously swat and fan mosquitoes away. The buzzing wings of one of the blood-sucking insects flying close to an ear interrupts the orchestra of the droning clouds of mosquitoes and ends with a wave of the hand or a slap at the ear. The boys soldier on experiencing a challenge they never imagined.

As Nate falls back, Daniel provides encouragement, "You're doing a great job. We'll get some food in an hour. When we see Ma and Pa, I'm going to tell them how tough you've been."

The darkness conceals the smile Nate bears. It was just the right time to boost him, and his steps quicken, at least for the moment.

*   *   *   *   *

A small grove of trees seems to materialize in from the silvery reflection of a pond. The boys navigate the edge of the pond to the trees that run steeply up a hill. "This is it. This is Uncle Nicky's. These are his trees," Daniel whispers.

They move slowly, weaving through the trees. "We have to be quiet now," Daniel hisses to his brother as they shuffle through the decomposing leaves of the previous year blanketing the forest floor. They crest the hill still in the cover of the trees, "I can barely see the barn over there," Daniel whispers and points.

The steep climb up the hill has winded both boys, and they breathe heavily. The climb combined with the excitement of being close to safety has pumped adrenaline into their bodies and they are alert and on the lookout. "Let's get to the edge of the trees and watch for awhile," Daniel whispers between breaths. They crawl on hands and knees, remaining in the trees. At the tree line they stop and observe, "I can see the house. No lights. Nothing. I don't see anything at all."

Nate stands, "Let's go."

"No," Daniel grabs Nate's shoulder and pushes him back to the ground. "The Indians didn't burn it down, but they might have run Uncle Nicky and his family off, and they could be sleeping here." Daniel stares at the house. "We'll wait ten minutes and just look for any movement."

Daniel positions himself on his belly facing the house and staring, looking for any sign. Nate mimics his brother and lies on his stomach, chin resting on the column of his two fists, just like his older brother. Two minutes pass and Daniel can hear deep breaths, the tell-tale sign of sleep. Daniel turns this attention back to the house, letting his brother sleep. Ten more minutes, then we'll get to the barn Daniel mulls in his mind.

Chapter 38
Hearing

Fort Sisseton

The early light of sunrise pours through the window of the commander's office. This is the residence of Lieutenant Colonel Edwin Hagen. The modest stone and wood, two-story structure is the commander's quarters and head quarters of the post. The first light of day has brought Chief Red Iron, Blue Feather, Captain Hillmann, and Major Taber to the parlor of the residence section of the quarters. With coffee served by Katy, the colonel's housekeeper, the first order of business begins. "Chief Red Iron, I must first thank you for bringing calm to your people," Colonel Hagen addresses Chief Red Iron formally, and the chief bows his head in deference to the words.

"These are very difficult times," Colonel Hagen continues. "I have men scattered across the Territory and into Minnesota. The peace being held in the Upper Agency is noted and reported to Fort Snelling and onto Washington, D.C."

The colonel gestures for everyone to sit. The shabby furniture with worn cushions reflects the untamed territory of the West. The guests shuffle to find a seat, but it becomes obvious that the furnishings are inadequate for the groups needs. "Well, then," the colonel remarks as he centers himself in front of the group, "We shall stand and discuss these matters. I want to first repeat my thanks to the chief. The Upper Agency is the only stable area in the region. I am grateful. We are in your debt." Colonel Hagen sips the last of his coffee and sets his cup aside. "Who would like to begin?"

Major Taber clears his throat, "Colonel, I too would like to extend my thanks to Chief Red Iron." The major waves a hand directing the attention to the chief. "As I understand the reporting, Chief Long Feet and Chief Little Crow are still wreaking havoc all over the Lower Agency. South of Fort Ridgely into Minnesota we are hearing reports of many settlers being killed."

Chief Red Iron halts the conversation with a raise of his hand and a look to Colonel Hagen, "Pardon me, Colonel," the chief turns to Major Taber and acknowledges him, "Major…" Chief Red Iron pauses as he gathers his thoughts. He looks to the light of the new day spilling into the room through the open window. Finally, turning his attention to Colonel Hagen, "Colonel, you know why I am here. My son has been arrested."

Colonel Hagen nods slowly affirming the information. "I am familiar with much of the story about your son, Curved Wing, and Indian agent Jon Coverdale, but please fill in the details."

"Colonel," Captain Hillmann speaks for the first time, turning to Chief Red Iron, "Chief Red Iron, if I may?" The chief gives a wave of his finger from his folded arm and a bow of his head to the captain. "Colonel, I have explained to Major Taber and anyone that will listen that Curved Wing was with me the entire time in question."

"Tell me then," Colonel Hagen flinches in true question, "why do I have multiple soldiers reporting, not only reporting, but giving sworn statements that identify Curved Wing attacking and killing Jon Coverdale? Every eyewitness account is the same. They all identify Curved Wing and his distinct horse, a paint, as confronting Coverdale as he retreated, along with the soldiers, back here to the fort after the initial confrontation.

Silence blankets the room. Blue Feather fidgets. She rocks on her feet before exploding with her pent up story. "Don't you see? They are all mistaken! If someone is responsible, it is me. I should be in jail. I was the Indian they saw with my brother's horse that day." Blue Feather's eyes search the room, bouncing from face to face pleadingly, hoping for an indication of understanding. "Please….please talk to the corporal from the stables. He can verify my story!"

Colonel Hagen folds his arms. His eyes narrow as he casts his gaze to Blue Feather, "Young lady, I know he is your brother, and you want to defend him, but I don't think you understand the gravity of the situation. Are you saying you killed Coverdale?"

The words are barely out of the colonel's mouth before Blue Feather is speaking a mile a minute, "The horse! Don't you understand? It was Jobba, the horse!" Blue Feather's hands flail at her sides. "The horse was frightened by Mr. Coverdale when he tried to grab the reins." Blue Feather's tone changes quickly as she talks, soothingly, pitifully about Jobba. "Jobba has been nursing a bad hoof. I have been exercising him with long walks." She shakes her head in disbelief as she mimes the event. "Mr. Coverdale pushed me." Her tone rises with the excitement of her recitation of the story, "As I fell, I yanked the lead rope turning Jobba, the horse bucked at the sudden commotion. He was spooked, he kicked. The hoof caught Coverdale square in the face." Silence rings through the room. Blue Feather whispers, "He was dead."

Captain Hillmann puts his arm on his wife's shoulder. Blue Feather stares out the window in a daze. She shakes her head and returns her eyes to meet the colonel's. "I had lost my grip on the lead rope after Jobba started bucking. I spent the next several hours chasing and tracking him down."

Colonel Hagen straightens. He places his hands behind his back. He looks at Blue Feather and begins with a monotone laced with the gravest of tones, "That...is an interesting story." The colonel pauses, reviewing his thoughts. "I examined Mr. Coverdale's body. He was beaten beyond recognition. From head to toe. Grass was stuffed in what was left of his mouth." The colonel looks around the room. "Now tell me, does that sound like a horse kicked the man and killed him?"

Blue Feather shakes her head in disbelief. "Are you listening? There was a mob coming after him. He was retreating with the soldiers. That's why he wanted the horse. Coverdale was kicked and killed by a horse!" Blue Feather punctuates her declaration with a finger pointed at the ground. She continues through gritted teeth, "When I left to chase after Jobba, who is to say what the mob did to his corpse. They were angry!" Blue Feather narrows her eyes, "You tell me, did any of those eyewitness soldiers stick around and see the results of the mob's actions? Burning the warehouse? Maybe mutilating a dead man?"

Captain Hillmann steps in front of his wife but picks up her argument losing calm himself. "What is my word worth? What are the orders on record worth? The orders show Curved Wing was with me. I swear to you he was with me." The captain shrugs. "He was assigned to my command escorting the supply wagons, the munitions delivery. He was with me...Sir!"

Chief Red Iron nods to Captain Hillmann. The emotions have boiled over. Blue Feather dabs at her eyes, wiping tears with her buckskin sleeve. Major Taber provides a linen handkerchief to her, and she accepts. Colonel Hagen looks to Major Taber. "What of his supply wagon, Major?"

"Sir, I have sent Lieutenant Jenkins to escort the wagons back," Major Taber confirms.

Captain Hillmann chimes in, "Colonel, Curved Wing and I left the wagons with orders to stay where they were. We noticed smoke on the horizon, right at sunset. We had just made camp. I made the decision that I would not bring the munitions into a potentially hostile situation."

Major Taber and Colonel Hagen nod as they listen to the captain. "I ordered Sergeant Chaffee to stay with the wagons and not venture back until noon. Curved Wing and I rode through the night to investigate."

Captain Hillmann recounts arriving to the Indian encampment and finding Blue Feather scared and alone; Jobba was hobbled outside her tepee. The arrival of Major Taber and the arresting party was detailed by both Taber and Hillmann.

Colonel Hagen listens carefully. He rubs his chin, "It was at that time that you informed Major Taber of the wagons."

Major Taber speaks up, "Colonel, when we apprehended the scout, I immediately ordered Lieutenant Jenkins and Bravo Company to intercept the supply train and provide an escort back to the fort."

"Very well, then," Colonel Hagen concludes. "Hearing that the scout Curved Wing was in the area based on your account of riding through the night, I feel Curved Wing should stay with us in the fort. It is for his own protection."

Chief Red Iron nods.

"Major Taber," the Colonel continues, "I will need to speak to Sergeant Chaffee upon his arrival."

"Yes, Sir,"

"Curved Wing will remain with us at the fort," the Colonel declares. "If there is nothing else, you are dismissed."

Chapter 39
The Mess

Fort Sisseton

As the summer's evening takes hold of the fort, the officers are enjoying coffee in the officers' mess. The mess, or dining area, is for the officers' quarters. There is a limited number of commissioned officers assigned to the post. On this night, all officers are present, except for one. Lieutenant Jenkins is in the field with his company of soldiers on his patrol mission to escort the munitions wagons. Colonel Hagen has joined the junior officers from his residence next door for supper. The other officers include Major Taber, Captain Hillmann, Captain Kelsey, Lieutenant Torrance, and Lieutenant Morrison.

The conversation included business but was for the most part casual and wide ranging. The tension of the Indian revolt seemed distant on the pleasant summer night with a fine meal prepared by the officers' housekeeper, an Indian lady called Jasmine. The final coffee was poured and discussion moved to the front porch to soak in the cool evening air along with the changing palette of the prairie sunset.

The quiet comfort was severed by the commotion of a lone rider galloping at full speed approaching from the fort's gate. The officers, previously sitting, were on their feet watching the horse and rider glide toward them. The dusty soldier reined the horse hard in front of the steps. The horse glistened in the waning sunlight, a sheen of sweat and froth blossomed forth from the horse as it blew and stamped its hooves, trying to recover from the journey. The bedraggled soldier was a private. He held the reins of the horse and stiffened in salute to the gathering of officers above him on the porch. Colonel Hagen steps forward and salutes, "What is it, Private?"

"Sir," the private quickly drops his salute and reaches into his pocket, "I have an urgent message from Lieutenant Jenkins." He extends his shaking hand offering a folded note.

Colonel Hagen nods to Major Taber who steps forward and snatches the note as he orders the soldier to stand at ease. He hands the paper to the colonel. The colonel unfolds the paper and reads the note to himself. "Damn it," he says offering the note to Major Taber.

Taber reads the note aloud, "Twenty-two men killed in action. Charlie Company all dead. Supply wagons gone."

Captain Hillmann staggers at the news. That was his company. His patrol. His men. Friends. All dead. He leans on the railing afraid he may collapse. His head spins. The tin cup of coffee falls from his hand and clanks to the porch spilling its contents.

Colonel Hagen rubs his chin as he contemplates the news. He moves his hand and pinches the bridge of his nose as he closes his eyes tightly. When he finally opens his eyes, he looks to the disappearing sun just now falling behind the horizon. He stares at the empty sky as he makes his pronouncement, "This is enough," he growls. His voice is low and intense, "We are going to clean up this mess now!" He looks at the officers before him. "This revolt ends immediately. I want Alpha Company, Delta Company, and Foxtrot Company mounted and ready first thing in the morning."

"Yes, Colonel," Major Taber nods.

"You will command this mission, Major," Colonel Hagen continues. "I want the Indians that attacked this supply wagon hunted down."

"With pleasure, Colonel," a sneer curls across the Major's lips.

The major turns and focuses on the officers standing in stunned silence, "You heard the colonel, men. Get the word to your men and get your gear ready. We will be on the move at first light!"

The officers scramble back inside to their quarters to prepare. Major Taber waves away the private still standing before him, "Get your horse to the stables then alert the men in the barracks."

The private salutes crisply. Taber casually returns the salute and the soldier mounts his horse and hustles to the stables. Taber disappears into the officers' residence, leaving the colonel with Captain Hillmann still holding on to the porch railing and staring at the ground below him. "You gotta let me go with them, Colonel. Those were my men." Hillmann softly demands without looking up from the railing.

Colonel Hagen approaches the captain and puts his hand on his shoulder, "I need you here for the moment. Your time will come."

Chapter 40
Prisoners

Upper Agency – Chief Red Iron's Camp

Under the cover of darkness, the leaders of the rogue band of Indian warriors have come to seek counsel with Chief Red Iron. In the tepee of the sage leader, Red Iron, Chief Single Eye and the warrior Long Feet are welcomed and entertained. Chief Red Iron smokes in a deliberate manner. He carefully waves the tobacco smoke to his face, eyes closed and drawing deeply, he breathes slowly and steadily. He takes his time, meticulously demonstrating the ritual. Single Eye and Long Feet are impatient, longing to break the silence, but respecting their elder leader and his home, they wait.

Finally opening his eyes and passing the pipe to Single Eye, Chief Red Iron speaks, "You have come to see me in the darkness. What brings you to my home?"

Single Eye rushes to inhale the smoke from the pipe and hand it to Long Feet. He is eager to reply, "Grandfather," Single Eye uses the highest term of respect in addressing Chief Red Iron, though they are not directly related. "We have come to ask you to join us. Join us in our fight. We need your warriors to assure victory on the attack on Fort Ridgely. We have warriors, many warriors. Little Crow…Hollow Horn. They have asked for you. With you we can assure complete victory."

Long Feet passes the pipe back to Chief Red Iron, "We have already had victories! We have many prisoners."

"Yes, so I have heard," Chief Red Iron smokes the pipe and sits silently, eyes closed. The low, flickering fire in the tepee dances and casts stark shadows about the room. Red Iron sits motionless holding the pipe in a pose offering it forward, eyes closed. Minutes pass. Single Eye and Long Feet look to each other, not understanding. More time passes. It is an agonizing wait for the warriors seated with Chief Red Iron.

Chief Red Iron's eyes snap open, and he stares past the two men seated across from him in a trance-like state. The warriors shift uncomfortably, but wait silently. "You will bring your captives to me. I will take custody of all prisoners," Chief Red Iron declares as he looks at the men and hands the pipe to Single Eye.

Long Feet raises an eyebrow, encouraged by what he hears, "You will join us in our fight then?"

"Bring me your prisoners."

"I don't understand," Long Feet is puzzled, "Why do you want the prisoners?"

"I will relieve you of the burden of the women and children you hold captive. That is all I will do."

Chief Single Eye queries, "You will help us?"

"I will take your prisoners," Chief Red Iron repeats, "They are nothing but a burden for you. My tribe will not join in the fight. This war is over, but I will not interfere with your endeavor."

Long Feet and Single Eye look at each other and start to rise. Chief Red Iron holds up his hand and signals the men to remain seated. "You have come here in haste. You do not respect the ritual of smoking the pipe and have rushed to smoke with me as you have rushed to battle. You are making irrational decisions. There was no discussion, no consideration by the elders to declare war. This is a foolish war."

Chief Single Eye bolts to his feet and moves to the flap of the tepee. He does not look back, "Fine. You will have the prisoners." He exits.

Long Feet glares over his shoulder at Single Eye and then back to Red Iron. He rises slowly to his feet and stares down at the elder chief. He extends his arms and hands the pipe to Red Iron and without a word, turns and exits the tepee.

Chapter 41
Refuge

Uncle Nicky's Farm

It is the first light of daybreak. Daniel has nodded off. All his efforts to stay awake and observe the house and barn for activity fell short. A jolt from a dream startles Daniel awake. He suffers the stiff, cold ache in his body from lying on the hard ground in his wet clothes. He feels strange as he does not immediately know where he is, but he quickly gathers his bearings in the low light of dawn. He sees his little brother Nate asleep beside him. Nate has not budged in the night, and the regular deep breaths of slumber continue.

Daniel observes the house from his tree-line position. The boys had settled into the cover of the trees during the night, and the camouflage of the foliage has served them well. He decides that, bearing no indication of movement in the farmyard by sunrise, they will venture to the house for food. The half-hour until sunrise creeps by with Daniel on high alert. He gets more nervous as the time approaches for the move. The orange sky gives way to the yellow orb in the east. The brand new day has begun, and the dingy gloom of dawn is burned away, replaced by the contrasting shadows cast by the rising sun. "Nate, wake up," Daniel shakes his brother, rousing him from his sleep.

Nate lifts his head. He blinks rapidly trying to make sense of where he is. Daniel whispers, "We're going to go to the house and try to get some food."

Nate sleepily stretches, "What?"

"Are you ok?"

Nate starts to get up, "Where are we?"

Daniel pulls his brother down to the ground, "Not yet. Stay down. We're going to make a run for the house, grab whatever food we can, and get to the barn."

Nate is awake. He feels his empty stomach and nods approval of the plan. He waits for Daniel's signal, accustomed to the drill repeated over and over from the previous day, hop-scotching from cattail slough to cattail slough. In a mad dash to the house, the boys break from the tree line and hustle to the one story wooden structure. Bursting through the door, there is no knock or casual greeting; it is in and out for the two boys. Shuffling through cupboards, the quest is successful, a half a loaf of bread and salt pork are confiscated by the hungry pair.

Quickly out of the house and across the open yard, the boys scamper to the barn. In the shade of the barn, backs pressed against the rough board siding, the boys catch their breath searching the surroundings for anything or anyone in the area. After a minute the boys edge their way around the corner of the barn. Daniel finds the latch to the main barn door and pushes his brother through the opening. He follows, quietly closing and latching the door. Inside the darkened barn, the morning sun plays with the clouds of dust kicked up by the boys as they make their way through the hay. The small barn is full of the first cutting of the season's hay. The boys climb into the loft where last year's straw is stored. The straw, used as bedding for the livestock, is an inviting refuge for the boys. The boys flop down in the brittle oat stalks and dig into their food. With a chunk of bread torn from the loaf stuffed in his mouth, Daniel starts to remove his wet clothes, "Get your clothes off. We'll get them hung up to dry."

Nate gets the garbled message from Daniel's mouthful of food and follows suit. Daniel finds a chunk of twine and ties it in the rafters constructing a makeshift clothes line and soon all the clothes are draped and drying. "Why can't we wait in the house?" Nate asks as he relaxes in the straw, gnawing on a chunk of salt pork.

"We can't risk it. If any Indians come, that will be the first place they look. Up here," Daniel points to the open window of the loft, "We can see anybody coming."

Nate accepts the answer and looks out the open window for a few moments, "Danny?" he queries.

"Yeah?"

"Where do you think Uncle Nicky is?"

Daniel stares at the bread in one hand. His glance goes back and forth between salt pork in one hand and bread in the other. He avoids eye contact with his brother. "I don't know," he finally answers. He takes a bite from the bread and shifts his gaze to the window. "I suspect they were warned of the Indians in the area and gathered with the other neighbors." He glances at Nate, who lies in the straw, hands behind his head staring at the rafters. Daniel rips off a chunk of the pork with his teeth. He chews and eases back into the straw, assuming the same position as his brother. "I guess the Indians never came here...otherwise they probably would have burned everything down. Just like our farm."

The boys sit quietly a few moments, each boy lost in thought. Daniel finishes his pork and bread. "What are we going to do?" Nate questions.

"I don't know. I guess we just hide here as long as we can. Soon, Uncle Nicky will come back."

A clunk emanates from below, "What was that?" Nate asks with a low, rasp.

The noise echoes below them again, metal on metal. The barn door creaks open. "Get back. Dig into the straw," Daniel orders his brother.

Nate does as ordered. Daniel scoots to the rail, pressed to the floor of the loft; he peers at the floor of the barn. A shadow darkens the opening of the door. A loud familiar bellowing of a cow rolls through the barn. The cow bawls again to signal her presence. Daniel perks up, "Nate, you want some milk?"

"Yeah!"

The cow enters the barn. Her bag is full of milk and the teats nearly drag on the dirt floor. The fullness is causing discomfort, and she has come to the barn per routine, looking for relief.

The boys scramble down the ladder and find a stool and bucket. They milk the cow and enjoy the fresh, warm, nourishing liquid.

Chapter 42
Pursuit

Outside Fort Sisseton

In the Indian encampment just outside the boundary of the military post, Chief Red Iron's band is still camped. The once desolate camp, void of men is now bustling with the settlers taken prisoner during the many raids over the last few days. Red Iron has worked with the Army to account for the captives, but the Indians have taken to housing, feeding, and caring for their guests. The Army commander has ordered a buffer zone of a half-mile distance between the camp and the post. The fort is not a fort in a traditional sense. It's naturally defended on three sides by water and the open side is guarded by large berms of soil and the companion trench that provided the earthen material. Access to the fort is controlled by the two gates on the prairie side. In the dark of early morning, Captain Hillmann passed through the guard post exiting the fort. The captain rode out on his horse headed to the Indian camp.

*　　*　　*　　*　　*

Before the first hint of light, Captain Hillmann entered his tepee. Inside, Blue Feather senses the movement and stirs from her intermittent sleep, still in the throes of frequent feedings of her baby; her thresholds of sleep are at peak sensitivity.

In a groggy state, but conscious, Blue Feather props herself up on an elbow, "You're here. What has happened?"

In the darkness of the tepee, lit only by the gray starlight of the open flap, Blue Feather can see her husband packing his saddlebag. "I have orders," he announces.

"Orders for what?"

Captain Hillmann moves from his packing to his wife. He wraps his arms around her. "I told you about the supply wagon. Sergeant Chaffee...All my company was lost when Curved Wing and I came back."

The captain still chokes on the words. He can't bring himself to use the word "killed;" instead "lost" seems to be less painful. "I have been assigned to command Lieutenant Jenkins' company. I will be riding with his men," he explains.

"Yes?" Blue Feather questions, still not understanding the orders.

Her husband squeezes her tightly and buries his head in her hair, "Colonel Hagen is sending out all the cavalry. We're getting reinforcements from Fort Snelling and Ridgely. They want this revolt put to an end and justice for those that attacked the wagons." He pushes her hair aside and kisses his wife's cheek, "I'll be back as soon as I can."

Blue Feather pulls her husband and kisses him on the mouth, "Please...just come home."

The captain pulls away, "I have to finish packing. We are leaving at first light." He returns to filling his saddlebags with the necessary equipment in the faint light. Captain Hillmann finishes packing, moves to kiss his wife goodbye. The baby coughs, momentarily distracting the farewell, but an exchange of whispered, "I love you's" punctuates the departure. In the opening of the flap, Blue Feather can make out the half-hearted, crooked smile of her husband and the silhouette of a hand waving goodbye.

Chapter 43
The Brig

Fort Sisseton

In a dark, dank cell, one of three for the military post, Curved Wing sits on the stone floor. The brig, as the jail is referred to in military terms, is truly a penal situation. Barely civilized furnishings of a straw-stuffed mattress, a can for a toilet, and a windowless cube take a mental toll on any detainee. A prisoner of the facility is rarely a repeat visitor. It is a lonely, scary, intimidating place. The iron bars and doors clunk, clank, and thud in the most cold and uncaring fashion.

In a rare situation of human contact for the day, a soldier appears behind the metallic clangs of the outside door opening. He brings a plate of food and a bucket of water. The soldier is Corporal Mancuso. Mancuso's assigned duties as the horse expert, including blacksmith and stableman, have expanded to jailor. "Here you go, Scout." Mancuso opens the slot on the door and slides the tray into the cell. He squeezes the tall narrow bucket of water through between iron bars.

Curved Wing accepts the food and water without a word. Corporal Mancuso continues his one-sided conversation, "Sounds like they are going to stop the revolt once and for all." He turns his back to the iron door and leans on it. "I heard the colonel sent out three cavalry companies, and we're getting support from Fort Snelling and Fort Ridgely." Mancuso turns back around and leans on the bars, facing the door. "It's no fooling around. They are trying to stop the uprising here and now."

Curved Wing nods. Through grate of the iron door, Mancuso can barely see the obscured eyes of the prisoner. The soldier awaits any sort of verbal acknowledgement. None is forthcoming. Mancuso shoves himself away from the cell door. "All right then. I'll talk to you later," the soldier quietly says as he departs.

Corporal Mancuso leaves and the door thumps shut, followed by the click of the metal lock activating. Curved Wing is alone again. He hunches over his plate; he eats the cold food slowly, methodically...keeping his strength.

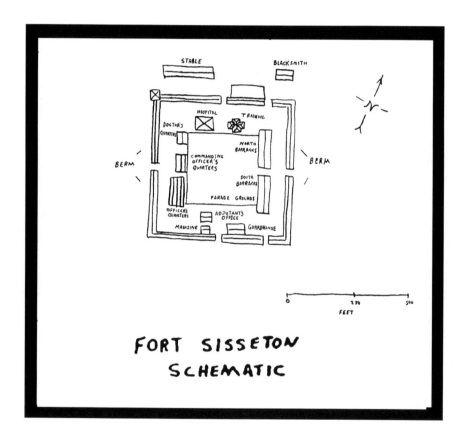

FORT SISSETON
SCHEMATIC

Chapter 44
Tell All

Uncle Nicky's Farm

The days passed slowly for the boys. The boredom of hiding in the barn for two days wore thin on the patience of two active boys. Daniel was lying on his back, hands behind his head in the soft straw. He stares at the rafters, boring holes in the roof with his eyes. Nate plays with a new found toy, a strand of twine. He weaves brittle stalks of oats into the twine. He is engrossed in his task.

Daniel turns his attention to his brother for a moment, then back to his focus on the ceiling. Daniel considers telling his brother about their mom. He had caught a glimpse of her bloody body by the chicken coop. The image was burned into Daniel's head. There would be nothing gained from sharing the fact that their mom was dead. Maybe he would feel better, sharing the burden of knowing this terrible fact. He keeps it to himself, but a tear trickles from his eye. An unconscious reaction to his thoughts, he doesn't cry or whimper. He just can't prevent the welling up of tears, the products of his emotions springing forth. "Are you ok?"

Daniel hears the voice of his brother. It surprises him, and he wipes at the drops on his cheeks. "Are you crying? What's wrong?" Nate queries further.

"I'm fine," Daniel sits up still wiping his eyes. "It's the straw and the dust. It's getting in my eyes."

"Where do you think Mom and Dad are?" Nate asks. Not waiting for an answer, he questions further, "What about Uncle Nicky?"

Daniel knows the truth. His father and uncle would not let Indians stop them from getting to their families. Something has happened to them. He forces himself to lie to his little brother. Daniel shrugs. "Probably watching out for Indians. Pa probably stayed in Ridgely when the Indians attacked." Daniel's head shakes side to side, not believing his own explanation. "Listen, what do you say about going out in the trees?

We can stay hidden in the trees just as good as here, and it gets us out of this dusty old barn."

"Yeah!" Nate cries out.

"We can come back later and milk the cow again. It will give us something to do for awhile."

Daniel smiles. He gets up and moves to the ladder. He climbs down from the loft, followed by his brother. Out of the barn and into the bright sunshine the boys squint. "Race you to the trees," Daniel challenges.

Nate does not wait for discussion; he bolts up the hill toward the trees leaving Daniel with a whining protest, "Hey!"

Chapter 45
Clash

Prairie

The Plains cover more miles than the eye can see. It is often compared to a sea, an ocean of grass. The U.S. Army was not going to be denied in its pursuit of the renegade Indians. Failure for this mission was not an option. The cavalry was assigned the task of squashing the rebellion. They were up to the challenge, and it was apparent immediately. The three companies of cavalry sent from Fort Snelling moved immediately to the southwest, out of their St. Paul, Minnesota location. From Fort Ridgely the three companies of cavalry moved south. From Fort Sisseton, the cavalry pursued south and east. Through the waves of grass the soldiers pursued the Indians. Superior horses, supplies, and the secret weapon, the Indian scouts, dominated the initial skirmishes against the Lakota from the Lower Agency. The Indians were on the run nearly immediately. It was not shaping up as the revolutionaries had imagined. A unified Indian front was never realistic. Chief Little Crow was killed early on in battle. With the head of the snake severed from the serpent, leadership of the warriors was absent.

Now on the run from a motivated cavalry, the Lakota were pushed toward territory of sworn enemies, the Yanktonai Indians and the Winnebago Indians. Options were evaporating, as were the warriors unsatisfied with the leadership. Deserting men, realizing the long odds, disappeared from the ranks of the Indian army.

Barnstorming across the countryside may not have originated in this pursuit, but the Indian warriors in full retreat burned homes, barns, and any structure in their path after pilfering the required supplies. With the aid of the Indian scouts the mounted cavalry was one step ahead of the warriors. The level playing field, based on the strategy advised by the scouts, tilted to the cavalry. There was no where to run for the warriors. The tenacious cavalry had worn the natives down to nothing. Black

Teeth's band made their final stand at the Battle of Oakwood Lake. Chief Single Eye had been wounded early on in the first week of fighting. His left arm hung uselessly by his side. He was one of several injured warriors still pressing on in the fight. The original thirty-plus warriors had dwindled to half that number, and not all were able bodied.

The Battle of Oakwood Lake was to turn the tables on the cavalry. Fifteen Indian warriors were on the offensive now. Moving at night they had come across the camp of Major Taber and his command of three companies spread across the comfortable shoreline. The Indians proposed to strike, resupply, and retreat under the cover of darkness. The confusion of a night fight would aid the aggressors. It was a massacre, but not as the warriors foresaw. The cavalry was taking no chances. Under the advisement of the scouts, each night was a baited trap. And this was the night the trap would be sprung. The cavalry camp had purposely been presenting a seeming vulnerable aspect of the formation. Guards posted, triple the standard number each night, had taken a toll on the men for the last week or so, but it was to pay off.

Black Teeth led his warriors quietly through the oaks surrounding the lake, straight into the quiet camp. It should have been a warning to the Indians, the easy advance through the trees with nary a challenge from a guard post. Blame it on the fatigue of battle over the past seven weeks. Blame it on the running, the constant retreat the warriors faced. It did not register; the lack of resistance the Indians came against should have been an alert. The first volley from the soldiers felled ten out of the fifteen attackers. Dead were Chief Single Eye and Medicine Man, Rain Tree, both were the primary leadership remaining, and now they were gone. Black Teeth escaped initially, but was cornered. When Major Taber arrived on the scene, he witnessed the final fury of a true warrior, the last of its kind. "I want him taken alive!" the major ordered.

Armed with only a knife, Black Teeth had held soldiers at bay for several minutes. The soldiers closed in, and Black Teeth slashed wildly at the troops in the flickering light of the campfires. Multiple soldiers were nicked and wounded by the flashing blade. "You will hang, you savage!" Major Taber yelled at Black Teeth.

Soldiers bobbed and swayed looking for an opening to attack and subdue the Indian. "Alive! I want him alive!" again, Major Taber commanded.

It was not to be. Black Teeth screamed at the soldiers, "You will not take me alive."

Minutes passed in the standoff. Lieutenant Jenkins hustled forward to the side of Major Taber. "Major," Jenkins barked, "We have one. We have a prisoner." The lieutenant gestures toward the Indian scout behind him. "Scout says he recognized our prisoner as Long Feet."

"Good. Good." Taber nods satisfied. "We'll kill this one then." The major shouts to the soldiers, "Kill him!"

Soldiers fall back away from Black Teeth disappearing into the darkness, making way for several armed soldiers to step forward, pistols in hand. Black Teeth relaxed as he saw the fight play out to an end. He stiffened. The hail of gunfire ripped his body to shreds. The burst of fire from the blazing guns strobed the area, and the warrior was dead.

"Bring me the prisoner!" Major Taber shouts.

"He's unconscious, sir." Jenkins answers. "We have him in chains loaded in the wagon with the other prisoners."

"Very good," the major nods satisfied, "We'll head back north to the fort tomorrow. Send a messenger with a scout. Tell them we're headed back with prisoners."

"Aye, Major," the lieutenant affirms.

Chapter 46
Imprisoned

Fort Sisseton

The rebellion was quelled, and the troops returned to their posts. Victorious, Major Taber returned to Fort Sisseton triumphantly, many prisoners in tow. Soldiers had worked quickly to construct a detention facility for the glut of warriors now held as prisoners at the post. All the wire fencing available was strung on large posts encircling an eighty feet by one hundred feet area. The open air detention center held forty prisoners. The minimal security was bolstered by chains. The chains attached to leg irons connected two prisoners together. No detainees were going anywhere under these conditions. Token guards patrolled the "box" as it was referred to by the soldiers.

One particular prisoner had been troublesome from the time he had regained consciousness. Long Feet fought the irons and everything else the soldiers did. Long Feet was going to get special treatment. He was hauled away for custom accommodations.

Inside the fort's brig Curved Wing sits in his cell. He is alone in the building. It is defacto solitary confinement until now. A jingling of keys and echoes outside the outer iron door. The stone building traps all sounds, and they die an echoing death off the walls. The familiar metal on metal tumbling of the lock opening pierces the cool, dark jail. Curved Wing can't quite see the outer door from his cell when he strains to see what is making the noise he is not familiar with. After the clunk of the iron door, he hears a rattling of chains and shuffling of feet. *Another prisoner?* Curved Wing ponders the thought after having been alone in his cell, alone in this building for over a month.

The effervescent Corporal Mancuso announces, "Hey, Scout! I got you some company!" He laughs. The corporal shoves the uncooperative prisoner forward. The question in Curved Wing's mind is quickly answered, provided by the revelation of the prisoner's identity. The new detainee shuffles in front of Curved Wing's cell. Curved Wing peers through the iron bars at his roommate. The iron door of the adjacent cell creaks open.

Long Feet recognizes his fellow prisoner, "Curved Wing?"

"Long Feet," comes the reply as Curved Wing acknowledges his fellow tribesman.

"What did you do? Did you join the revolution? Last I knew you were working for them."

Curved Wing answers slowly, lowly, "It's a misunderstanding."

Long Feet scoffs, "That's a Hell of a misunderstanding. This is where they put the hard cases. They assured me I am going to hang. I assume that's your fate as well."

Curved Wing shakes his head, "You are proud of this?"

Long Feet straightens, "I did what I did to try to help the people. I am proud of that!"

"What did you do?"

"I fought them!" spit flies from his mouth, Long Feet is enraged. "It's more than can be said of your father! Chief Red Iron is a coward! And you...a traitor! Working as a scout for the enemy. You make me sick!"

Long Feet draws his bound hands across his neck as if slitting a throat. Curved Wing stands as his hands curl around the bars of his cell. He pushes forward, scowling at Long Feet through gritted teeth, "Shut your mouth."

"Or what," Long Feet forces a laugh. He looks pitifully at Curved Wing. "This is how they reward you, a *good* Indian. We killed many soldiers. We gave food and supplies to the people! And you? Look at yourself."

Curved Wing shakes his head, irritated, "For what? What did you accomplish? You. You look around. Nothing's changed!" Curved Wing pushes back from the bars against the wall. He slides his back down against the stone wall as he drops to the floor. Long Feet shakes his head pitifully at the Scout, "What did you do?" gesturing to the walls. "Why are you here?"

"I told you it was a misunderstanding."

Mancuso speaks up, "This is the man accused of killing Indian agent Coverdale."

Long Feet's face tightens in surprise as he looks from Mancuso back to Curved Wing. He emits a low whistle as his eyes widen. "Impressive. Congratulations. I'll give you that one. He was a White man that definitely needed killin'." Long Feet lets go an evil laugh. The laugh lasts too long and is uncomfortable.

"I did not kill that man," Curved Wing defends himself.

"No matter," Long Feet shrugs. "It is funny. I would kill you myself, you traitor, but the White man will do it for me." Long Feet laughs again.

"I didn't kill him!" Curved Wing shouts. "You'll see. I'll clear my name."

Long Feet just laughs louder, "Sure. Sure. Sounds like we'll be enjoying each other's company on the gallows. The only regret I am going to have is that I never had a chance to kill that coward father of yours." Long Feet continues to laugh.

Mancuso draws his pistol, "Take it easy, laughing boy."

Corporal Mancuso holds the pistol as he stands away from Long Feet with the gun trained on the middle of the Indian's body. He throws the key to the shackles at the warrior's feet. "Get in your cell and get your chains off."

Long Feet moves into the cell with the shackle key. Mancuso closes the iron-bar gate behind him and locks it. Long Feet bends and works to remove the chains on his ankles. "Don't try anything," Mancuso warns, "I have been told you are a troublemaker. They also told me not to worry about finding a reason to shoot you. Play nice. I let you live."

With the leg irons removed and the wrist shackles away, Long Feet knows the drill. He tosses the chains to the middle of the open floor outside his cell. Mancuso reaches for the chains and hangs them on the wall. "Very good," Mancuso comments as he locks the outer iron door. "Gentleman," Mancuso gives a nod as he departs.

Chapter 47
Uncle Nicky

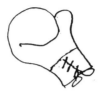

Uncle Nicky's Farm

The dozen or so days the boys had endured had become routine. There was plenty of food. Eggs from the chicken coop; they milked the cow twice a day for fresh milk. The bread had gone quickly, but there was still salt pork. Daniel had paid enough attention to his mother's cooking that he was able fry eggs and salt pork for almost every meal. They had started to use the kitchen in the house for meals, but still bunked and spent most of their time holed up in the loft of the barn. Daniel had even been adventurous enough, and desperate enough for variety, that they had butchered a chicken and attempted to cook it. They had tried this on a couple occasions. After dark they built a fire in the woods and met with limited success of cooking the bird roasted on a spit constructed out of a pitchfork. The second attempt worked much better over the hot coals of the fire, avoiding the flames that charred the skin of the chicken.

The boys passed the time doing chores on the farm. Feeding the chickens and milking the cow were necessary for immediate survival, but pulling weeds and hauling water to the large garden not only passed the time, it provided the future meals for Daniel and Nate. Much of their conversation was spent talking about how they would feed themselves on the thriving vegetables. In short order they would be feasting. But, first were the berries ripening in the scattered woods surrounding the farm. In nearly every direction you traveled from the farm in just a short distance, there was a slough. Near the water on the surrounding slopes you would find shrubs and trees intermixed with the summer's crop of fruit. Berries of all kinds were making themselves available. Every day the boys ventured out with a bucket and returned with enough sweet fruit to satisfy their taste.

There's always some work to do on the farm. Nate and Daniel found they had time to attack the weeds growing in the ten acre stand of wheat. It was ripening and Daniel eyed the scythe in the barn, but refrained from attempting any harvest. The boys pulled the weeds interloping in the green-turning-gold waves of wheat. Daniel made the decision that they would start cutting the wheat and hauling it to the barn in five more days. He had begun marking off days in the barn. He wasn't even sure how long they had been alone, but they now had eight hash marks carved into the rafter in the loft.

The work on the farm was a healthy distraction from the fears: the fear of Indian attack; the fear of never seeing their mother or father again; the fear of being found and taken to an orphanage. The orphanage was a fear that loomed as a fate worse than death. In the stories, rumors, or the threats from angry parents when the boys were acting up, the orphanage had to be the scariest place on earth.

The evening before, the boys had taken to laundering their own clothes. After more than a week, it was decided they probably should wash themselves and their clothes. That was the last order of business of the day. They would bathe and scrub the clothes. They could dry everything overnight in the barn. The evenings had threatened rain nearly every night with successful showers about one out of three nights. The plan was to lounge around until late morning in the barn to make sure the clothes were dry before starting the day. Waking up with the sun, but dozing on and off for a couple hours, Daniel finally checked the clothes. "Dry enough," he told Nate. They were anxious to pick berries and get some food in their stomachs.

In the loft, buttoning the last button and ready to descend the ladder, the routine came to a halt. The distinct squeak of the barn door opening sent the boys scrambling to the safety of the straw piles of their makeshift beds. Daniel held his finger to his lips to shush Nate. Nate followed the order. He was too scared to make a sound, and his eyes were as wide as saucers as he sought comfort and reassurance from his big brother.

A gruff voice said, "Check the barn."

Daniel peered carefully over the mound of straw. When the darkened door released its occupier, it revealed a heavyset man in suspenders and a large floppy hat. Another shadow darkens the door. Another man with a large hat obscuring his face joins the first man. The man with the floppy hat shakes his head, "Nothing in here, Nicky. I can't believe they didn't burn your place down."

The commotion in the hay loft catches the men off guard. "Hey, what's that?" the man with the floppy hat shouts.

"Uncle Nicky! It's us!" Daniel shouts as he makes his way down the ladder followed by Nate.

"Nate? Daniel?" Uncle Nicky crouches down and grabs the boys in his open arms. "What are you doing here?"

"We've been hiding here," Daniel explains. "The Indians burned our place down."

"I know. I just left your pa there," Uncle Nicky smiles. "I'll take you back there right now. He's been sick with worry." He stands lifting and hugging the boys. "I can't believe I found you."

Uncle Nicky is cut from the same bolt of cloth as his brother, Paul Kauffmann. The older of the two, Nicholas, or Nicky, since no one called him by his formal name, was the kind-hearted uncle that every niece or nephew needed or wanted. He was thicker and shorter than his brother, and he had always sported a full beard from the time he could grow one. He represented a Santa Claus figure to his young nephews. Surprisingly light on his feet and the strongest, toughest man in the valley, he consistently amazed his brother and nephews with his antics whether dealing with irritated livestock or simply lifting timber or equipment. He was a man in all sense of the word. His athletic prowess was known to even a wider audience thanks to some sanctioned boxing in his youth along with some ornery roustabouts that overstayed their welcome in the valley. Nicky had sent them "cheerfully on their way" as he described it. The scar on his knuckle, a product of an imbedded tooth told a different tale regarding the unwelcome visitors' decisions to move along. Nicky worked and worked, and then he worked some more. He was a widower at a young age and never found another wife that suited him. He had taken to his nephews as if they were his own.

He lowers the boys to the ground, and the boys still cling to his side. "Come on. Do you guys remember Dave Johnson? He's our neighbor to the north. They burned his place too."

Dave manages a weak smile as he receives a wave from the boys. Everyone moves outside into the mid-morning sun. "Let's get the wagon and get you back to your pa. He's gonna be surprised!" Uncle Nicky shouts.

"The Indians didn't get him?" Nate questions.

"No, son. He's fine. I'll take you home right now," Uncle Nicky assures.

Dave retrieves the horses and wagon. Everyone loads up, and the horses are directed back to the Paul Kauffmann farm.

*   *   *   *   *

Uncle Nicky pushes the horses, and the wagon bounces and groans over the rough terrain. He prods the horses onward, faster than he normally would. The boys are oblivious to the teeth rattling trip over mounds of soil excavated by gophers. Uncle Nicky points out the mounds to Daniel, "We'll have a new chore for you, gopher trapping."

Daniel excitedly nods, "That sounds fun."

The wagon crests the last hill between the two farmsteads and below them; the boys can see their farm. "There's Pa," Nate points with such enthusiasm he nearly falls out of the wagon. Daniel and Uncle Nicky both grab at Nate as he nearly spills over the side. Nate's eyes practically pop out of his head as his face feels the rush of the air the wagon wheel pushes toward him. The momentary hovering near the wheel silences everyone as they gasp a collective breath. The revelry is put on hold for only a moment.

Nate and Daniel yell to their father at the threshold of his hearing. He spots the unexpected wagon and moves toward the vehicle rushing down the hill. The children's voices are a siren's song, luring him quickly towards the wagon. He lopes, calling out, "Daniel? Nate?"

Paul Kauffman can finally see his sons in the wagon, and he runs faster to the wagon, calling out their names and moving as fast as his legs can take him. Uncle Nicky pulls up the reins on the horses, and they shuffle to a halt. There will be no incident marring this reunion. He wants the wagon at a standstill and nobody falling out, especially after what just happened to Nate. The wagon stops, "Get out. Go see your pa," Uncle Nicky orders.

Paul Kauffmann makes an expert running scoop of his boys, and they spin in an ecstatic reunion. "I though I'd lost you guys," the father says as he buries his head into Nate's hair. His tears of joy stream from his eyes. "Uf-dah, you are heavy," he smiles at Daniel as he eases him to the ground and shifts Nate in his arms. He looks to Daniel, "You took care of your brother good, didn't ya." He tousles Daniel's hair. "How did you survive?"

Daniel smiles weakly, "We saw the Indians, and we hid. We snuck over to Uncle Nicky's in the dark. We've been staying there."

Paul nods, "Come on. Let's look at the farm." He turns and walks back toward the ruins carrying Nate in his arms.

Daniel is still very conscious of his mother and did not want to speak of her in front of Nate. Uncle Nicky and Dave pull along side him in the wagon. "Hop up here, kid. Why walk when you can ride?" Dave calls down from the wagon.

Daniel climbs aboard, and the wagon lurches forward. "Uncle Nicky?" Daniel questions mournfully.

"Yeah. What is it? What's wrong?"

Uncle Nicky looks back and sees Daniel staring down at the boards of the wagon bed as he sits, holding the rail to keep from being bounced out of the back. Daniel does not look up, "Did you see my mom?"

"No," Uncle Nicky responds, "We were expecting to find her with you."

"You didn't see her body? When you were here earlier?" Daniel looks up.

Uncle Nicky looks back again at the boy. He is puzzled, "Body? What are you talking about?"

"I saw her. Josey killed her. I saw her body covered in blood by the chicken coop. Nate and I were still hiding on the island. We were fishing when Ma went back to make supper." Tears fall from his eyes as he continues the story. "We heard the gunshot earlier. We came through the brush carefully. I saw the three Indian warriors aways back, and Josey was standing over her body. He was holding a pistol. Then he just took off with the Indians. Nate doesn't know. He couldn't see over the scrub oaks. He doesn't know."

"We didn't find no body," Uncle Nicky reins the horse so he can observe Daniel. "We woulda found her body if she was dead."

Daniel points to the chicken coop, "She was laying right by the coop. I saw her. Dead."

They get down from the wagon and move to investigate the coop. It is empty, "Somebody came by and took all the chickens," Dave observes.

Paul carries Nate toward the group standing near the coop. Uncle Nicky puts his hand on Daniel's shoulder, "Don't say nothin' yet. I'll talk to your pa. Rumor has it that the Indians picked up lots of prisoners. Your mama's a tough one," Uncle Nicky nods. "She probably got swept up in the prisoner group; that's why all the chickens and livestock are gone. The Indians fed 'em to the prisoners."

"Hey, Nicky," Paul offers a smile as he approaches. "You found 'em! Where were they?"

"Hidin' in my barn."

"It's a miracle," Paul shakes his head in disbelief as he squeezes Nate in his arms.

"Come on. I'll show you a miracle," Uncle Nicky gestures to the wagon. "We can all stay at my place. The Indians didn't burn my place at all."

"No sign of Amy?" Paul questions.

"Nothing," Uncle Nicky responds with a shake of his head and a shrug. "Dave, here, said that word has it that the Indians are holding lots of women and children prisoner."

Paul nods in affirmation, accepting a positive spin on the news, "We'll find her."

Chapter 48
Butch

Agency Village

    Colonel Thurman "Butch" Howard was the man put in charge of sorting out the situation. He had inherited a mess. The political time bomb was ticking. Meting out justice was the cry from the East; it resonated 1500 miles away. "The Indian uprising could not be tolerated. A clear message had to be sent to the savages."

    Those were the verbal orders he had received the night before the train departed from Washington, D.C. The written orders assigning him to Fort Snelling were more generic: "You are hereby assigned until further notice to provide legal counsel at Fort Snelling, Minnesota."

    Colonel Howard read and reread his orders a hundred times as the train rocked back and forth, carrying him to the end of the line in Minneapolis. He was a lifelong soldier and lawyer for the Army. He had a thousand military court martials under his belt, but this was going to be new to him. Prosecuting deserters and ne'er-do-wells of the Army was a far cry from treason and the death warrants of civilians he was faced with. He had received a special appointment by Congress to execute his duties as explained and attached by letter to his orders. He was to find full cooperation with whomever and whatever military assistance he deemed necessary.

    Colonel Howard arrived at the Sisseton Indian Agency saddle weary and worn. He was not a field soldier. He was not a horseman by any means. His mind was preoccupied by his sole duty at the moment: sorting out innocent Indians from the suspected rebels that instigated and carried out the revolt. He led his contingent into Fort Sisseton, having visited Fort Ridgely and Fort Abercrombie previously. The case work was staggering. Over three hundred Indians had been condemned to death by his investigations and ensuing tribunal as prosecutor. There was an expectation that another one hundred Indians would face a death sentence at the Sisseton Agency.

The traveling party for Colonel Howard was about two companies, equivalent to about sixty men. Howard had about thirty staff assistants and aides to manage the case work. Roughly thirty men were support and logistics; feeding, protecting, and escorting the legal personnel through the Territory.

After reporting to Colonel Hagen at Fort Sisseton and being appropriately welcomed, Colonel Butch Howard's band of lawyers set up camp within the confines of the corner of the parade grounds. They would be under the protection of the cavalry and enjoy all the luxuries of life at the post compared to life lived out of a wagon. There was not a discernible difference for the most part.

Settled at the fort, Butch rode with his team to the Indian agent's office. Next to the rubble of the burned out warehouse, the office was in disrepair, but a day's organizing and cleaning made the building habitable. This would be the colonel's headquarters for his investigation. He liked the stone building. It had its own regality and sense of place on the prairie. It seemed to the colonel that the natural stone structure fit the gravity of his work. "Whoa!" he cried out dramatically in front of the building, reining his horse to a halt and dismounting.

He threw the reins toward an assistant who took care of the mount. Colonel Howard was in his element now. The past two months had given him the experience and honed his expertise for this unique task.

"Come on, men!" the colonel continued his dramatics as a Shakespearean actor would perform. "We have work to do! Guilty from the innocent, separate the guilty from the innocent, that's our charge!"

Colonel Butch Howard is an aging soldier. He is fifty, but looks almost seventy. His hairline has receded and thinned. He is of slight build and the lines on his face are carved deeply. His stage acting persona continues, he swipes his hat from his head, stands with hands on his hips, and orders the takeover of his new base of operations. "Get those files in here. I want to be reviewing the cases within the hour!"

Assistants scamper to and fro hauling crates full of papers from the wagon. "Hup, hup, hup! Move it! I have testimonies to read!"

*   *   *   *   *

An hour and a half later Colonel Howard sits at his desk. He is surrounded by stacks of papers. "I want to hear the Curved Wing testimony tomorrow," Colonel Howard says to no one in particular without looking up from the papers in his hand. "Major Kechen. You hear me?"

"Sir?" Kechen responds.

Major Philip Kechen is Colonel Howard's top assistant. He is the right hand man for the colonel. He is in charge of all the legal wrangling and maneuvering required to get the cases expedited in the impossible timeframe imposed by the powers in Washington. Ashen blonde, pale, and of medium build, Kechen is of Nordic descent; the major has taken a shine to the life on the prairie.

"Curved Wing. Testimony. Tomorrow," Colonel Howard blurts out the order as a repeating rifle would speak its bullets.

"Yes, Sir," Kechen moves directly in front of the desk of the seated colonel.

Colonel Howard sets his papers down, leans back in his chair, and removes his bifocal glasses. With a deep, melancholy sigh he addresses Kechen, "I was waiting to say something, but I have decided to share some information with you...now."

Major Kechen cocks his head, intrigued by the colonel's odd demeanor.

"I have it on good authority our cases will be reviewed by the Secretary of War and the Senate Committee on Indian Affairs. I understand we have caught the attention of the President."

Kechen nods, "I had no idea, Sir."

"My point is they want their information, and they want it now. We have until the end of the month," the colonel continues. "Have a seat, Major."

Major Kechen's brow furrows as he sits in a chair opposite the desk from his boss, "That's only fifteen days. We still have almost a hundred cases to review; we'll have to be trying almost ten cases a day. How can we do that?

"We'll make do." Colonel Howard leans forward extending a finger toward Kechen. Your name...and my name will be all over these cases...get my drift, Major?"

Major Kechen shrugs, puzzled by the question, "No, not really, Colonel."

"Our names will be put in front of the most powerful men in the world. We do this right, and we will...we will have bright futures in the Army and beyond." Butch relaxes again, lowering his arm and folding his hands on his desk. "Tell me, Major, do you have political aspirations?"

"Not really, Colonel," Kechen shrugs.

"Well, you should," Colonel Butch snaps back. Kechen flinches at the unexpected outburst. "What I'm trying to tell you is that you can make a name for yourself. Opportunity has knocked, so open that door."

The message is received. Kechen and Howard stare at each other in silence, each pondering the future. "Where is this Corporal Mancuso?" Colonel Howard finally queries breaking the silence,

"Hmm?" is the only response from Major Kechen, still lost in his thoughts.

"Mancuso!" Butch scowls at the major. "I want to talk to him about his testimony in the Coverdale murder."

Snapping back to the business at hand, Major Kechen recovers, "Uh, yes, Colonel. Coverdale. Let me see."

"Come on. Come on," Butch is back demanding information. "Indian Agent Jon Coverdale had some friends in high places in Washington. They want somebody to hang. The sooner the better."

Kechen has sorted through the files on the colonel's desk and found the proper information. "I have it here. Mancuso. He is a guard at the fort's brig."

The men stare at each other in silence. The colonel is losing his patience, "Well?"

Major Kechen stares blankly at his commander. "Bring me Mancuso!" the colonel shouts.

Kechen bounces to his feet and turns a circle as he spins out the door to retrieve their star witness from the fort.

Chapter 49
Testimony

Agency Village

Major Kechen cursed himself as he took off across the grasslands separating the Agency from Fort Sisseton. *How could I not get the hint from Colonel Howard.* Kechen chastised himself as he rode his horse on a gallop across the open land, gliding through the tall grass. "Stupid, stupid, stupid," he said aloud. "He wanted Mancuso, and he had to yell at me to do it. I know better."

In just a few minutes he passed through the fort's gate and was at the brig. No Corporal Mancuso was to be found. A soldier directed the Major to the blacksmith shop. It was here that Major Kechen found Mancuso. The corporal was in his leathers, working the forge and hammering out a fresh set of horseshoes. He was sweaty and soiled from the work. Nonetheless, Mancuso listened silently to the summons order. He set aside his work, donned proper uniform, and rode back to the agency office with the major leading the way at a trot.

The pair arrives at the stone Agency building and a soldier from the support contingency gathers their horses. "The old Agency office, eh? Ironic, don't you think, Major?" Mancuso comments coolly.

The major eyes the corporal. He reaches to brush the dust from the corporal's jacket and straighten his collar. Corporal Mancuso flinches and pulls away from the officer. "I'm just trying to make you presentable for the Colonel," Kechen puts his hands up in retreat.

Major Kechen leads Mancuso into the building where the corporal proceeds to the front of Colonel Howard's desk, snaps to attention, and salutes, "Corporal Mancuso reporting as ordered, sir."

The colonel does not look up from the papers he is reading. Several moments pass, and Mancuso holds his salute and stands rigidly waiting for acknowledgement. Mancuso's eyes move shiftily as he faces forward, but scans the room suspiciously, drifting to the side of the room catching view of the major watching the scene. The major shrugs and points stiffly with his concealed thumb toward the colonel. The message of trying to indicate to the soldier to keep at attention is received, and Mancuso waits. Corporal Mancuso waits and waits.

"At ease soldier," Colonel Howard drawls quietly without looking up. "I can smell you. Have you no respect for the military?" Colonel Howard cocks his head as he finally looks at the man standing before him. "No need to answer the question, Corporal. I can see by looking at you and your dirty uniform where you stand."

Mancuso relaxes and drops his salute to his side. He stands at parade rest in front of the colonel's desk, feet shoulder width apart, hands clasped together behind his back. Mancuso manages to glimpse the major standing near a window casually checking the goings-on outside, seemingly not paying attention to the proceedings.

Colonel Howard leans back in his chair, "Tell me what you know about Coverdale's murder."

"Sir, I was working at the stables that day but was called over by Coverdale's assistant to help hand out supplies to the Indians."

Colonel Howard looks at his notes, "Jackson James...that is the assistant to which you refer?"

"Yes, Sir."

"Do you know what happened to Mr. Jackson James, Corporal?"

"Sir, I believe he was also killed in the revolt."

"Yes, he is deceased. Otherwise, we'd probably be speaking to him and not you."

"I have an unrelated question," Colonel Howard rises from his chair and repositions himself with his rear sitting partially on the corner of his desk as casually as this stuffed-shirt of a man can make it appear. "You are a jailer, a stable worker, and..." The colonel gestures at the disheveled and dirty uniform.

With a weak attempt to straighten his jacket, Mancuso responds, "I also work as a blacksmith. That's what I was doing when the major came and got me."

Colonel Howard nods knowingly. An unconscious frown paints his face. He nods without saying anything for an uncomfortable amount of time. "Well, then, Private Jamison testified earlier that the Indian scout, Curved Wing, killed Agent Coverdale. He said he recognized Curved Wing's horse...a one-of-a-kind paint."

Corporal Mancuso shakes his head side to side, "That's not true sir. Jamison was helping hand out supplies, but I was at the stables earlier. I gave that paint horse out previously that day. I signed out that horse to an Indian woman named Blue Feather, Curved Wing's twin sister."

Colonel Howard's brow furrows, "You are sure about this?"

Corporal Mancuso relaxes to his usual extroverted self. His hands come free from behind his back, and he waves his hands in synch with, and to aid his words. "Absolutely, Sir. There I was. It was crazy." Mancuso' hands flail, "Riots broke out right in front of us. We couldn't wait to get out of there, and we retreated. By the time we were highsteppin' back to the fort, I happened to look up and see that woman chasin' after that horse. I didn't see Coverdale." Mancuso shrugs, "He was probably already down. The grass was tall. I couldn'ta seen him with all the grass if he was down." Mancuso points out the window and dips his head, "It was right out there where they found Coverdale's body. That's right where I had seen the horse and the woman."

Colonel Howard waves Corporal Mancuso away, "Thank you, Corporal. You are dismissed."

Corporal Mancuso comes to attention, does an about face, and marches out the door. Major Kechen quickly moves to Howard's desk, "What are we going to do, Sir? His testimony is in direct contradiction to Jamison."

Colonel Howard returns to his chair at his desk and sorts papers into a file. "We don't need Mancuso. Private Jamison will do just fine. In fact we have two other eye witnesses that testify the same as Jamison. Private Rendell. Private Hasty." Howard smiles, "Last I looked, three privates are worth more than one corporal."

The color drains from Kechen's face, and his head spins as the truth is buried.

Chapter 50
Tribunal

Fort Sisseton

On a crisp fall day the military tribunals began. Lieutenant Colonel Hagen's office had been converted into a makeshift courtroom for the hearing. The small office of the commander was more than adequate. These weren't legal trials; these were military tribunals. Enemies of the United States did not have the consideration a common civil or criminal trial might entertain. The rules were simple, a military officer acting as a judge would listen to the case and make a decision. In this instance the sole determinant of guilt or innocence rested in the hands of General Skelly. General Skelly was a portly man. His remaining hair was a shock of untamed white strands. Skelly had a non-threatening grandfatherly-appearance. But, as benign as he looked, he was a towering figure in the military justice ranks with his 25-years of service to his country. Graduate of West Point and later detailed by the Army to attend Harvard Law School, he was the Army's expert when it came to legal matters.

There was no nonsense when you stepped in front of General Skelly as Long Feet, in wrist and ankle irons, moved forward, shuffling, bound by his restraints. "You are the Indian, Long Feet?" the General queried.

Long Feet stood silent but finally nodded. "Do you understand English?" General Skelly continued his line of questioning.

"Yes," the reply came tersely.

Beside Long Feet stood his token counsel, Captain Earhard. If there were a question surrounding these hearings, it was the lack of representation and little chance to mount a defense for the accused. There had been no counseling provided by Captain Earhard. He was a token lawyer provided by the Army for their records and for nothing else.

The case had been heard earlier in the day and after a short recess, the hearing resumed as judgment would be passed. "You understand the charges that have been presented?" Skelly follows his script of questions.

Long Feet again nods. "Do you have any final words with which to defend yourself before I hand down my verdict?"

"I fought for my people," Long Feet pronounced sharply.

General Skelly waited for any follow up statement but realized he had heard all that was to be said by the Indian. "Long Feet, on the charge of treasonous acts against the United States, I find you guilty based on the evidence presented at this tribunal. I sentence you to hang." Skelly bangs a gavel on the desk in front of him.

Two soldiers move forward to escort Long Feet from the chambers. The soldiers grab Long Feet's arms and direct him to the exit. With lightning quickness, Long Feet wrests himself from their grip and moves toward General Skelly. He spits in the face of the surprised man and moves to club him with his bound wrists. A third soldier intervenes quickly, and with the butt of his rifle, he lays a blow to the side of Long Feet's head. Long Feet is unconscious, sprawled on the floor, a trickle of blood from the blow spills to the wooden slats.

With a scowl directed toward the two soldiers attempting the escort followed by a nod of appreciation to the quick thinking soldier with the rifle, General Skelly pronounces, "Well, now, wasn't that exciting. Next case!"

The two escort soldiers move forward and grab Long Feet's arms. They drag the large man out of the building. Skelly stands and removes a handkerchief from his pocket and wipes the saliva deposited on his face. He finishes cleaning up and returns to his seat at the desk. "Colonel Howard, you may proceed."

Colonel Howard stands from his desk to the side of the cramped office. The acting prosecutor of the cases clears his throat, "Your honor, I summon..." Howard's voice cracks and he clears his throat.

"Are you alright, Colonel?" the General asks.

"Yes, your honor. Just something in my throat," Howard clutches at his neck. "I summon the Indian known as Curved Wing."

"Proceed," Skelly growls.

Curved Wing is escorted by two soldiers into the building. He is shackled at the wrist and ankles and shuffles forward, taking his place before the judge. Following Curved Wing into the office, but remaining at the back of the room, his family lines the wall. Present are Chief Red Iron, Blue Feather, and Captain Hillmann.

Colonel Howard stares down at his files for a moment, "Your honor, we have presented the sworn testimony of eyewitnesses that Curved Wing was instrumental in the murder and mutilation of Indian Agent, Jon Coverdale. As you recall, Coverdale was beaten beyond recognition, grass was stuffed..."

General Skelly holds up his hand cutting off the speech of the colonel, "Yes, yes, I am familiar with these details." He turns his attention to Curved Wing standing before him. "And you, Scout, you speak English and understand the charges and these proceedings?"

Curved Wing nods in the affirmative. He stares at the judge seated before him.

"Very well then, Scout," General Skelly leans back in his chair, "I am curious to hear what you have to say in your defense."

"I did not commit the crimes that they are accusing me of," Curved Wing states succinctly.

From the back of the room, Blue Feather steps forward, "It was me! I held the horse that killed that man! Not my brother!"

General Skelly scowls and grabs his gavel. He looks to the back of the room and raps the wooden hammer sharply on the table several times, "Order! I will have order!"

Captain Hillmann puts his arm around his wife to calm her.

"One more outburst like that, and I will clear the room," the judge announces as he sets the gavel aside, "Colonel Howard, is there anything else?"

"Yes, your honor," Howard's voice again cracks and he composes himself and takes a swallow of water. "Not only have we tied the Indian scout, Curved Wing, to the beating death of Mr. Coverdale," the colonel snaps his fingers and is handed a piece of paper by a young lieutenant seated at the prosecutor's table. "It is a fact that Curved Wing's assigned company as scout was wiped out by a group of Indians lead by the Indian Long Feet." Colonel Howard holds up a piece of paper. "The names on this sheet of paper are the names of the two dozens soldiers brutally murdered in the attack on the wagon train."

Howard dramatically steps forward, brushing past Curved Wing, and hands the paper to the judge. "It is our belief that Curved Wing provided Long Feet the information needed for the attack."

"That is not true!" Captain Hillmann calls out. "That is a ridiculous accusation!"

"Captain," General Skelly's voice booms, "you will remain silent or be escorted out. I have warned all of you."

Captain Hillmann is beside himself with disbelief, "General, have you not seen my sworn testimony? Curved Wing was with me! He had no part in the Coverdale death. Now, the prosecutor makes a wild accusation based on no evidence..."

General Skelly holds up his hand again, cutting off the captain, "I have considered your testimony, Captain. Frankly you are not objective or credible. You are in fact Curved Wing's brother-in-law."

Captain Hillmann shrugs, "I don't understand. You are calling me a liar?"

Skelly waves away the statement, "Careful, Captain. I have considered your testimony, now please let us continue."

"No!" Captain Hillmann steps forward. He begins to approach the judge. Blue Feather pulls on his arm to hold him back. Two soldiers step forward to intervene. "I will not be slandered in this sham of a trial!" Hillmann tries to push his way through the two soldiers. They drag the captain toward the door.

"Get him out of here!" General Skelly stands and points to the door. "I don't want to clear the entire courtroom, but I will. One more peep from anyone and that's it."

The General returns to his seat at the table. A wave of his hand toward Colonel Howard indicates he is ready, "Continue!" he orders brusquely.

Colonel Howard retreats to the side of his desk near the wall. From this position he is able to address everyone in the room. He balances himself on his index finger resting on the table. He emphasizes each word with a tap on the table as he makes his statement, "Your honor, based on the evidence, I ask you to find the Indian, Curved Wing, guilty of murder and treason."

General Skelly's eyes turn toward the back of the room and locks eyes with Chief Red Iron. "Chief Red Iron, would you like to make a statement?"

"I only ask for justice. Justice for my son," Chief Red Iron bows his head.

General Skelly nods ever so slightly as he pauses and turns his attention toward Curved Wing before him. Silence blankets the room for a minute before the General moves his focus back to Chief Red Iron. "Chief Red Iron, I thank you for your instrumental work to restore peace. You single-handedly saved hundreds of women and children."

Skelly's eyes search the room. First looking at Colonel Howard who looks as if he may collapse. He is shaking nervously and sweating profusely. His future relies on this decision. Next, the General inspects the young man before him. He looks him up and down before falling back to meeting eyes with Chief Red Iron. With a sigh and a shake of his head, seemingly to his own disbelief he makes his pronouncement, "I dismiss the treason charges that purportedly involved you in connection with the decimation of your fellow soldiers. They are without evidence or merit. But, it is with a heavy heart that I find you, Curved Wing, guilty of inciting the insurrection and the murder of Jon Coverdale. You are hereby sentenced to death by hanging."

General Skelly banged his gavel on the table, and the sound was like a rifle shot through Blue Feather. She dropped to her knees clutching at her father's leg. Chief Red Iron placed his hand on the head of his daughter as he stoically faced the judge. Curved Wing turned his face skyward looking for a respite that might be held by the Great Spirit as the soldiers grasped his arms and steered him out the door. The fluffy cumulus clouds had raced across the sky all day, intermittently shadowing the area and then moving on their journey to allow the bright sun to bathe the prairie. It was an affect that a person noticed as the light and dark slowly pulsed through your visual senses. The verdict and sentenced were handed down in synch with the darkest phase of cloud cover, a symbolic condition of the day's proceedings.

"Next Case!" General Skelly ordered.

Colonel Howard was relieved and sickened all at once. He saw the inconsolable Blue Feather on the floor. He questioned everything in his life that had led to this point. This conviction would quench the blood thirst of those in Washington, D. C., that wanted revenge for their fallen man, Coverdale. Howard would live with his part and be haunted the rest of his life.

Chapter 51
Clocked

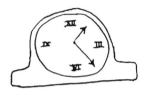

Fort Sisseton Brig

Kitty-corner across the parade grounds from Colonel Hagen's office and makeshift courtroom, the fort's brig fell in line. It was part of a row of non-descript brick, stone, and wood buildings assembled to serve their designated purpose. The jail was not accustomed to seeing the kind of alleged criminals it housed as of late. Sure there was an AWOL or drunk and disorderly soldier now and again, but detaining hardened, treasonous, and murderous criminals was not in the building's make up.

Curved Wing was escorted from the courtroom to a wagon. He had brief contact with his family, a quick hug from Blue Feather, a hand on the shoulder in an attempt to comfort from his brother-in-law. Solemn promises of appeal were made. The distance across the parade grounds was a mere two hundred yards or so, but with leg irons, the walk would have been quite arduous. Soldiers lifted Curved Wing into the back of the conveyance. The wagon bore the drips and drabs of blood from its previous trip to the brig hauling an unconscious Long Feet back to his confines. There was no conversation between prisoners or the appointed guard soldiers, or between the soldiers themselves. The mood was quite solemn. A man had been sentenced to death. Whether Indian, White, or other, he was still a man. Being in the presence of such a condemned man gave one pause, and the soldiers reflected on their own lives in the short trip across the manicured parade grounds. The clouds darted and dodged the sun, still whipping in the high altitude winds not felt at ground level. The lights and darks of the shadows cast by the clouds provided an unearthly feel to the mostly pleasant and mild day. The racing clouds typically predicted a change in weather. The high pressure pushing through would destabilize the air; rain was likely to precede the cool air being pushed down via the high pressure from the north.

Chief Red Iron, Captain Hillmann, and Blue Feather trailed the wagon across the parade grounds to the brig. That was as far as they were allowed to go. They were ordered to stand back as the prisoner was unloaded from the wagon. A knock on the outside iron door brought forth the click-clack of lock and key and when the door swung open Corporal Mancuso was revealed. He accepted custody of the prisoner. As he did so, he frowned and acknowledged the family, standing afar, with a nod.

The outside iron door was shut with a screech of rusty hinges and locked. Inside the brig Mancuso spoke in low tones to Curved Wing as he led him to his cell, "Sorry to hear about your sentence."

They moved by Long Feet sprawled unconscious on a blanket on the floor, still in his chains. Curved Wing stops. He motions with his chin, "Is he going to be alright?"

"I think so. They clocked him good." Mancuso pauses and looks down at the Indian on the floor of the cell. He gives a shrug, "He's still breathing."

The men move into the empty cell adjacent to Long Feet. The corporal bends down with a groan, "Let's get the shackles off."

He works the iron locks from Curved Wing, freeing the prisoner from the restrictive chains. 'There you go, Scout." Mancuso moves outside the cell and locks the door. "Stay strong, buddy. I'll bring some food later and check on your friend." Mancuso gives a nod toward Long Feet. "Make sure you eat. Ya gotta keep that strength up. There's always an appeal."

Curved Wing grabs hold of the bars and leans against the iron door. He stares at his jailer, puzzled by the one-sided conversation. Mancuso gives a wink and a nod to the prisoner as he leaves, locking the middle door of the three doors separating the prisoners from freedom.

Chapter 52
Josey

Fort Sisseton Commander's Office

    The court proceedings pressed on in the makeshift courtroom. There was a deadline to stick to and more cases had to be heard. General Skelly tediously, incrementally dissected the cases presented by Colonel Howard. The stacks of papers piled on the General's desk slowly melted away as they made progress in the crude court of military justice. "Call the next case, Colonel," General Skelly barked, growing shorter in patience by the hour.

    "I summon the Indian known as Josey," roared Colonel Howard now emboldened with his conviction of perpetrator of the Coverdale killing.

    Josey is led into the room in chains by soldiers. He shuffles to the desk of the judged, being centered before the General. Colonel Howard reads the writ indicting Josey, "The Indian known as Josey, also known as Cuts the Cane, is charged with inciting the insurrection and terrorizing."

    "I see in the file that there is a witness for Mr. Josey's defense?" the General questions, eyebrows arched in surprise. "There is a defense for this man?"

    The counsel representing Josey, Captain Earhard is equally surprised at the news as he shuffles through the papers on his desk. "Your honor," Colonel Howard interjects, "Yes, a woman. One of the captive settlers has come forward with information."

    This delay tests the tolerance of the General, "Captain," the judge addresses the lawyers in the room first glaring at Captain Earhard, then turning his wrath toward the colonel. "Colonel, I suggest you produce this witness as quickly as possible. We will recess until the witness arrives."

    "Yes, General," is all that Colonel Howard dares reply.

Soldiers escort Josey out the back door. Captain Earhard moves to discuss the matter with the colonel. It is a short conversation as Colonel Howard spit fire through gritted teeth at his lieutenant and Captain Earhard. The officers take leave from the colonel's presence as droopy as a pair of scolded puppies. The sergeant at arms escorts the officers out of the building and waits for horses in order to retrieve the witness from the refugee camp still home to many displaced settlers waiting to return to their farms.

As the disorder from the recess settles and personnel depart to take care of business, General Skelly stands and waves his hand to summon Colonel Howard to a corner of the room. "We only have a couple more cases. I want all the condemned Indians to be available for transfer to Fort Snelling tomorrow," the General casually orders an attentive Colonel Howard.

"Very good, General," Colonel Howard bows his head in acknowledgement. "We will have wagons and a cavalry company for escort at first light tomorrow."

The General shares a final word, "See that it happens, Colonel."

Chapter 53
The Message

Fort Sisseton

Between the fort and the Indian camp the woods surrounding Cattail Lake provide a calming refuge to regain a sense of control. Here Blue Feather finds therapy as she carries her baby in her arms, her husband, Captain Gary Hillmann at her side. Her eyes are red and swollen from crying more tears than can be counted. The mature oak trees have begun to shed some early leaves as fall settles on the prairie. The blanket of leaves crackles under foot. "Gary, can't we do something?" Blue Feather pines, her voice thick with her tears of anguish.

"There will be an appeal. That is automatic for any man sentenced to death. There will be time as another judge reviews the case."

The captain and his wife stroll at a snail's pace with no destination in mind, crunching through the leaves. Blue Feather stops walking. She rocks her baby in her arms, "I can't lose him. I can't lose him. I can't lose him." She stares into the dense stand of tree trunks that block the open prairie and provide the seclusion she seeks at the moment. "I just can't lose him! He's my twin brother." She breaks down into sobs, planting the crown of her head into the chest of her husband as he tries to console her. Her body is wracked with sobs, and the baby swings in her arms with each heaving breath. Captain Gary Hillmann takes the baby from her arms and pulls her close and tight, in an attempt to thwart the sobs.

Blue Feather can only collect herself when a strange voice echoes through the woods calling, "Hello?"

Corporal Mancuso winds his way through the tangle of oaks dipping under branches, then straightening as he marches forward. He stops short of the surprised couple. They are puzzled and annoyed by this intrusion. Mancuso approaches, closing the distance between himself and the couple. He salutes crisply, "Good afternoon, sir." Mancuso bubbles forward, true to his spirit.

Captain Hillmann does not know what to make of this meddling soldier. He hands his son back to his wife, who stares at the man standing rigidly before them. Hillmann returns the salute. "What is it, Corporal? You are disturbing my wife and myself."

"I deeply apologize, sir. I...I just wanted to give you a message." Mancuso hands a folded piece of paper to the captain and salutes.

Captain Hillmann accepts the note and returns the salute. "Have a good evening, Sir," Mancuso bows ever so slightly. He turns to Blue Feather and tips his cap, "Ma'am."

"You too, Corporal," the captain calls out to the backside of Mancuso who has already disappeared into the maze of oak trees, leaving only the sound of crunching leaves under a casual pace and the whistle of a happy tune from the lips of the soldier.

The mysterious intrusion has distracted the couple for a moment or two. Blue Feather scrunches her face, "What was that about?"

The captain stares into the woods in the direction where Mancuso disappeared, "I have no idea."

Blue Feather shifts her baby on her hip, "What does the note say?"

The captain unfolds the paper and reads it, shaking his head, "It just says 'Brig Midnight'."

Chapter 54
Final Hearing

Fort Sisseton

Late in the afternoon, the converted commander's office was bustling as court reconvened. General Skelly had ruled on the final cases remaining, except for the Indian Josey. Now the witness had been located, and the accused stood before the judge. General Skelly looked exhausted and small as he sat at the makeshift judge's bench, a desk with only a few scattered papers. Josey had once again been marched, more correctly, shuffled, into place front and center of Skelly. The chains rattled holding Josey's arms and feet clattering at every movement of the encumbered man. "Colonel Howard! Is the witness available?" Skelly bleated with renewed energy as the finality of the seemingly endless hearings was in sight.

Colonel Howard pushed himself to a standing position, leaning heavily on the table. He was also worn by the non-stop string of cases. His eyes were weary, and his bifocals perched precariously on his pointed nose as he read from his papers. He gave a look to the judge, "Yes, General. I present Mrs. Amy Kaufmann."

Amy Kaufmann is escorted gently into the room by a soldier. She is wide-eyed and disheveled as she absorbs her surroundings, eyes dancing across the room. She spots Josey in the room, breaks free from the soldier holding her arm. Her shabby shirt and skirt bounce as she runs to Josey. She nearly knocks Josey off his feet as she throws herself at the broken Indian.

"Josey! Thank you! Thank you! Thank you!" Amy calls out in a voice of husky shock and disbelief.

"Order! Order in my courtroom!" General Skelly rumbles from his chair as he bangs his gavel unabashedly on the desk. "Ma'am, please..."

A look from the judge to a soldier brings the young man forward. He approaches tentatively and tries to pry her free from the death grip she holds on Josey. Tears stream from her eyes. General Skelly relinquishes and waves the soldier back to the wall, "Ma'am, if you please, could you tell us what happened?"

Amy composes herself as she relaxes her grip on Josey. She uses the heels of her hands to wipe her tears and makes a feeble attempt to smooth her tangled hair and ruffled clothes. She pushes away from Josey, standing before the judge, "This man is a hero," she says shakily as he points a finger toward Josey. "He saved my life with his quick thinking. I beg you to set him free. I need him to help me track down my family."

"Your honor," Colonel Howard interjects, pointing to the desk, "I believe you have the woman's statement,"

General Skelly shuffles through the papers on his desk. "Yes." He silently reads for a moment before looking at the woman. "According to your statement, the Indian Josey works for you?"

Amy Kaufmann nods adamantly, "That is correct. He is our hired hand on our farm. A good worker."

The judge cocks his head, interested "You said this Indian saved your life. How did that happen?"

Amy breathes deeply and begins, "A band of Indians came to our farm. They said they were hungry and wanted chickens." The tears well up in her eyes again and the first tear breaks free and rolls down her cheek. Amy does nothing to stop the following tears as she continues, "I had left my boys near the lake. They were fishing, and I wanted to start supper. Josey was there with the Indians when I showed up. He ordered me into the coop to show the Indians he was in charge. He had pretended to be on their side." Amy shakes her head and chokes back a sob. "Josey got me in the coop, quickly explained the situation and covered me with chicken blood. He fired a gun and pushed me outside. He fired into the ground next to me. The war party could see I was dead; covered in blood." Amy sniffles and looks upon Josey reverently. "Later I was swept up by another band of Indians that held many prisoners. I have been here...for I don't know how long."

Amy moves back to Josey's side and puts her arm on his. "I pretended to be dead. I lay there motionless until dark...afraid to move. But Josey had led the Indians to another farm, away from me and my boys....he saved me..."

Amy fans herself with her hand as she tries to catch her breath, "...and hopefully my children."

Amy has fought hard to keep her composure, but she is overwhelmed and breaks down into sobs, leaning heavily on Josey. The judge and Colonel Howard look at her pitifully. For the first time the bedraggled Josey speaks, "I saw the boys. They disappeared into the trees. I am sure they are fine. Those boys are tough."

Amy snaps to attention on hearing the words from Josey and grips him tightly. General Skelly stares at the odd reunion before him. "Well, then, Colonel, based on this testimony, I do pass judgment that the Indian Josey is exonerated of all charges and ordered released...immediately." The judge waves the soldiers standing guard along the wall forward. "Release the man from his chains,"

Josey slumps in relief. Amy Kaufmann leans into Josey, and they provide support for one another. "Further," General Skelly continues, "the court orders a horse and supplies be provided to Ms. Kaufmann to return her to her farm in the company of Josey."

"As you order, General, so shall it be," Colonel Howard acknowledges stoically.

Josey stands swaying gingerly to avoid obstructing the soldiers enabling his freedom as the irons are removed from his hands and feet. He rubs his wrists in disbelief. His stoic expression is defied by his tears.

Chapter 55
Escape

Fort Sisseton Brig

At night in the weakest light of a kerosene lantern, the jail could not look more ominous. The long shadows darken every corner, hiding the unknown. In the dark it is hard to picture a prisoner present in the facility, the deep breathing would give away a body's existence, but the mind could easily be fooled. An unconscious Long Feet lies in the middle of his jail cell still in shackles. A bucket of water through the bars courtesy of Corporal Mancuso jolts the Indian. He stirs, and the rattle of the chains' echo assures Corporal Mancuso that the man is awake. He leans against the iron door where he can peer through the bars and see his prisoner. Long Feet rolls to his side and groans. His hands go instinctively to his head and the chains on his wrist slap him in the face. "Ohhh," groans Long Feet as he struggles to sit up.

"Look who's awake," Mancuso's sing-song voice sounds like he's talking to a child. "Get up!" he orders with a new, harsh tone.

Long Feet holds his head. Finally he reaches blindly for anything to help push himself to his feet. "What happened?" he questions hoarsely, his throat dry.

"You tried to attack a General. You are lucky to be alive with a headache. I would have thought they would have shot you on the spot."

Long Feet gingerly gets to his feet. He pushes the heels of his hands deeply into his eye sockets in hope of unscrambling his brain.

Mancuso smiles as he reaches in his pocket for his ring of keys. "The good news for the Army is that you're alive and they can still hang ya. The bad news for the Army is that you're a lucky man; your family came through. They bought you your freedom...at least freedom from my brig anyway."

Corporal Mancuso holds up his hand and shrugs, "Like I said, lucky you."

With the key located, the corporal opens the cell door. He enters, pushing Long Feet back. "Sit," Mancuso commands, "Give me your hands."

Long Feet crumples to the raggedy, straw-stuffed sleeping mat and holds up his hands unsteadily, still groggy. He leans forward and looks into the empty adjacent cell, "Where is Curved Wing?"

"Never you mind. Just sit," Mancuso focuses on the shackles and removes the restraints. "If you must know, I had to send the scout to the infirmary. Something he ate I guess." Mancuso lies. He does not want Curved Wing to see the bribe, so he had soldiers escort the prisoner for some fresh air; the corporal had called it a last gift for a condemned man.

Corporal Mancuso turns his attention to the ankle irons and has the chains off in no time as Long Feet strains to focus in the darkness. As the restraints fall away, Long Feet poses a question, "How much?"

"Hmmm?" Mancuso responds as he stands. The corporal straightens, twisting and loosening his back in discomfort.

"How much did my family have to pay to bribe you?"

"Let's just say I won't have to worry about having a horse for the rest of my life."

"Ten ponies?" Long Feet arches an eyebrow.

"Hmm. More," Mancuso's corners of his mouth twitch toward a smile.

"Twenty ponies?" Long Feet is aghast.

"Twenty-five, but you're worth it...right?" Mancuso smiles and shrugs. The smile quickly turns to a frown, "Now for the not so good part."

Long Feet recoils, "What do you mean?"

Corporal Mancuso holds up a hand, "Nothing like that. I mean bad for me, good for you!" He emphasizes the last three words with a manic smile again. "You are escaping after all. You are getting no pardon. You leave here; you are going to be a wanted Indian. I have to make it look good, so you get to punch me in the face. It's all part of your elaborate escape." Mancuso frowns again as he thinks about getting hit. He draws his pistol and points it at the Indian.

"What's going to happen?" Long Feet questions.

"Well," Mancuso rubs his jaw, "Everyone is in their racks for the night, so let's get to it. You punch me; I wait fifteen minutes, then I report to my sergeant that you assaulted me and escaped."

"I only get a fifteen minute head start?" Long Feet whines.

"You'll take what I give you."

Long Feet holds his head with both hands trying to get the throbbing to stop. Mancuso shakes his head as he looks down at the Indian, agonizing over his head injury. "Listen, just get to the trees and get as far away from here as fast as you can. You likely won't be missed since we got a hun'erd other Indians sentenced to hang sitting in the compound. Why would they miss you? Just disappear."

Corporal Mancuso extends his hand to Long Feet who grabs his forearm. Mancuso pulls the Indian to his feet. Mancuso waves the pistol at the prisoner, "It's time. Give me your best shot. Make it look good...but not too good. You try anything more, I'll shoot you dead in this cell." He spreads his feet apart and puts his chin forward. He waves his hand to beckon the Indian. "Bring it on." He bends his knees and braces.

Long Feet smiles and cocks his fist behind his ear, "This is gonna be good." He holds nothing back and brings a crushing right fist crashing to the left side of the corporal's face.

Mancuso staggers back and falls on his backside. He gets to his hands and knees and stares at the ground in front of him. Drops of blood fall to the floor from a small cut below his instantly swollen eye. He points the gun at the Indian but doesn't look up at his assailant. "Get out of here," Mancuso orders.

Long Feet stands over the corporal still holding his clenched fist, admiring his work. He eases toward the door keeping an eye on the downed soldier. He opens the door cautiously and surveys the outer room. He moves through the door and cracks open the unlocked outer door. He inspects the surroundings shrouded in darkness through the slit of the open door. He sees nothing to thwart an escape and makes a run to the shadows of the trees along the lake bordering the fort's perimeter. Nobody notices as he disappears into the night.

Chapter 56
Infirmed

Fort Sisseton Brig

Corporal Mancuso spent five minutes on his hands and knees, breathing deeply, and waiting for the pain to subside. The next five minutes brought relief. The soldiers returned with Curved Wing to find him on his back, eyes closed, finding some easing of the pain thanks to the cool, concrete floor. The shocked soldiers throw Curved Wing into his empty cell. He had been free of his ankle irons, but he sported the wrist restraints. After securing Curved Wing, the soldiers took action to provide aid to their fallen comrade. The questions were fired quickly from Mancuso's Samaritans. "What happened? Did he get away? Are you ok?"

"Get the sergeant," was Mancuso's only reply.

The soldiers scoop up Mancuso and haul him to the infirmary where the doctor and Sergeant Cornin meet the debilitated corporal. Cornin is a large framed, heavily bearded, intimidating man. "Wha' happened, laddie?" the sergeant quizzes Mancuso in a strangely accented tongue.

"I'm sorry, Sergeant. He jumped me. I let my guard down for a moment, I guess."

The Doctor inspects Mancuso's eye. "I think you'll be alright."

"That is good news," Sergeant Cornin nods. "Don' worry aboot it son. Deese tings 'appen. Deese Injians, dey have noowheer to ga. We be roundin' hem up soon enoof."

Mancuso eases off the doctor's table. "I better get back to the brig."

"Nay, laddie. We be gittin' you back the Indian camp and yer wife."

"I'm fine, Sergeant."

The sergeant looks to the doctor who shrugs a disinterested shrug.

"I'm fine. The brig is my second home. Besides, I had a little fight with my wife; I could use the night away from her screeching...especially when she sees my eye."

"Ho-ho-ho," Sergeant Cornin laughs roundly, "Aye. I udderstan compleet-lee. A little peas and quie-et."

Mancuso musters a smile for the sergeant.

*   *   *   *   *

Back at the brig, alone in the darkness and shadows just outside the prison building, Corporal Mancuso waits. His dark blue uniform hides him perfectly in the gloom of night. He listens to the night sounds and picks up the measured steps of someone walking in the shroud of darkness, wanting to be undetected. It is midnight. Right on time Mancuso's visitor arrives as instructed. "Very punctual, Captain," the corporal's voice pierces the night silence.

The unseen voice startles Captain Hillmann, and he staggers back, "You scared me," he remarks as casually as his racing heart will allow. He steps closer and makes out the faintest silhouette of the corporal.

Corporal Mancuso smiles and nods in the dark. His parted lips and wide eyes glint in the faint light, cutting through the darkness. "Come then, I got something for you."

The two men enter the unlocked outer door of the jail. Inside the outer room, a kerosene lantern burns, providing minimal illumination. Even with the dim light the captain can see Corporal Mancuso's damaged, and swollen eye. "What happened to your face, Corporal?"

Corporal Mancuso touches his swollen cheek and eye. "You haven't heard?" He pushes open the unlocked door to the reveal the jail cells. "We had a prisoner escape earlier. Long Feet jumped me and got away."

"Maybe you should be in the infirmary?"

Mancuso waves this statement away with his hand, holding the keys to the cell and they rattle on their ring. "I'm fine. I was just there." He looks down at the key ring in his hand like he notices it for the first time.

The corporal looks up and sees the captain measuring him. He tosses the keys to Captain Hillmann who fights the darkness to capture the keys in his hand. A puzzled look darkens his already shadowed face as words slowly come. "What is this?"

"I think you know," the corporal moves aside.

Captain Hillmann stares at the man in front of him. Finally he directs only the slightest of nods to the corporal. "I do," he whispers.

"Captain," Mancuso says dryly in a monotone, "I am married to a native...just like you. Her name is Chasing Star. Our wives know each other." The corporal's head shakes and a frown crosses his face. "I know what is going on in these sham trials."

Mancuso waves the captain forward as they move to the locked iron door. The corporal takes the keys back from the captain, locates the correct key on the ring, and opens the lock. "You see, Captain, I was there. I saw what happened. I handed out Curved Wing's horse to your wife as she stated. I saw Jon Coverdale die. I saw the revolt start." Mancuso shakes his head from side to side, "I saw it all."

The corporal pushes the door of the jail cell open. "Colonel Howard called me in, and I gave sworn testimony. Yet, they ignored the truth...my story wouldn't work in order to fix blame and show people back East that justice is being served in the Territory." Mancuso shakes his head, shrugs, continues his commentary dripping with sarcasm, "See how civilized we are?"

The men step into the lone occupied cell as Mancuso pushes the door solidly against the wall, and it clangs, waking a sleeping Curved Wing with a start. "He's all yours. Take him. Send him to Canada. Anywhere far away from here."

Captain Hillmann does not hesitate. He moves forward, grabs Curved Wing by the arm and pulls him to his feet. He exits the cell, brother-in-law in tow. He stops and looks back, "What's going to happen here?"

"Just go!" the corporal orders. "This is justice!"

"But, what about the General? The Colonel?"

"Captain, this is what justice looks like. Just go."

Captain Hillmann and Curved Wing move out of the brig and disappear into the darkness as Mancuso moves to the door and as they vanish from the threshold of his sight, trailing the similar path of Long Feet just an hour before. Mancuso shuts the door and rubs his aching cheek and eye. His hand moves to his jaw, the swelling has moved into his jaw, but he still manages a grin, satisfied with his effort.

Chapter 57
Two For One

Fort Sisseton

The defenses of Fort Sisseton were not accustomed to being exploited as they were on this dark night. Earlier Long Feet had disappeared into the abyss of the prairie, a prisoner freed on a bribe, vanishing from the fort. It is a simple route, crawling over the berm and melting into the nearby trees of the bordering lakes.

Now it was Captain Hillmann and Curved Wing, cut loose by a disgruntled jailer. Curved Wing was now free; and Captain Hillmann, a very good brother-in-law indeed, was assisting in the escape. The pair followed a similar path to freedom away from the fort. A low crawl over the berm into the ditch, and a sprint below grade and out of any sightlines that were not available in the darkness anyway. The run through the bottom of the ditch was muddy. Puddles from recent showers gathered in the trench and slowed progress. It was a silent trip for a better part of twenty minutes, fearful of giving away their position. Once out of the ditch and into the trees bordering the lake, it was a quick dodge around the outpost of a perimeter guard. From there they were free. Varying between a fast walk and a lope, the men picked their way through the trees. Nearly three-quarters of a mile from the fort the captain called a halt to their advance. They speak in hushed tones, barely above a whisper. Captain Hillmann looks at the silhouette of Curved Wing; it's all he can identify in the darkness. "You all right?" the captain manages between breaths.

Curved Wing gasps for air, "Sure...never better."

Unseen in the darkness the captain smiles, "You know you gotta get out of here...far away."

They kneel in the cover of the trees as they recover their wind and breathing normalizes. "North to Canada is where I'll go," Curved Wing finally rasps.

The adrenaline still courses through their bodies. Compounded with the exertion of the trek through the trees, recovery is taking time. "We are near Chief Red Iron's camp. You stay right here. Don't move. I'll go get Blue Feather and send her with the news."

Curved Wing nods affirmatively. The captain can see the indication in the dark, but he presses for more. He places his hand on Curved Wing's shoulder. "Take my knife." Hillmann hands his leather-sheathed blade to Curved Wing. "I'd give you my pistol, but a gunshot would alert the whole fort. You know how to use the knife, but promise me you'll stay hidden right here, and you won't have to do anything. Say you'll stay here."

Curved Wing repeats the words, "I'll stay here."

With a final order through gritted teeth from Captain Hillmann, "Don't move!" the captain disappears into the darkness leaving Curved Wing alone. The scout drops from his knees to flat on his stomach. He rolls to his back and breathes deeply, still trying to catch his breath. He focuses on his breathing and listens to voices in the distance. He thinks he recognizes voices from his father's camp, but they are fleeting and faint. Noises are twisted by the echoes through the trees. Curved Wing rolls on to his front and edges closer to the tree line; crawling on his belly, he moves all the way to the edge of the tree line. He can see into the clearing from his position now. The tepees are aligned. He spots the largest canopy silhouetted amongst the rows of tepees. He knows it is his father's domicile. Chief Red Iron is less than one hundred and fifty yards away.

A voice cuts through the black curtain of darkness behind him, "Well, well. It looks like it is my lucky night. I will get two for one."

Curved Wing is startled by the voice in the dark. He twists to try to see anything through the shroud of trees. *The voice, I know it.* Curved Wing's mind races, and it registers...it is Long Feet.

"Who is there?" Curved Wing calls out. He knows who it is, but the scout is stalling for time and trying to locate the position of this new adversary.

A branch snaps to the left, and Curved Wing strains to detect something...anything. "Now I get to kill your coward father and you...the traitor."

"Long Feet, no..." Curved Wing is cut off. The warrior Long Feet is up to the task; he is on top of Curved Wing, pummeling him with his only weapon, his heavy fists.

Curved Wing breaks free of the immediate attack. Long Feet is surprised that he has over estimated his advantage. "You are quick." Long Feet laughs sharply, "Where do you get your energy?" Long Feet steps forward and kicks something loose at his feet, even in the faintest light he can make out that it is a sheathed knife. Curved Wing had dropped his only weapon.

Long Feet, the much bigger man, chases after Curved Wing. They crash through the trees, and Curved Wing is on the defensive. The fight moves into the clearing of the Indian encampment, but is still shrouded in the black veil of night.

Chapter 58
Exit Strategy

Chief Red Iron's Camp

Captain Hillmann surprises his wife in their tepee, stealthily moving through the entry flap announcing with a low hiss, "It was as I told you earlier. Corporal Mancuso released Curved Wing!" Hillmann is pulling his wife to her feet, "He called it justice." The captain's words come rapid fire as his adrenaline has rekindled. He unrolls a buffalo hide to find his rifle and bullets. He checks the rifle with a quick flick of his wrist, assuring the weapon is loaded. "Come, we have to get to your father." Blue Feather is on her feet, baby in hand, "Come on, Curved Wing needs supplies. He's heading north to Canada as quickly as he can! Hurry!"

The captain pulls his wife through the tepee flap before she can respond, hand-in-hand the couple silently sprints the one-hundred yards to Chief Red Iron's home. They arrive in front of the Chief's tepee. "Get in there," the captain whispers to his wife, "Get in there and stay there with your father. Prepare some supplies for your brother's travels. I will go and retrieve your brother, now, while it is clear." He moves Blue Feather with their son into the tepee as he heads to the trees to find Curved Wing.

*   *   *   *   *

Blue Feather pushes through the flap and into the fire-lit tepee of her father. "My daughter, is that you?" Chief Red Iron's voice resonates as he puffs his pipe and peers through the smoky haze hanging in the tepee.

"It is me, father, Blue Feather."

"Oh, good. Your mother is here also. It is good to see you." Chief Red Iron smokes his pipe, churning more haze. "What brings you here tonight, so late?"

Blue Feather moves close to her father. He smiles and raises a hand to brush the cheek of his grandson in her arms. "It is Curved Wing, father. He is free. It is like the captain said. He has gone to get him...to bring him here to say goodbye. He is going to Canada."

Chief Red Iron contemplates the statement for a moment. He taps the tobacco from the bowl of the pipe into the fire and returns the pipe to its decorative leather sheath. "Very well then." He rises and hands the encased pipe to his daughter.

Blue Feather accepts the pipe, puzzled. She watches her father move toward the exit. "Father, no! We must wait here. Curved Wing will come to us."

Chief Red Iron ignores his daughter and exits the tepee. "Mother! Mother, take the baby!" Blue Feather calls out. She hands the baby to her mother and follows her father out of the tepee.

Chapter 59
Duel

Chief Red Iron's Camp

From the tree line the hand to hand combat between Long Feet and Curved Wing raged into the clearing. Curved Wing was on his heels, not a good match against the older, larger, stronger warrior. "I didn't want to get my hands dirty, but your skills have surprised me." Long Feet produces the knife he plucked from underfoot and pulls it from its sheath.

Long Feet whips the knife through the air. Curved Wing ducks and dodges the wild lunges of the blade from Long Feet. The scout takes evasive action and dives into the tree line and comes up with an arm-sized branch to brandish. He hacks at Long Feet's knife with a blind swing and connects. The blow drives the knife from a shocked Long Feet. The knife flutters away into the darkness.

Long Feet shakes his head in disbelief as the men stand apart. He leans with his hands on his knees catching his breath, "I have really underestimated you, Scout."

Long Feet ducks out of the way of an attacking Curved Wing as the branch whistles by his ear. The blow to the head that Long Feet suffered earlier at the hands of a soldier in the court room has dampened Long Feet's reflexes; his condition has leveled the playing field in the confrontation between the men.

Captain Hillmann moves toward the trees with a purpose, but he hears scuffling and kicks to a full sprint. "Curved Wing?" The captain can make out two shadowed figures dancing a fighting waltz as they circle each other, exchanging blows. Hillmann shoulders his rifle and moves forward more deliberately.

*   *   *   *   *

Chief Red Iron converges on the commotion he hears in the darkness. He moves toward the tree line curious as to the rustling in the night. Blue Feather chases after him. "Father, please...please wait. Stay here and wait for Curved Wing and the Captain."

Blue Feather catches her father's sleeve, and he halts momentarily, "It is a beautiful night. Go get your brother's horse. He will need to depart immediately to get a start under the cover of the black sky."

Blue Feather lets go of Chief Red Iron. "Yes, father."

Chief Red Iron reaches for his daughter's hand in the pale gloom of night as she turns to carry out the order. "Also, prepare a bundle for his journey. He will need food and supplies. Now, hurry. Bring it as fast as you can."

"Right away, father." Blue Feather hustles away as fast as her feet will carry her.

Chief Red Iron homes in on the commotion in front of him as he moves forward to discover the source of the jostling of the trees. With his focus diverted to the noise in the bushes, Chief Red Iron nearly crashes into an equally surprised Captain Hillmann. The men move forward together. "Curved Wing!" the captain calls out again.

At the tree line the duel between Indian brothers, Long Feet and Curved Wing raged on. They were not brothers by birth, but brothers of the Lakota band now in a battle to the death. Curved Wing is spent. He gasps for breath. His head pounds and muscles ache in fatigue, starved for oxygen. He hears his name in the darkness, a faint familiar call from his brother-in-law. The distraction is enough for Long Feet. The warrior charges forward and puts his shoulder into Curved Wing's stomach. The wind is driven from Curved Wing in a resonating gasp, and the crash projected to Chief Red Iron and Captain Hillmann. "This way!" Captain Hillmann calls out; the crash of Long Feet tackling Curved Wing has defined their position.

The captain and Chief Red Iron are quickly upon the battling men. Long Feet is on Curved Wing's chest, hands around his throat. With rifle shouldered, but unsure of who is who, Captain Hillmann hollers, "Curved Wing!"

The gasps and gurgles from the choking man are unearthly. Captain Hillmann holds his rifle trained on the man on top of the other. Unable to determine the identity of either combatant, the captain stands frozen with indecision. Chief Red Iron sweeps the rifle from a surprised Captain Hillmann. "Out of the way!" Chief Red Iron orders.

He shoves the perplexed captain, who stumbles away, unprepared for the assault. Red Iron aims and fires at the silhouette in front of him. The crack of the single round sizzles and splits the night air.

"No!" the captain cries out, uncertain of the target presented before them.

The bullet strikes Long Feet squarely between the shoulders. The impact of the slug and its momentum flattens Long Feet to the ground atop Curved Wing. Long Feet is dead, the bullet has separated his spinal column and penetrated through the warrior's heart. "Curved Wing!" Captain Hillmann cries out again.

*   *   *   *   *

The gunshot ripping through the night freezes the sounds of the darkness. Birds and bugs are silenced. The eerie calm was momentary. A ripple of movement within the Indian encampment a few hundred yards away made itself known as curious members of the Lakota band investigate the disturbance. Slowly the ambient sounds of nighttime return; first with the chirps of frogs and crickets, then with other members of the biological orchestra eventually chiming in.

Captain Hillmann was paralyzed; stunned by the events his eye bore through the darkness at the man of peace standing before him; rifle still trained in the direction of the fighting men. The captain's eyes can discern nothing from the murky expression cast by the chief. When finally able to command his muscles to move, he leaps forward, bounding through prairie grass and rushing into the brush. He is finally able to ascertain who is who when he is standing over the men. He drags the dead man off Curved Wing who is gasping and flailing wildly trying to regain his breath. Unsure of what to do, he pulls Curved Wing into a sitting position and raps the wheezing man on the back with an open hand.

Captain Hillmann looks back to see Chief Red Iron slowly approaching. The rifle is still in his hand, but now hanging limply at his side. He trudges forward ever so slowly, seemingly dazed himself. "Are you crazy?" Captain Hillmann calls to the Chief. "You could've killed Curved Wing!"

Chief Red Iron arrives and stands over the men. "A father knows his son."

Curved Wing emits animal-like wretching noises that pierce through the night. "Come on, let's get you on your feet," Hillmann orders.

Curved Wing is unable to speak, but he nods and the captain stands and pulls the Indian to his feet. Curved Wing stoops. He rests his hands on his knees and is finally able to turn the corner of recovery. As he stands bent over at the waist, blood drips from his hair and clothes...Long Feet's blood.

"We got to get moving!" the captain hisses. "That gunshot will bring lots of attention."

Chief Red Iron stares at the body of Long Feet in front of him. He unconsciously points the rifle at the corpse partially hidden in the knee high grass. The night's shadows wreak havoc with the eye's perception and the brain's comprehension of what it sees and interprets. At his feet, Chief Red Iron imagines, it is a monster, but a monster no more. Curved Wing raises his head, still hunched over, hands on his knees. He sees his father mesmerized at the dead man sprawled at his feet, the work of his own hand. Captain Hillmann moves to Red Iron's side and removes his rifle from the grasp of the chief. The Indian chief is oblivious to the release of the gun as he gazes down.

The first words from Curved Wing are spoken in a barely audible, hoarse whisper, "Some men just need killin'."

The words break Chief Red Iron from his trance. "Come," he motions to the men. "To the tepee. Hurry."

Captain Hillmann practically carries Curved Wing as they hustle to the encampment. The captain gives a quick visual survey of the few on-looking Indians, before whisking Curved Wing inside the tepee. The calming voice of Chief Red Iron sounds, "My people, all is well. It is night. Time to rest." With a wave of his hand, the chief scattered the Indians. Those who witnessed Curved Wing's return were directed to retire to their tepees.

Chapter 60
Get Away

Chief Red Iron's Camp

Blue Feather enters the tepee of Chief Red Iron. She is caught off guard as the dying firelight illuminates her blood soaked brother flanked by her father and husband. The men are hunched over; Chief Red Iron scratches a map into the earth with a stick. He indicates the route of Curved Wing's travel's north, highlighting landmarks to guide him. Blue Feather drops the bundle she has prepared for her brother. "Brother!" she calls out as she rushes forward. The men straighten. Ignoring the bloody mess of threadbare linens hanging from Curved Wing's body she hugs her twin. "All this blood. Are you ok?"

Curved Wing nods, as the captain fields the question, "He's doing fine. It is someone else's blood."

Blue Feather breaks her hug and wipes some of the crusty blood from Curved Wing's cheek. Her brother grabs her arms and directs her to the side. He smiles, "You're standing on my map," he manages in a weak voice. "I am going to Canada. North as fast as I can. Father is drawing me a map..."

Blue Feather ducks away, embarrassed. "I have Jobba outside," she points to the bundle she dropped by the door flap, "...and some supplies."

The group moves outside. "Thank you, sister," Curved Wing whispers. Blue Feather fastens the bundle to Jobba's saddle.

Curved Wing turns to his mother. She holds his nephew. He touches the sleeping baby's cheek and meets his mother's eyes. He hugs her. "Goodbye, Mother. Take care of my nephew. Take care of everyone."

"Thank you, brother," Curved Wing extends a hand to Captain Hillmann before turning to his father. "Thank you, Father, for saving my life."

Chief Red Iron nods and extends his arm. The men grab each other's elbows and embrace. "Have a safe journey north, son," the chief instructs. "Find Chief Fox Tail with the Chippewa and give him this."

Chief Red Iron hands his favorite pipe to his son. "He will take care of you."

Curved Wing nods and hands the pipe to Blue Feather. She quickly wraps the pipe in buckskin and stows it with the bundle strapped to the horse.

"We will see you, "Blue Feather affirms with authority.

"You will," Curved Wing bows his head. "I will see my nephew, and he will be a chief like his grandfather. Goodbye."

"Go fast and hard," Captain Hillmann orders. "Go as far as you can. Until Jobba needs to rest."

Curved Wing salutes the captain and mounts his horse. "One more thing," the captain orders holding up his hand. Blue Feather hands the captain's rifle to her husband. He tosses it to Curved Wing who catches it with one hand.

With a final nod to his family, Curved Wing digs his heels into Jobba's ribs. The horse lurches forward into the darkness. Curved Wing gives one last look over his shoulder as the darkness swallows them, and he disappears from their view as they vanish from his. Jobba is fresh and hardy. Curved Wing searches the clearing sky and finds the North Star. He directs the frisky horse due north.

Chapter 61
Minnesota River Valley

Prairie

    Courtesy of the U.S. Government, a wagon and horse were provided to Amy Kauffmann with her promissory note to return the assets in due time. Josey, her farm's hired man drove the horse and wagon that bounced stiffly along, trailing through virgin, tall-grass prairie. The culmination of a nine week ordeal was nearing an end. Amy was wracked with nervousness as she finally recognized the Minnesota River Valley area she was familiar with. She had never strayed more than the ten or so miles to the village in her years on the prairie, much less the eighty plus miles the prisoners had marched to the Indian reservation. "We're here, aren't we Josey?" Amy questions.

    "Yes, ma'am."

    They crest the last rolling hill and what is left of the farm is at the bottom of the shallow valley below. They peer down the slope where Mr. Kauffmann and his brother are working to clear the burnt shell of the house. The boys sit atop the horses hooked in their harnesses and hitches in turn attached to charred beams and wreckage as the animals drag the scraps from the home site. Undeterred by the Indian attacks, Mr. Kauffmann had quickly decided to rebuild. The burned out house and barn had been originally laid out with a precise plan. Strategic and scenic the house had been located on a flat bench before the final slope to the creek. The barn, now in ruins, was on this same bench, close and convenient to the house. No, these were the locations where the heart of the farm was and must be. The chore of moving the rubble was a small price to pay to have the desired and memory laden locations.

    The wagon on the hill is quickly noticed and work pauses. The boys recognize their mother. "Mom!" Nate cries out.

    The boys slide from the backs of the horses and run to the wagon. Never had there been a slope of a hill as easy to climb. The boys ran toward their mother gliding up the grade separating them from a completed family. Amy exits the wagon and runs down the slope breathless, not from the sprint, but from the fulfillment of two months of prayers for such a reunion.

Chapter 62
Lincoln

Washington, D.C.

In November of 1862, 303 names of condemned Indians were forwarded to President Abraham Lincoln's office. President Lincoln personally reviewed each case. After careful consideration of each file for every condemned man, and much internal deliberation, the President concurred with the conclusion to execute thirty eight Indians for their part in the Indian revolt.

On December 26, 1862, thirty-eight Santee Sioux Indians were hanged near what is now Mankato, Minnesota, the largest mass execution in U.S. history. It was the grisly conclusion to the Lakota Uprising overshadowed by the Civil War.

Nearly 800 settlers and soldiers as well as an estimated 3,000 Indians were killed in the 1862 Lakota Uprising. The number of dead for all parties might have been significantly higher, if not for the efforts of Chief Red Iron, an advocate for peace.

Epilogue: Reunion

1867 – Canada

    North of the Turtle Mountains in Chippewa country, deep in the middle of the continent, where the waters head north, draining into the Hudson Bay, is where Curved Wing settled. In the sparse population known only to fur traders and the nomadic natives of Assiniboin to the south and west as well as the Chippewa to the south and east, Curved Wing made a home with his wife, Morning Sun. She is a beautiful, tall, young lady. She is light-skinned reflecting her French-Assiniboin heritage.

    The couple shares a weather beaten shack perched on the edge of one of the many gravelly-bottomed lakes dotting the area. Unofficially, the lake was referred to as Bad Medicine Lake. The name was a deterrent for many, especially natives travelling in the area who would insist on giving this particular jurisdiction a wide berth. There was no sense in tempting fate they reasoned and steered clear, except for the occasional lost hunting party. Curved Wing preferred the solitude. The ache left in his soul from his departure from his home nearly five years prior was nourished by the silence and desolation. The ache of missing family was also fueled by fear. It came and went, the feelings of fear. He would be absorbed in his chores, and the thoughts of being hunted by the U.S. Government would leave his mind, but they would sure enough return when thoughts of home and family prompted the memories. Oh, there was no doubt in his mind he would be a wanted fugitive; he had been convicted of murdering an Indian agent. The government wanted justice for the death of an American official carrying out his duty and killed in action. No, the bitterness felt by Curved Wing would never cease. He was content to stay isolated, work and build his fortune and family in Canada where he was left to his own devices.

    The one room shack might as well have been a castle on the Canadian prairie. It was the only structure within a fifty mile radius. He had built it himself and was its king. The logs of the cabin stood solidly, and the porch was sturdy. The family lived in the tepee adjacent to the wood structure, but the cabin was the key to life in this outpost. It held the cache of supplies and the valuable goods for trade. The porch was also the workshop, and Curved Wing today toiled here. He was carving on a flat piece of wood. This was a stretcher, a tool for drying the furs he trapped and traded. Preparations were being made in the summer for the fall trapping season, and crafting the tools of his trade was as critical as the trapping itself. Surrounding Curved Wing on the covered porch were the pelts prepared for the rendezvous. Morning Sun accompanied Curved Wing today on the porch. She nursed the baby while she kept her eye on their two-year old boy. The nursing of the baby had interrupted her task of working the hides over a rope to make them soft and supple.

The mid summer morning was progressing towards noon when Morning Sun watched her toddler chasing a butterfly. "Looks like we have company," she smiled turning to her husband.

Curved Wing turns his attention to the horizon. The open plains to the southeast reveal the visitors. Behind the cabin to the northwest, the intermix of hardwood and pine forests contrast the open plain. The family has made their home on this dividing line between the eco-regions and has enjoyed the benefits of both. The forest provides the furs, the plains providing a modest crop of grains and vegetables in the short growing season, as well as pasture and hay for the stock.

Curved Wing inspects his work with a close eye; he blows on the plank in his hand to remove the dust and shavings. He runs his finger across the grain, checking the smoothness. Satisfied he sets the stretcher aside and focuses on the wagon in the distance. "Who do you think it is? Some lost soul?"

Morning Sun smiles, "That's all we ever get around here."

Curved Wing cocks his head as he focuses, "I don't believe it."

"What is it?"

Curved Wing's expression of surprise raises Morning Sun's heart rate, "Who is it? What's happening?"

Curved Wing's jaw hangs, his mouth agape, "I think it's my sister and her family." Unconsciously, drawn by some primitive instinctual connection, he lifts his arm and waves it to the strangers in the distance. The visitors mirror the signal in return.

"It's them."

Curved Wing and his family move across the prairie to the wagon where they intercept his sister and company. Hugs, disbelief, and introductions punctuate the happy reunion. "How did you find me?" Curved Wing puzzles.

"Just asked around," Captain Hillmann responds with a smile. "Everyone we asked pointed to the northwest, and said, 'the only shack in area. Nobody but that crazy Sioux and his family would live near Bad Medicine Lake.' I knew we were on track."

Curved Wing shakes his head and laughs, "You came all this way? Why?"

Captain Hillmann shakes his head and shrugs. He points to his wife, "Blue Feather wanted to see you...and you know your sister; how could I refuse when she gets an idea in her head?"

Curved Wing slaps at his knee and chuckles roundly, "Some things never change." He moves to grab his sister in a hug and kisses the top of her head.

The captain moves to the back of the wagon, "Curved Wing, come! I bring good news!" He stretches his full length and grabs the handle of a trunk, dragging it to the rear of the wagon. With a grunt and some brute force, Hillmann moves the heavy trunk into a position to be opened. Lifting the lid exposes clothes beneath a leather saddlebag. He extracts the saddlebag, closes the trunk, and rests the bag on the trunk. Unclasping the saddlebag, the captain sifts through some papers and pulls free a decorated parchment and presents the document to Curved Wing.

"What is this?" Curved Wing accepts the paper from Hillmann as he inspects it.

"That is your ticket home, brother," Captain Hillmann beams. "It is a full Presidential pardon. Thanks to your father and a few others, your case was reviewed. Your name is cleared! You can come home!"

Blue Feather shakes her head and smiles. "Gary is modest. He went to Washington and spoke on your behalf. He is very persuasive." She shrugs, "Nonetheless, you can come home...that is, if you like." Blue Feather stops shaking her head in disbelief and changes to an affirming positive nod. "I see you have a home here...maybe come just to visit?"

Curved Wing looks far away to the south, miles away toward the corner of Dakota Territory and his upbringing. He is quiet and contemplative. Silence falls upon everyone as they observe Curved Wing and soon join him in looking south. He nods, "Yes, maybe a visit home."

The End

ABOUT THE AUTHOR

Greg Heitmann originally hails from South Dakota, but has resided in Santa Fe, New Mexico since 2004. Greg currently works for the Federal Highway Administration, but other occupations have included or currently include, novelist, screenwriter, actor, rancher, and soldier

This is the second novel in his Western series, *Dakota Territory*. You can find out more about Greg at his website: **www.thegmann.com**. Contact him via email at **g_mann_jr@yahoo.com**.

Made in the USA
Lexington, KY
01 December 2019